An Ocean of Jewels

Thank you,

Judy C. Andrews

An Ocean of Jewels

Judy C. Andrews

The Harlem Writers Guild Press
Literary Excellence Since 1950
New York   Lincoln   Shanghai

An Ocean of Jewels

Copyright © 2006 by Judy C Andrews

All rights reserved. No part of this book may be used or reproduced by any means, graphic, electronic, or mechanical, including photocopying, recording, taping or by any information storage retrieval system without the written permission of the publisher except in the case of brief quotations embodied in critical articles and reviews.

THE HARLEM WRITERS GUILD PRESS
an imprint of iUniverse, Inc.

iUniverse books may be ordered through booksellers or by contacting:

iUniverse
2021 Pine Lake Road, Suite 100
Lincoln, NE 68512
www.iuniverse.com
1-800-Authors (1-800-288-4677)

This is a work of fiction. All of the characters, names, incidents, organizations and dialogue in this novel are either the products of the author's imagination or are used fictitiously.

This novel is a work of fiction. The names, people, places, and things mentioned belong to the author's imagination and were not based on any one specific person, place or thing. The names Jewel Park, New York, Eva Creek Island, and Creeksville, Georgia belong to the author's imagination and were not based on any one specific person, place or thing. Although, many aspects of the author's Gullah/Geechee culture were incorporated into the novel's plot.

ISBN-13: 978-0-595-40030-0
ISBN-10: 0-595-40030-2

Printed in the United States of America

This novel is dedicated to:
Catherine Andrews and Walter Underwood, my precious parents.
Tengky fuh de tenduh mannus fuh lub.

Acknowledgments

Thank you, members of The Harlem Writers Guild, Inc., for your loving and unwavering support. Your wisdom strengthened me. Blessings to Grace F. Edwards and Eugene L. Hobgood for the astute expertise and thoughtfulness you offered so graciously; and to Betty Anne Jackson, your enlightening words about Jewel Avenue in New York were very much appreciated. Thank you: William H. Banks, Rachel De Aragon, Alfonso Nicks, Karen Robinson, Sarah Elizabeth Wright, Bob DesVerney, Diane Richards, Sheila Doyle, Olubansile Abbas Mimiko, M.D.; Dr. Angela Lynch-Clare, Funmi Ossaba, Gammy L. Singer, and Andrea Broadwater for your encouraging words. Thank you Mr. Jon D. McWilliams and the staff of iUniverse.

For uplifting my spirit to publish this work, thank you, Michael Anthony Belton.

I would like to acknowledge two important resources that I am grateful for, which I used to help provide me with a better understanding of Gullah/Geechee culture as I wrote this novel:

Brown, Alphonso; **Web site links:** *The Twenty-Third Psalm; Some Things In Gullah; A Glossary of Gullah Words taken from The Black Border by* Ambrose E. Gonzales *(The Black Border: Gullah Stories of the Carolina Coast,* by Ambrose E. Gonzales, Pelican

Publishing Co., U.S., February 19, 1999); Web site: gullahtours.com

Jarrett, Charles W., Ph.D and David M. Lucas, Ph.D; *Introducing Folknography: A Study of Gullah Culture;* A paper presented at the 65th Annual Meeting of the Rural Sociological Society, August 14-18, 2002 at the Congress Plaza Hotel, Chicago, Ilinois; page 2, 3, 26; Web-Site: Jarrett@ohio.edu.

Chapter One

The Early Times Old Style Kentucky Whiskey tasted good for breakfast. I took another sip as I worked on my third glass and reread a passage from an article my father wrote in a newspaper the year I was born. It was five o'clock, Christmas morning, 1999, and I waited.

People, places, and things never really die because my mind holds them when I'm not paying attention, like gene pools or circles or photographs connecting to the beginning of my life.

My hands danced across my face wiping tears away as I read the last poem I'd written in my journal, after Blue Greene went home to take care of business, a prayer for my own healing. Birthday's have a way of making me pray.

I observed photographs of my parents, myself, and a love letter my father had written to me on the day I was born that I found hidden beneath my mother's mail in a top dresser drawer when I was eight and discovered the scent of *Chanel No. 5* perfume on my fingertips.

Last night, the hospital had called me before Blue Greene had. My father's pressure had been dropping all evening. Daddy had been in a diabetic coma for two days.

Waiting for death a day before my birthday when I was 12 gave me anxiety every birthday after that because I was always waiting for a phone call telling me that someone had died. For 17 years, I've been waiting, only to find out that now, at age 29, I can't handle it. I placed the phone's receiver back on the machine anyway.

I let the photographs and a love letter fill a cave in my soul overflowing like the Gullah/Geechee heritage of Georgia I owned, but had never learned. Inside the cave lived a dark mix that reminded me of tough roots, cypress forests, and peat moss that thrived on the shores of the Okefenoke Swamp as well as the Ogeechee and Savannah Rivers that surrounded low country living. I never learned the language my mother and father spoke whenever they wanted to share a secret about a murder in 1901 that kept my father from sleeping comfortably most nights when he came to visit Mama and me when I was a child. But the language of photographs and a love letter kept appearing on the walls of the cave that had grown in my soul along with the oak trees, especially on my 12th birthday, when my mother's sweet whispers of her love for me disappeared.

That night, I learned the art of dancing people used to wipe tears away.

It was Christmas morning, 1999, and now I knew in advance what I was waiting for as I longed for a warm familiar family quilt with the design of a holy river named Eridanus that my grandmother used to cover me with whenever I was cold.

To calm my nerves I sipped whiskey for breakfast, something I began doing around this time last year after a shower of champagne hit my face.

"Please God," I whispered, "I need some answers soon."

I wiped away the tears as I tried to forget that while I was wrapped in paisley sheets scented with White Musk oil, Blue Greene, a man with skin that reminded me of a red maple tree with comforting hands, had kissed my lips, neck, breasts, stomach, and then had worked his way up again to my ear to say, "Sweet, I have to tend to some business. You know that, don't you?"

His lips moved across my face to my lips again.

I then watched him watch all two hundred and fifty-seven pounds of me. He apologized again by kissing the handprint he had placed on my face, a swollen bruise on the left side that remained from last night's slap for reminding him that I needed his love more than jewelry. He called me "unappreciative." He then calmly repeated, "Got to tend to some business in the morning, understand?"

Yes, I did. He had made being with his common-law wife, Linda Cree, on Christmas, business.

But I had smiled, given him another gift of fine cologne, quietly made him breakfast, and sipped my cup of coffee in the living room as I watched him leave at five in the morning to go over to The Blue Zephyr, the tasteful nightclub he owned on Dandelion Street and Simpson Avenue, which was five blocks walking distance from my home. Then I had returned to the paisley sheets, then to my father's chair, then back to the sheets to continue my modern dance of wiping away tears, and waiting.

Terror lived in my stomach as I listened to the sound of the ringing phone and a message that made me pray.

"Ms. Henderson?" After I let Dr. Lateesha Clarke know that I was listening well, she told me that my father died at 4:45 A.M., never recovering from his diabetic coma.

I sipped more whiskey.

Dr. Clarke on the other end kept talking, "I'm so very sorry to tell you this news. Ms. Henderson?"

"Yes, thank you for calling," I whispered.

Dr. Clarke continued, "Call me, Ms. Henderson, if you need to talk. Any other information I receive later, I'll be sure to give to you," she said.

I lied, "I will call you if I need anything. Thank you, doctor."

I listened to the dial tone until I heard an operator's recording informing me to hang up, and then I heard loud, uninterrupted beeping, and then silence. The waiting was now over.

A haunting memory kept me so still after I got the news of my father's death that all I could do was move my eyelids to limit the flow of water I tried unsuccessfully to control. My tears forced me to remember what Autumn did the night the devil took my mother, the night I became a foster child. It was Christmas Eve, 1982, the day before my 12th birthday. The same night, God took Nana Zola Jewel. And the same feeling I had then of loneliness, I have now.

I, along with the police thought the most logical place for me to be was with my father. Autumn detested the idea. No other woman's child would move in and mess up *her* marriage.

My hand held the image of a party, hers. On the evening of my mother's suicide, Autumn celebrated her 35th birthday, and I was waiting to celebrate my 12th birthday the next day.

Photograph: *I was put in a police car with our neighbor Mrs. Greta Johnson to ride to Autumn's house where Daddy was living on Dandelion Street, just off of Robinson Boulevard. The policeman rang the doorbell. He gave Autumn the news about Mama because Daddy wasn't home. Although I stood behind the policeman, I could smell beer on Autumn's breath.*

She laughed at the news and said, "Ruby Jewel Weaver? She's really dead? Nana too! Good!" More laughter. I lunged forward and jumped on her.

She ran to the kitchen, got a butcher knife, and started swinging and calling me names, "Just like your Mama. Come on. You wanna' fight me? You think you're woman enough?"

Yes, I thought, adjusting the coat over my pajamas. The knife had left a cut on my right arm and on my shoulder, only slightly visible now, thanks to cocoa butter.

There was a lot of blood.

The knife also left a cut on the policeman's hand. He began yelling into his radio, "Backup! I need backup."

The knife fell to the floor. Minutes later another policeman dragged me to the police car.

The ambulance arrived, and I was dressed in pajamas and bandages. Autumn told me, "Next time, I'll kill you."

The terror she planted in my stomach that night has never left me.

The news made me ask, "But my Mama is dead? Nana, too?"
That's when I learned the art of dancing people used to wipe tears away.

Now, Daddy was gone.

My tears were interrupted by the voices coming from my next-door neighbor, Valerie Jacob's house. She had been calling me or banging on the door all night as Blue slept peacefully. She had given up on waiting for me to answer her around three in the morning.

Guests from Valerie's Christmas Eve party that I had been invited to, but had turned down for a night with Blue, were streaming out of her three-family brownstone and piling into luxurious cars. I heard Redd, Valerie's husband, offer to give familiar voices that belonged to familiar people rides home. I recognized the voices of the only family I had, Cayenne, Mark, and Bless Brown; Angela Montgomery, Cayenne's new girlfriend was there also.

The haunting memory of Autumn's breath took me deeper into the cave of my soul where Christmas Eve, 1982 lived, and I placed my father's article back into my journal along with nine pictures. The tenth was the most recent.

That night, Nana died peacefully at the age of 82.

That night, Mama killed herself after she got the news. She was 45 years old.

After midnight, I became 12. Every birthday after that I have been waiting for someone to die not realizing that each year something inside of me died as I waited.

Both Nana's and Mama's funerals were held one week apart from each other. That week I learned the art of hiding. And I learned how to talk to God about what confusion does to the photographs that linger on my mind.

That night in 1982, I was taken to a Catholic group home in Jewel Park named St. Mary's Place for God's Children where I lived for two years. After that, I was placed in foster care, and from ages 12 to 21, I lived at eight different places. Each time I entered a house, I searched for mansions and jewels, holding on to each celebration of hope that

Daddy would find me, but he never did find me the way I wanted him to.

Now Daddy was gone, just like Nana and Mama, on my birthday.

That night, in my soul, I found many mansions filled with jewels from Mama's tree. That is what I imagined at the age of eleven on Christmas Eve, 1982 when Mama whispered to me through slow, slurred, strange speech, "Imani Jewel Henderson, I love you." She then kissed me goodbye.

That night, Mama swallowed a handful of Valium pills and washed them down with an eight-ounce glass of rum, no ice. Her cirrhosis could no longer be hidden. She slipped into a coma, and then death.

That night, I found a cave in my soul filled with roots that I must clean out. I knew the cave was there at age 12 after Mama's death, but I did not know that it had grown each year. Occasionally, I found roots within that I could not see clearly.

These roots are oak trees in my soul: long, dense and heavy.

I have a cave in my soul filled with photographs.

Since the waiting was over, I moved from the paisley sheets to the chair in the living room. There I sat embracing Daddy's thin, russet phone book, a love letter, and ten photographs. Nine of them I hadn't seen in a long time. One photograph was of him and my mother that Daddy had found in my journal and had asked for without an explanation. He had placed it in the back of his phone book on a top shelf of my bookcase in the living room. The photograph fell out when I picked up the phone book, next to my journal of poems, which lay on a small photo album that I kept with pictures I had collected before foster care, of my parents.

Daddy had left his phone book, which also doubled as a daily planner, a week ago when he had visited for Sunday dinner. We had shared sarcastic words because I had corrected his grammar for an article on Orphan Train survivors from New York he was about to publish for a weekly college newspaper he regularly contributed to. He calmly let me know that he felt his correction was better. When I asked him why he was doing research about Orphan Train survivors, something I had read about in college, he gave me an uncomfortable smile. Why?

Monday morning he was rushed by ambulance to the Jewel Park Medical Center to treat the diabetes that had been responsible for the dark circles under his eyes and a second heart attack. He was admitted that day and never returned to me. His uncomfortable smile was now on my mind.

The photograph of my parents was framed in an antique, mahogany glass case embraced in Kente colors of the earth: gold, blue, green, and red. Daddy was married at that time to Autumn, someone who despised Mama because my mother was the color of white chocolate, and Autumn was brown like the volcanic ash from Mount Nyiragongo, brown like me, and brown like Daddy. Back then, Daddy spoke Geechee regularly.

I observed the photograph of my parents again through water as I sipped whiskey and ignored the world. Daddy's molasses colored eyes glanced at Mama, as his delightful teeth brightened the blurry background during the kiss. The look on her face surrendered to the kiss, and seemed to indicate that she had been offered the most delicious chocolate she had ever experienced. The kiss barely touched the left side of her lips. Daddy seemed to be whispering something to her with the smile, teeth, kiss, and lips. Daddy's eyelashes were curled beautifully as they rested over his lower eyelids. Only the photographer knew the secret they shared.

Another photograph stemmed from a one year old birthday celebration, mine, from last Christmas where I found my self in an extraordinary place, the arms of my best friend's husband, Mark Brown, in a pose similar to that of my parents' in the photograph. Only, I had to leave the birthday celebration that my best friend, Bless Brown, had given me because we got into a fight over the pose.

That night I lost her love. Until that night, she had been my sister/friend.

It was a night similar to the one I remember on the night of Mama's suicide.

The eight other pictures of my grandparents, parents, and Autumn haunted me.

All morning I sat alone in my two-family brownstone my father used to own, where an ambulance and a policeman had to remove me from when I was eleven. I craved for Nana's laying on of hands.

The waiting was over, but the search for my love was just beginning. It was buried in the cave of my soul waiting for me to find it and hold on to it. I have not moved from my father's chair to wash my hair, dress, eat, sleep, talk, walk, jump, scream, call, hear, answer, chant, curse, pray, sway, or glare, but whiskey helped.

Chapter Two

I fought to forget that it was Christmas day, my 29th birthday, and that in a week the 21st century would begin. I had read through Daddy's phone book four times, finding only a handful of appointments and names, none of which I knew, and a heap of services from restaurants to dry cleaners, but no kin, except for a note scribbled on the last page that read, "In case of emergency, call Autumn, Imani."

A Brooklyn, New York area code and phone number followed. I also found an old picture on the bottom of that page that Daddy had drawn with a black marker of the constellation Eridanus, the mythological river, engraved on another picture of a familiar family quilt. I never knew that Daddy had an interest in astronomy. Under the constellation, written also with a black marker, in capital letters were the words, LOOK UP ORPHAN TRAINS/1854-1930. That was followed by three exclamation points.

I glanced at my simple black and white composition notebook (I had about fifteen of them—journals), where I now kept the pictures also, along with my own daily planner as I remembered the family quilts I had seen on Eva Creek Island in Georgia when I was a child, and I had written about them in my journals; Nana made quilts back then that just about everyone on the Island had.

Daddy wanted me to call Autumn Brook Taylor? Why? They had divorced when I was 21. Why was there a picture of the same constellation that was on our family quilts? After Nana's death, I never saw them again. Why? Did Daddy give them away? Did Autumn have them? What was an Orphan Train? I remembered his uncomfortable smile.

Hate really had set in with Autumn and me when my father gave me the house the year they divorced. She has never forgotten it. I guess she thought that a foster child was not supposed to have a house.

I pushed the questions into the cave and stared at the photographs as I listened to my doorbell. I continued hiding.

For eight years, from the time I was emancipated from foster care until his death, once a month, Daddy visited me in this house for Sunday dinner. We regularly ate in silence. When we did talk, it was always about work, the weather, news or my life.

Silence and avoidance had delicately wrapped themselves around him over the years after Mama's death, and the embrace grew tighter after his divorce from Autumn. He would never answer my questions I wanted to know about him or Mama. Now I had to contact a woman who had threatened to take my life when I was eleven?

I ignored the doorbell's music along with the voices shouting my name behind it. I glanced at the shadows behind the cracked shutters in my living room windows of my neighbors Cayenne and Valerie. I listened as a car pulled in to Valerie's driveway. It was Mark, Cayenne's brother. I listened as they whispered. Joy, Valerie's 12 year old daughter, had not learned the art of whispering and she shouted, "I don't think Imani's home, Ma. I'm hungry."

"Go on in the house, baby." Valerie told her, annoyed. She went on, "I still can't find the damn keys Imani gave me years ago. Damn it!"

I heard Valerie's door slam as Cayenne's shadow passed by my living room window.

All afternoon I sat in the dark with the shutters cracked, thinking. Somewhere in the cave of my soul is an image of a mansion filled with jewels I am still searching for. Mama took her jewels with her or gave them away, and Daddy left me a brownstone.

The night of my mother's passing, Autumn was arrested, and she never forgot why. Years later, I understood her threat of murder for me was just a threat. That Christmas Eve in 1982, Autumn had settled for hate to haunt me.

I resembled a slow modern dancer as I wiped the tears from my face and shoved the memory into the cave.

I will not call her, I thought. *I will hide.*

I refused to look at the second photograph again. I hid from the others.

I placed the phone book and photographs on the coffee table in the living room as their images crept into the cave along with the tough roots, cypress forests, peat moss and a constellation of a river named Eridanus that resembled a familiar family quilt.

I sipped whiskey with ice.

I cried, and then hate took over as I moved. I beat up the walls of my house. I kicked them and threw dishes while I moved from my father's chair stumbling throughout the house as I wiped tears from my face and resembled a slow modern dancer. And then I tried to forget the darkness that reminded me of syrup and red maple trees with fingers scented with White Musk oil, and a handprint.

Chapter Three

"Imani, are you home? Girl, open up this door!" Valerie shouted. She continued, "Please open the door, Imani. I know you're home. Come on, girl. We love you. Please open the door, Imani."

I watched her shadow through the curtains behind the door. She was carrying a plate of food.

I ignored her.

She rang the doorbell one last time, and then threatened me with, "If you don't open this door, I'm going to call the police and have them break it down, understand?" Then I heard her door slam as she entered her own brownstone.

I didn't care who she called.

The photographs that rested on my mind now left me with anger and fear. I sat in silence and kept blinking to make the photographs disappear. Each time I blinked, I saw a photograph clearly. But information was always missing from it.

The phone rang. It was Cayenne.

"Jewel, if you're home, please pick up." He waited. "We love you. You don't have to go through this shit alone. Please, baby, pick up the phone." I waited for him to hang up and then I pulled the phone cord from the wall.

I remembered a conversation.
"Where's my Daddy?" I asked.
"Oh, he's fine. You'll see him soon."
"When?"
"Soon."
"How soon?"
"Very soon."
"Later on?"
"Yes."
"Later on, today?"

My first group home was St. Mary's Place for God's Children the evening Autumn was arrested. The police and a black woman who was a social services administrator, Mrs. Marie Hayes, a woman my father knew, wouldn't let me live with Daddy because of Autumn.

Why couldn't they take me? I have wondered since age twelve. Most children I knew had relatives like Autumn.

When I arrived at St. Mary's Place for God's Children, this huge, white, rectangular building just off of Austin Street in downtown Jewel Park that resembled an office building and a holy dungeon for homeless or abused children, it was after midnight, and I vomited. It was my birthday. I remember falling into it and then running past a dining room as a policeman chased me because my father was "detained."

I screamed, "I want Daddy."

They put me in somebody's office. I threw up again. Mrs. Hayes wiped my tears with a wet cloth and told me St. Mary's Place for God's Children was my family and new home. Daddy argued with her to let him take me home after he saw the vomit.

Years later, after I became a teacher at Jewel Park High School, I learned that Mrs. Hayes, a social worker, worked with the school social worker there along with my father, and she had assisted some of Daddy's former students.

I had to stay, someone agreed.

Another mystery.

Mrs. Hayes escorted me into her office. I screamed, "Family? I have a family!" I had relatives, didn't I? I had aunts, uncles, cousins, nieces, and nephews, didn't I? My family had found this town. They were buried in my soul. As we entered the office, Mrs. Hayes sat behind a huge desk. A glass vase of red roses and pictures of herself and her family were on the desk. Mrs. Hayes stared at me and smiled. I didn't like her. She liked small talk and said my name, "Imani Jewel Henderson." That it was pretty. When I tired of crying, she sat me down across from her, opened a large folder and read it for what seemed to be a long time. She sighed.

I interrupted her. "Will I see my Daddy later today?"

"You'll see your father soon," she said, and then she flashed me a quick glance.

After that, Mrs. Hayes looked up from her folder to smile at me, I remember. She said, "You're very smart," and she tapped the folder with her one inch long red fingernails, like the back-up singers for Barry White did. I used to watch him on *Soul Train*.

With a smile she said, "I see you're in the ninth grade. Skipped twice! And what lovely names you all have." She looked puzzled as she quietly mumbled Mama's name, "Ruby Jewel Weaver," and the words, "Depression, diabetes, psychosis, anxiety, alcoholism, beautiful woman, though." She must have had a picture of Mama in that folder.

I was smart enough to know that her mumbling was a form of psychology. She wasn't supposed to say that to me, no matter how smart she thought I was.

I said, without flinching, "Yes. Hallucinations. Lots of pills. Yes. Alcoholism. She was a famous fashion model."

Most of the time, I had been very frightened of my mother, especially on the days when it rained or snowed. After making me believe that she was taking me shopping, she liked to take me to Jacobs Street and Clarke Road instead, in downtown Jewel Park and stand at the main intersection talking to the sky as cars whizzed by us. Across the street was a bagel shop, and the owner, a beautiful Jewish woman who was always stylishly dressed would offer me protection as she would shout at me in a thick accent to come over to her. She waved her hands frantically to make sure I understood her. A policeman usually rescued us, taking us, wet, to a nearby police station to be driven home or to the bus that led home. For years I had a fear that I would grow up to be just like Mama, but I buried it in a cave with darkness the color of syrup.

I remember her smell of alcohol and our favorite perfume.

During winter, I dressed in layers of clothing whenever she took me outside, just in case. It wasn't until I was 12, during Mama's wake, that I heard whispers from church members, neighbors, and friends who knew pieces of my mother's life and were often puzzled by my father:

"You know, Ruby tried to kill that child. And herself several times!"

"What?"

"That's right, honey. Sho' did."

"Yeah, girl, she use ta' walk right out in traffic. Pitiful sight!"

"I seen em' once, myself. Holdin' hands by a bagel shop. Ruby be staring right up at the sky like she talkin' to it, just like Nana Zola Jewel used to. Sho'did! Seen her with my own eyes. Yes, Lord, sho' did!"

I never remembered the names that went along with the voices. I remembered the toasted cinnamon raisin bagel with cream cheese I got often whenever I found the courage to let go of Mama's hand and run toward the bagel shop into the arms of the Chantilly-laced lady with the thick accent who wrapped warm, loving words around me. She waited with me for the police while I watched Mama talk to the sky. I used to tell Daddy about the bagel shop lady all the time. He would just smile and repeat the same phrase: she was an angel from God. Then he'd never explain exactly just what he meant by that.

Hearing someone whisper that my mother tried to kill me has never left me, no matter how hard and fast I've spent my life running from the whispers. My parents' neighbors have moved away, and the only new folks are twenty-something's with wealth. No one from my mother's neighborhood is around anymore, except Mrs. Greta Johnson. And the bagel shop is now a café with a new owner.

I spent a lot of nights crying myself to sleep in St. Mary's Place for God's Children, often wondering why my mother wanted me dead. I know now that she wanted to die, but she wanted to take me with her, not get rid of me. My father placed me in the group home to keep me alive, not knowing that Mama was already dead until after he had signed the forms to turn me over to the state. I learned years later, that he had been planning to remove me from my mother's home at least a month before her death. Did Mama know that he was planning to take me in on my 12th birthday?

I know on the night of her death, Mama hoped I would die right along with her. Mrs. Johnson had told the police officer that six sleeping pills along with a glass of water had been placed beside my night table in my room. I guess in my mother's confusion from the Valium and alcohol, she had forgotten to give them to me. Or had she changed her mind about taking me with her? Or did I just tell her that I wouldn't take them when she had asked me to? I couldn't remember. For that entire year at the group home, I prayed to God for me to go where Mama was. Astonished that I talked about it, Mrs. Hayes pretended not to hear me and uncomfortably changed the subject to my father. She mumbled, "Matthew Henderson."

I said, "My father. Normal. Famous. He's a history teacher at Jewel Park High School, a journalist and a scholar. I love him too. He wrote a book about my mother's family, *The Children of Eva Creek Island*," I said, proudly.

Mrs. Hayes smiled.

For 29 years, my father taught social studies at Jewel Park High School, where I now teach English, and my mother, for ten years, taught math before her modeling career expanded. Alcoholism didn't look pretty in photographs in famous magazines, so when I turned ten, Mama stopped working. And we lived off of crumpled hundred dollar bills, then crumpled twenty dollar bills, then crumpled dollar bills and plump coin wrappers.

As a child, Daddy was labeled a prodigy; he entered college at the age of 14.

I remembered Mrs. Hayes. We shared the same eye color, hazel, and weight. I was just as curvaceous as she was when I was 12. She closed the folder and then placed her arms around my waist.

More anger surfaced as I saw photographs.

She said, slowly, softly, "This is your new home. You're..." She never got to finish her sentence. Mrs. Donahue, her assistant, knocked on her door just as the phone rang. Mrs. Hayes got the phone and whispered to Mrs. Donahue to take me to the dining room for a snack, and then she gave me a handful of Kleenex.

I remember I walked down a long hallway past a big game room with toys wrapped beautifully under a seven-foot tree. None of the children were asleep. We stopped right in front of the middle of the room. Mrs. Donahue introduced me to about fifteen or twenty children playing loudly in the room. The children were mostly my age and brown like me. She tried to get them to sing "Happy Birthday" to me, but I had competition with the tree. I didn't fit in. The children wanted to know why I "talked white," and one of them almost hit me for correcting her "ain't" to "isn't."

I remained at St. Mary's Place for God's Children for two years before I entered foster care. No one ever explained why.

Photograph: *Mama is on the floor. The emergency medical technicians put her in a black bag.*

I hear the zipper closing off her body to the living as the emergency medical technicians put her on a table and wheel her to the back of the ambulance.

I feel the arms of the policeman holding my shoulders down, then my hands as he leads me to a police car.

I smell urine, mine.

I see Daddy's face staring into mine at the hospital as he kisses the bandages on my hand and gives me a stale doughnut and milk. I see Daddy breathing deeply along with tears as he waves goodbye to me at St. Mary's Place for God's Children. I ask everyone I see there if he's coming back. No one answers me. I sit on the floor and cry. They put me in a room with a bed and I cry all night holding nine photographs close to my heart. They are all I have.
I see Daddy whispering in Mama's ear.
I see Bless Brown and a glass of champagne.
Now I have to see Daddy sleeping in a coffin?
The photographs haunted me.

The banging on my front door forced me to jump. I heard keys. Someone was trying to get in, but couldn't. More banging continued.

"This is police officer Jenkins. Can you hear me, Miss Henderson?" Your neighbors are worried. Ma'am?"

I stared at Eridanus, a note about an Orphan Train, and Autumn's phone number as I wiped my face with my fingertips.

"Just a moment, please," I whispered. I placed the phone book on the coffee table and finished the glass of whiskey. I grabbed peppermint candy from a glass dish on the table. The candy slowly melted on my tongue.

Chapter Four

I thought of funeral preparations. "Get it together, girl, now!" I told myself.

A chorus of voices was shouting my name.

"This is Officer Jenkins, ma'am. If you're in there please open the door. There are some concerned neighbors out here. Miss Henderson?"

I had not adjusted the heat, and the house was still draped in darkness.

I had been awake for more than 24 hours staring at photographs on my mind, grieving for my father, and nursing anger and fear with a half empty liter bottle of Early Times Old Style Kentucky Whiskey. A half empty liter bottle was my limit for weekends. Throughout the week I sipped the liquid in six ounce orange juice glasses along with three cubes of ice until the bottle was empty. Every other weekend I was ready for a new bottle.

"Imani! Girl, open this door!" Valerie's voice.

"Jewel? You in there?" Cayenne's voice.

More banging. "Imani Jewel! Baby?" Yes, it was Valerie Jacobs.

"Jewel?" Mark Brown, Cayenne's brother.

I recognized the voices, especially the last one, and I vomited halfway between the dining room and hallway as I approached the door. "Damn," I said. "Just a minute," I yelled, as I wiped my face with a towel.

I slowly opened the front door as I watched my neighbor, Valerie Jacobs say, "Thank you," to the policeman, a nice looking black man.

"Lord, have mercy Jesus!" The plea for mercy came from Valerie, Jewel Park's finest caterer, who at only 32 years of age had inherited a two million dollar business left to her and her brother Andre by her parents, Alfred and Emily Jacobs, who now lived in Richmond, Virginia. She also owned The Prayerful Café Corner Restaurant that was part of the property of The Jewel Park Temple of Faith Church we often attended. But I hadn't attended church in a while. Valerie's voice was heavy from too much tobacco smoke. It was nearly 6 P.M., the day after Christmas, and I assumed she had been up all night partying.

My friend Cayenne Brown frowned at me. I glanced at his eyes that resembled purple/black grapes. He wore a jogging suit that complimented skin the color of clover honey, and he apparently had been working out in the basement gym of Valerie's brownstone, where he lived on the first floor. His beeper, attached to his jogging pants, beeped continuously, but he didn't read any messages. They were probably related to his job as a computer specialist. He seemed much older than his 34 years, a wise soul, but women loved to stare at him. He stood next to Valerie.

My best friend's husband and my former lover, Mark Brown, who had not acknowledged my presence until recently this year, stood behind them, but I saw him first. The sight of him provoked rage. He was still married to Bless.

"Imani!" Mark sighed.

I vomited into the towel.

"Let's get her inside!" Cayenne said, authoritatively. "It's cold out here." He took the towel from around his neck and gave it to me to wipe my face.

"Sure is," Valerie said, tightening her bathrobe that fit snuggly over 350 pounds of flesh, a cardigan, and stretch pants. She looked stunning with her manicured nails, shoulder-length Senegalese twists, and limited makeup that complemented the deep dimples in her mahogany face.

"Imani!" Mark said again, moving his head like a sad child recovering from a whipping. He was 38, but looked ten years older.

Valerie ushered everyone into the house past the kitchen, and on into the living room. She repeated, "Lord have mercy, Jesus!" After throwing a glance at Mark, then Cayenne, her gray eyes were transfixed on the vomit in the hallway, dishes in the sink, laundry scattered across the basement steps, a half pot of cold coffee, a Christmas tree sparsely decorated, a half-eaten birthday cake, wrapping paper from unwrapped presents, garbage that smelled like sour milk, the telephone upside down near the remote control in the living room, the television on mute, a cell phone disconnected from its battery, a jewelry box, a phone book, the photographs.

Throughout the night, rage had taken my hands and slammed appliances against the wall. Throughout the day, hate took my feet and kicked my living room chairs against the unit that held my CDs and stereo sound system. Fear took my fingers and swept the phone off the coffee table onto the floor, and then they had thrown food at the kitchen window, and a butcher knife was lying on the kitchen floor next to my own daily planner.

I brought my hands to my face and realized dried blood was covering a small cut over the back of my left hand. I felt eleven as I dropped to the living room floor and cried. "He's gone," I repeated it softly to myself.

"I'm calling an ambulance!" Mark said, searching for the phone. His voice was cotton candy sweet, enough to make me sick; yet, I craved more.

"Jesus!" Valerie repeated, fixing her eyes on me.

She glanced at the collection of my previous night's celebration with Blue as she investigated several items on the kitchen table hidden under colorful wrapping paper. They were gifts, and two of them were easy to see; a pair of small, box-shaped diamond earrings with a matching bracelet inside of a black velvet jewelry case, and on the kitchen chair, a Lenox China teapot with a pink rose petal pattern, all from Blue.

Valerie noticed the two leftover waffles I had made for Blue's breakfast still on the kitchen table swimming in AlaGa Syrup.

Anger returned to my soul. "No ambulance," I yelled, "I'm fine!" I forced myself to stand up. I reached the phone before Mark did. I snatched it and slammed the receiver onto the answering machine box.

Valerie kept her eyes fixed on me as she poured me a glass of whiskey from the collection of wines and liquors I kept in the kitchen pantry my father had turned into a mini liquor cabinet. I took a sip and set the glass designed for orange juice onto the coffee table.

Cayenne cleared his throat and said to Valerie, "I don't think she really needs any more of that. I'll make some coffee."

"That's right. You right. That's good," Valerie told Cayenne.

"No!" I said, again. "No ambulance. Please! And I don't want any damn coffee."

Mark sat next to me as we both watched Valerie put items in neat places; she breathed heavily and mumbled incoherently. She wore the gold bracelet I had given her as a Christmas present. Cayenne made coffee. Mark sat staring at the coffee table.

A year of resentment had festered toward him within me. I remembered and whispered, "I hate you."

His eyes talked to Valerie's and then Cayenne's before he carefully whispered to me, "Get over it!"

"Got to hell," I told him.

He forced me to focus on his dark green eyes. His skin was the color of brown leaves falling in the eye of an autumn sunset. His stare made me so uncomfortable that I turned away from him to sip more whiskey.

In the past year, after the affair, I had aborted the child he had planted in me. He had gotten a restraining order to keep me from following him around Jewel Park; the same way my mother had followed my father around when I was a child.

Photograph: *My mother is standing on the grass in my father's back yard watching Autumn and my father embrace in a warm home in Silver Row. It's raining and Mama's holding my hand. I think the raindrops are mixing with her tears. We go out at a nearby diner. She sips coffee. We share bacon, eggs, grits, and toast. She gives the waitress four rolls of fifty-cent penny wrappers along with four crumpled dollar bills. We go home to our pretty house that's not as pretty as the one Daddy shares with Autumn. Before bed, I taste the painted plaster from my bedroom wall. I am eleven. Mama sees me and gives me cereal because we really only eat one meal a day.*

Mark whispered, "I'm sorry, Imani." He offered me another taste of cotton candy. I took it.

When I met Mark, Cayenne, and Valerie, I was 14. Mark was 22, and Cayenne was 19. Our foster parents were next-door neighbors in Jewel Park; they received children from the same foster care agency. Although my mother lived on the southern part of town just off of Crescent Boulevard, and Daddy lived with Autumn on the northern side in Silver Row before moving to Dandelion Street, I lived on the eastern side in uptown Jewel Park, which is also where Cayenne, Bless, and Mark had grown up.

Back then Bless Brown and I were the same age and neighbors, and she, Cayenne, and Mark lived as foster children under the same roof. Cayenne attended Jewel Park's Technical College and went into business for himself as a computer specialist. Mark finished medical school at New York University. Cayenne had been Mark's foster brother since age two. Throughout the years they had often been separated, but they frequently managed to have their social workers place them in the same homes. Both men knew nothing about their biological parents, except that they were New Yorkers. Whispers about Cayenne's mother being a prostitute haunted him. No one ever dared to investigate the whispers. The only thing that Mark knew about his mother was that she was only 13 when he was born. We had all been born in Jewel Park.

Bless, Mark's wife, and I each knew our parents, but I was the only one who kept regular holiday visits with at least one parent through the years. Bless knew that her mother was a cafeteria aide in an elementary school and her father was a bus driver in New York City. Bless received a full scholarship to study music at Julliard at graduation. Since I had been skipped twice in high school, I was walking down the halls of New York's Columbia University's Teacher's College. Just about every year and a half before college, one of us was moving to a different home, but we always kept in touch through letters during college. Bless' last foster parents were Valerie Jacob's parents who had lived next door to my father for four years. He had moved from Silver Row after his divorce from Autumn.

Valerie and her brother Andre had spent most of their time in boarding schools in New York or with relatives in Virginia. After graduating from Howard University, Valerie and Andre moved to Jewel Park to live with their parents. Valerie took over the business right after college, while André disappeared from Jewel Park in hope of shedding the disappointment he felt toward his parents for shunning him because of his gay lifestyle.

From age 18 until the time Bless married Mark, she lived with Valerie's parents, but saw them less frequently when she realized that they would never stop introducing her as, "Bless Brown, their lovely foster child." She wanted desperately to be called, "Daughter."

Neither I, Cayenne, Mark nor Bless had any biological brothers, sisters or relatives who were willing to give us shelter, but somehow we seemed to form our own family unit. My father wouldn't take me in because of Autumn, but he always let people know that I was his daughter, because while I was in foster care, we lived only five blocks apart. I felt he loved me. He did tell me when he called me daily, but when he said it, it was as if he was reading it from a cereal box.

Fear kept us unusually polite toward one another as if we were good but not great friends. Actually, I don't remember ever having an argument with my father or him ever raising his voice toward me, or anyone. He had a profound calmness about him that made most people nervous. Yet, even though Autumn separated us, we, father and daughter, loved each other in ways that can only be expressed in spirit. I loved him as a daughter should.

On holidays and birthdays we celebrated with the relatives of our foster parents by sitting in corners holding paper plates of soul food, staring at strangers who stared back at us with polite laughter or with pointing fingers followed by the words: foster child. We didn't know that there were millions of children like us craving to be called, "My son," or "My daughter," or "Our beautiful child." I didn't even know what Gullah/Geechee meant until I went to college, and even then, I couldn't get anyone to talk about it, especially Mama or Daddy.

But I had a love letter, and I carried it with me everywhere along with nine photographs.

"Lord, Jesus. Have mercy!" Valerie said. Then, "I left the kids in the house alone. So I can't stay long. Let me just call Joy and make sure she's feeding the baby. Redd's at the store. He'll be back soon. Then I'll straighten up here." She gave Cayenne the garbage to set on the curb, and then reconnected the kitchen's phone to its wall outlet. She spoke softly to her 12-year-old, Joy. She whispered a few words to her, but the only word I heard was "Mess!!!" I watched Valerie eye a used a condom that had missed the kitchen's garbage can.

Jesus! I thought.

When Cayenne returned, he washed his hands and sliced a few pieces of cantaloupe that had been resting with other fruit on the kitchen table, and handed them to me. He took a seat in a cushioned chair next to the radio that rested on an antique table by the living room window. He poured himself a cup of coffee, and then sat opposite Mark and me, but he was closer to me and touched my hand. As he spoke, I listened and eyed the plate of cantaloupe, but reached for the glass of whiskey that tasted very good.

"You okay?" Cayenne asked me. His profound gaze instructed me to relax. I tried, but failed.

"How you feeling?" He asked.

"Fine," I said, getting another taste of the smooth honey colored liquid.

I watched his lovely brown fingers reach for my hands and touch them brotherly. "You need anything? I'm here."

I managed to show teeth, but no smile as I clutched the drink with both hands. For the past year I had learned to handle my liquor well.

Cayenne said, "Call me. I'll check in on you later." He stood, kissed my cheek, finished his coffee, and glared at Mark, who had been doing his own glaring at the photographs. Mark moved closer to me without looking at Cayenne.

"So, you still have this?" He asked me, referring to the picture of our 1998 kiss.

Cayenne sighed and raised his hand to point a finger at Mark. He said, "Look brother, don't go there, now."

They had an understanding the way brothers do on the street when knowing to fight, get schooled, walk away or quiet down.

Mark quieted down and watched Cayenne exit the kitchen confidently. I heard the jingling of Cayenne's keys and then the front door squeak.

Mark asked, "How do you feel?" because he couldn't think of anything else to ask for, I guessed.

My eyes said, *how do you think I feel?* Instead, I said, "Not too good." I finished the whiskey and began working on the cantaloupe. The cotton candy tasted sweeter.

He looked at his watch, and then rubbed his thighs, a habit he rarely noticed about himself.

Mark then pushed my braided hair away from my face. My extensions rested on the middle of my back.

Mark said, "Valerie called me early yesterday. Told me what happened. We thought you were at the hospital with him Christmas Eve, so we wanted to give you some space. Reverend Clarke called Valerie from the hospital yesterday morning around five or six because your line was busy. He and his wife, Winnie, spent Christmas Eve with your Dad. He had asked them to stay. So they stayed all night, along with their two children, Dr. Lateesha and Dr. Lawrence. He died in Winnie's arms as she prayed with him." Mark paused, and then said, "I'm really sorry, Imani."

I refused to cry in front of Mark. "I'm glad Daddy wasn't alone," I whispered, guilty that I was not the one with him.

"Where were you?" Mark asked. Valerie appeared interested also. I saw it in her eyes.

"I was tired, and I wasn't feeling well, "I said curtly.

Mark seemed to smell shit at that moment, and Valerie quickly coughed. Mark leaned closer to me, enough for me to smell the *Allure for Men* cologne I had given him as a birthday present when we were lovers a year ago, and asked, "What's up with the condom over there, and what happened to the side of your face? It's swollen."

I was more concerned with why he was wearing a scent I had given him that I knew Bless didn't like. "Go to hell," I whispered again. I was angry that he still wore that cologne.

Disgust appeared on his face as she said, "You still got issues, I see!"

I whispered, "Fuck you, Mark!"

The shit was gone, but he smelled something else as he continued staring at me. He ran his hand through his hair, a maze of freshly twisted dreadlocks that he referred to as African locks. They resembled tight curls. He wore them short and neat, never letting them grow, unlike Cayenne whose hair was cut so close to his scalp that if formed waves. He glanced at his watch, adjusted his sweatshirt, jeans, and down sports jacket, and then he stared at his designer sneakers and put his hands in the pockets of his jeans. At five feet, eight inches, he was able to look me in the eye easily, since we were almost the same height, only now, I weighed more than I did a year ago.

I avoided his eyes as he lifted his head to stare at me.

He rested the photograph on the coffee table, then he said, "Blue Greene. You better leave that brother alone." I quickly grabbed the photograph along with the others and placed them inside my daily planner, next to my journal.

He whispered, "I gave you more than what that brother could ever give you—but you killed it—and I never put my hands on you. I really am sorry about your father—and I'm sorry—for us. You need anything?"

"No," I lied, holding on to the sweetness he had just given me.

Mark stared at the floor.

I sipped more whiskey. He watched me carefully, then asked, "Since when you start drinkin' whiskey? I could never even get you to sip a Pina Colada!"

"Right after that shower of champagne at your house last year," I told him.

He continued to watch me, then said, "I'm sorry."

I remember the look Bless had on her face on Christmas day, 1998. Hurt. The way a kitten has been hit by a car, but is not hurt enough to die. She could only breathe deeply, and moan, having no tears to wet her face or mouth.

I waited for more of his sweetness, but Mark stared at the radio as we listened to Lenny Kravitz sing, "Black Girl," a song I loved.

I heard Valerie yell from my kitchen window that faced the backyard to Cayenne's window, "Tell Redd we're going to The Flower Blossom. I ain't cookin' a damn thing today!" Valerie came into my living room, crossed her eyes at Mark, then smiled at me. "You hungry, Imani? I saved you a plate: roast duck, stuffing, macaroni and cheese, yams, those French cut string beans you like, and some cornbread, and pecan pie. I even got some Teacola Tea, straight from Eva Creek Island. I remember when you was a little thing and you used to love that with that coconut cake you used to beg your Nana to make you all the time."

"No," I said. "Thanks, but I'm supposed to be starting a diet." I mumbled.

Mark smelled shit again.

I did want some pie, though, and her duck was not to be missed. I rethought my answer and then said, "Well, maybe just a little food, later."

"Oh, won't you stop frontin' girl! Look at me, baby. You see me complaining? I know I look good! Anyway, every man I know loves a little meat on the bone!" She threw a look at Mark. "Even you, Mark, with your skinny ass wife!" She then smiled at me, "I'm bringing you a *big* plate! You missed my Christmas Eve party. I have a gift for you, also. Don't worry about it though. Get some rest, Imani. Come on over soon. Joy got some kind of creative writing project to hand in. And you shouldn't be alone! She sure could get some help with writing it! I'm a math person myself. Can't stand English!"

I smiled.

With an edge of anger, she turned to Mark, "Tell your *wife* I said, happy Kwanzaa. I suppose you'll be in church Sunday?" Mark, who also worked as a youth leader in the church's Youth Ministry smiled. So did Valerie. No real ones, though.

It had been a year since I had been in church, and Sister Greta Johnson, the last person to hear my mother's voice, who was now the director of the Youth Ministry had given up on calling me to come back. She believed in minding her own business.

As all five feet, four inches of Valerie mustered a dignified strut down the hallway for the last time I heard, "Lord, have mercy Jesus." And then the slam of my door. She had never warmed up to Mark, and she hated the way he had treated Bless as well as me in the past. But when she found out that I had had an affair with Mark, she didn't speak to me for a month.

I looked at Mark. "Why are you really here, Mark?" I whispered, wanting him to say, "Because I want to hold you."

He explained, "Valerie's baby, little Mocha, has the flu. Redd asked me if I could stop by to check her out. And we were all worried about you, especially my brother. He has a thing for you. But I'll tell you now, and I'm sure you know he won't have anything to do with you until you get yourself together. Too bad I'm not more like him."

"So, you still make house calls?" I asked, ignoring his sarcasm, knowing that as a pediatrician, he did. But my question had a deeper meaning, and he figured that out immediately.

Mark looked at his watch. He said, "You need to throw that picture of us in the garbage, where it belongs! You really need to do that, you know? I have to go," he said. He walked to the front door.

"Go to hell," I yelled after him. I really wanted to tell him, *Please don't leave me all alone.* Instead, I just smiled fabulously fake. The cotton candy was gone. I sipped whiskey.

Chapter Five

The funeral for my father was held on the day I am named for, the seventh day of Kwanzaa, Imani. The year 2000 arrived quietly in New York.

I hoped 43-year old Reverend Dr. Lance Scott Clarke, the senior pastor of The Jewel Park Temple of Faith Church, would give a compelling eulogy, but he didn't. Sister Greta Johnson, the Youth Ministry director, provoked deep emotions all by herself that filled my soul as I, along with nearly one hundred people, remembered my father, the 52-year old historian, journalist, scholar, and teacher—January 1, 1947 to December 25, 1999. He would have been 53 this day.

As I sat in the congregation listening to the music, I talked to God silently about the photographs on my mind. I had to travel down into the cave of my soul to find where I had placed my father's generous bragging about a book concerning my family that he had died being ashamed of. Since age 12, I have wanted answers.

I learned from my father's research that my ancestors on my mother's tree were Golas from Sierra Leone, West Africa, who migrated from the neighboring country of Liberia. Gullah comes from the word Angola, a country in Africa. Geechee comes from the name of the Ogeechee River in Georgia, where many of my enslaved ancestors settled. Daddy had read a book about Gidzi people in West Africa and thought that that was where the Geechee name originally came from. I am the ninth generation of Golas in my family to live on the clay of America.

My first ancestor to live in America was named Malika. My father was able to trace my first enslaved ancestor back to 1787. I remembered the names my mother always mentioned, but never once elaborated on: Sally Baptiste, Jewel White, and Nana. How can I learn more, God, because this is where my mother stopped?

I had always asked as a child. I stopped asking after age 12 because no one I asked answered me. People went deaf, it seemed. The subject was usually changed with a smile or a frown.

I watched the pastor pray. Dr. Lance, as the congregation affectionately called him, had known my father for at least five years. He was a respected community activist, civil rights attorney, and father of eight children; four were even pastors or played a major role in church leadership; two were doctors; one was in the United States Marines and the other was a teacher.

He had moved to Jewel Park from the Bronx after receiving his doctorate from the Theological Seminary of Scholars in Jewel Park to assist his father with the ministry. His father, Reverend Scott Clarke, Sr., had founded The Temple of Faith Church in 1937 after moving here from Eva Creek Island. My father had told me that my Uncle Saul had worked with Mr. Clarke, Sr., from 1937 to 1944, but Daddy had never explained what Saul did for a living or why he had moved from Eva Creek Island. I gently stroked Valerie's Christmas present, a small diamond cross that hung around my neck. The cross was supported by a delicate gold chain.

Dr. Lance and his wife Winnie had been married for four years. His first wife, Gladys, died of alcoholism, and the four children she had that Winnie now called her own, didn't talk about that. The two doctors, the Marine, and the teacher belonged to Gladys. Winnie's four children, whom she had fostered before marrying Dr. Lance, but had never adopted, managed the church. Winnie was an accountant and had her own business. She and her husband were probably the only people in Jewel Park my father trusted, and Winnie had always been kind to me, often inviting me for Sunday brunch or to neighborhood cafes after I finished work to talk or pray. I had never accepted any of her invitations because the last thing I wanted to do was talk to a foster parent! I had never known Gladys.

Winnie was 35, looked 25, and was elegant, yet hip, and other women loved to look at her husband.

Daddy had stopped going to church regularly nearly fifteen years ago. He read the bible weekly and prayed often, though, usually with a bottle of Mr. Boston Raspberry Brandy mixed in with three or four cups of tea. He also had recently bought a bible written in the Gullah language, but when I looked for it the Monday after his death, I couldn't find it. It consisted of only one testament, The Gospel of Luke.

I asked Winnie to remind people to sign the guest book. She smiled and nodded to let me know that she wouldn't forget as she sat next to me in the sanctuary's front row, near the altar, along with my neighbors. It was strange to me that Jewel Park was founded by and named after my own relatives, and here I was at my father's funeral with no family members to grieve with me.

I glanced toward the back of the church. The lobby's expansive, marble floor was decorated with two mosaic-like quilts with patterns ranging from what resembled a step ladder leading to a cluster of twinkling stars to a labyrinth of colorful designs forming a long river to massive geometric shapes of repetitive circles, triangles, and squares. I remembered my father's drawings in his daily planner and wondered why the church also had the same drawings.

Delicate peach colored walls calmed me. They were covered with signature paintings of African American artists, but one favorite was the works of artist Jacob Lawrence, showcasing several masterpieces from *The Migration Series.*

I was watched carefully as church members warmly greeted me.

I wanted to yell, "To hell with you!"

All these damn people, I thought, and not one of them ever called me to ask how I was feeling.

Dishes that were distinctly mine as well as my father's favorites were being prepared in the church's downstairs restaurant, The Prayerful Café Corner, which was run by Mr. Jacobs on weekends and regularly by his wife Valerie.

The aroma of fried chicken, sweet potatoes, collard greens, corn bread, and coconut cake filled the sanctuary.

I re-read Daddy's love letter to me that I wasn't supposed to find when I was eight. Mama had caught me searching through her dresser drawer for *Chanel No. 5* perfume. It was her favorite and mine also, and I wanted to stare at myself in the mirror as I used my finger tips to gently tap the tip of the bottle, my neck, the back of my ears, and my wrist, just like Mama did. Instead, I found the letter, propped myself up against Mama's bed, and read it quietly with my perfumed hands.

December 25, 1970:
My dearest Jewel, Imani:
Welcome daughter!
You are a medley of beauty
with millions of melodies inside
waiting
Your loving father, always
I love you.
You are a melody of intricate pieces
finer than diamonds or gemstones
gold or silver
sparkling like sunshine
against a rainbow of color
more intense than Ruby,
your precious mother
I am a part of you
We are one
Your loving father, always

This is easy to write
Matthew.
  Mama said nothing and sipped rum with soda and ice. She seemed stunned. I remember the tears flowing down her face as she stood against the bedroom wall and watched me. Just calmness mixed with rum and soda. So, I kept the letter and showed it to Daddy the next day when he came to visit. He only smiled when I asked him if he had written me more. No words. We never discussed it again, me, him or Mama.
  The dance of tears began as I looked at the letter's well-preserved handwriting on stationery paper outlined with a border of roses with my baby picture scotch-taped to it. I gently placed it back into my journal.
  Winnie smiled graciously at her husband, who was standing at the altar preparing to begin the service as he waited for the deacons to finish praying behind him.
  She put her arm around my shoulder. Winnie was not darker than the color of the Caribbean sand that rests on the beaches of Negril. Winnie said, "It's going to be alright, girlfriend!" She patted my shoulder as she adjusted her gray designer suit.
  For almost an hour the mood changed from sad to happy, to blues, to jazz, to pop, and then finally to gospel as a gifted musician played the piano.
  I thought of my very fair-skinned mother whom Winnie reminded me of.
  For the first time since entering the sanctuary, I looked up at my father's rosewood casket. The reddish-brown finish reminded me of him. The velvet interior was a russet color.
  I noticed in the second row right behind me were Valerie and Redd Jacob's family, Cayenne and his girlfriend, Angela Montgomery, his brother Mark, and Mark's wife Bless and their daughter, Malika as well as an assortment of church members, five Jewel Park High School faculty members and community activists, most of whom were running for office sometime soon. Everyone was clap-

ping, dancing, and getting happy in the Holy Spirit. The orchestra advised the violins to take a rest, and the drums partied with the tambourines, horns, electric guitar, piano, and organ.

Blue Greene sat in the fourth row sandwiched between two women about my age, and was nearly blocked by another woman's hat. I couldn't get his attention because one of the women had engaged him in conversation. I did not see his common-law wife, Linda. I searched for her in the rows nearby, but there was no sign of her.

I considered the church too well organized. The Clarke family ran it like a conglomerate, multi-million dollar media organization with 15 ministries.

As the Doves of Glory Trio, an offspring of the church choir, sang an African American Spiritual, Dr. Lance stood at the altar and instructed the congregation to pray.

Dr. Lance began, "Well, beloved children of God, we come here today to comfort our dear brother, Matthew Henderson, on his way to the Kingdom of The Most High, and his wonderful daughter, Sister Imani Jewel. The Holy Spirit has instructed me at this most important hour to open up the sanctuary for Brother Henderson. The Holy Spirit has led me to ask you to turn this meeting into a Holy Ghost prayer meeting for Brother Henderson, and his friends. Turn this meeting to words of love and blessings. Turn this meeting to inspiration and happiness, not sadness. We thank Him. Hallelujah!"

Dr. Lance led the trio, along with Mrs. Johnson, into a chant of hallelujah.

The congregation joined in with the Doves of Glory singers to the impromptu beat of African drums that softened to set the mood for what Nana called a praisemeetin,' rather than a eulogy.

This reminded me of the time when I visited Nana on Eva Creek Island as a child with Mama. We met in a Prayer's House, a square-framed, one-story, brick house with folding chairs inside, an un-cemented floor, no pictures, no altar, and no musical instruments, except for a tambourine. It was next to Nana's house, and it was still preserved from the days of slavery whenever the elders went to what Nana called, a "washup" service.

No one stood up to talk about my father. A hush of soft weeping fell over the congregation instead.

Each time I closed my eyes, I saw pictures of him with me, with Mama, with clients, with students, with colleagues, and with Autumn.

But I never saw history or any of his close friends.

History: family.

The church said, 'Amen."

Two hours passed and the congregation formed a line to view the body. Each person then passed me and touched me gently, quietly whispering prayerful blessings.

I was last to see him. My eyes hurt as I cried quietly over the coffin.

African violets of Bethany, Blackberry Halos, and Bourbon Mists, white roses, and a dozen wreaths decorated in more white roses complemented the sanctuary.

I touched his hands. They were ice, brown, and seemed to have been dipped in chalk dust.

Daddy preferred suits to casual clothing. He was dressed in a navy blue suit and a silk tie the color of Sangria. He wore navy shoes that were well polished. His neat African locks resembled tight curls. The only jewelry he wore was a wedding ring. I looked closer. Why did he have on a wedding ring? It wasn't the ring he wore when he was married to Autumn. His ring at that time was shaped like an Egyptian ankh. Autumn had a matching one, and her tiny ring would never fit Daddy's fingers. And Mama never had a ring because she and my father were never married. The question stayed on my mind. *Why was Daddy wearing a simple gold band—a wedding ring?*

I could not move or let go of his hand.

I promised myself to never let him go, just like I had never let Mama go. I would never let them go. Not until I found them among the roots in my soul, like a daughter should.

Photographs: *His piggyback rides, our trip with Mama to Disney World, my first bottle of perfume, our love of coconut cake, and age 12.*

I did not feel the gentle touching of hands around my waist or my feet moving or the familiar breath of Valerie's laced with the whispers of "Lord have mercy, Jesus," until I was outside in the wind staring at the hearse. Nor did I notice Autumn Brook Taylor, who had dropped the name Henderson immediately when she divorced my father, and added the name Taylor when she married Leroy only a month later. She was across the street in a maroon BMW, glaring right at the hearse. I watched her spit and mouth the word bitch as she sped away.

I had not followed through on my father's wishes to call her. Somehow I had managed to sit down in an accompanying black limousine with gray, tinted windows. Valerie sat next to me holding a cup of water while Redd, her husband, looked out of the car's window.

The long, narrow, charcoal snake moved elegantly past the streets of Jewel Park to the banks of The Knowing River to my family's plot.

Chapter Six

After the funeral, I remained sober as I talked to God silently about questions I'd had all my life. I sipped Teacola Tea Valerie regularly had shipped from Eva Creek Island to the church's restaurant, and I ate sweet potato pie.

Why was Daddy wearing a gold wedding band?
Did anyone ever find the Klansman who murdered Jewel White's children back in 1901?
Why didn't my mother or Nana talk about that?
Why didn't my mother look like Nana?
Why did Autumn and my father get divorced?
Why didn't Autumn and my father have any children?
Where was Autumn from? Why didn't I ever meet any of her relatives either?
Why did my father marry Autumn instead of my mother?
What happened to my family?

Jewel, the middle name my maternal great grandmother gave to all of her children during Reconstruction to identify them if they were ever lost, stolen or illegally sold, was passed down through the generations to a town in upstate New York named Jewel Park and is all I seem to have left.

Whenever I asked Mama about Jewel White, it seemed as though the name Jewel White would get stuck in her throat. Seeing Daddy's phone book and remembering my conversation with Mrs. Hayes left me wanting knowledge as I looked at the guest book from the funeral.

The guest book was filled with the names of only sixteen people that I already knew: four school administrators, eight business people my father knew, and four former students from the Youth Ministry my father had taught history to.

When I was five, Mama told me about Sally Baptiste's "youth ministry." Sally gave us freedom. Her mother, Marie Baptiste had had her at the age of eight, but the birth killed her. Daddy said that her age was probably listed incorrectly because she was so small. He told me that no one believed the story about her age, and that her correct birthday was probably unknown.

Sally escaped by boat to Eva Creek Island, just off the coast of the Georgia mainland in 1858, where the Gullah/Geechee language was fluently spoken. Daddy told me that Gullah/Geechee people live off the coasts of the mainland from South Carolina, to Georgia, to Florida. He also said nearly one thousand islands exist like Eva Creek: Hilton Head, St. Helena, Lady's, Kiowah, Edisto, Sapelo, Daufuskie, Jekyll, and Wadmalow; they are jewels from heaven that the buckrahs want to take over and develop into wealthy real estate ventures. Daddy often said, "Haffuh hol on to we 'own land; haffuh hol on tuh we' own freedom, 'cause de buckrahs can tote it and abuse it forever and then bad mout' we!"

Today in Jewel Park, New York, two rivers, The Knowing, and The Horizon, are still both strong, cultural reflections of Sally's daughter, Jewel, and Jewel's husband, Horizon. Before migrating to Jewel Park, New York, my mother's family lived on Eva Creek Island from 1858 to 1916 with the Creek, Cherokee, and what my father called, "fostered free men and women," because he hated the words, fugitive slaves. The Island, named for an African slave woman who married a Creek chief, embraced the Savannah and Ogeechee Rivers as well as the Okefenoke Swamp with its vast array of wildlife, offered protection during slavery, and up until the Great Migration, provided a good living for my family.

I once visited the Island in 1975 with my mother for a family reunion and for the funeral of my mother's oldest brother, Savior. I also met my aunts Malika, and Sally (who was named after Sally Baptiste), but never Cecilia.

I was only five then, but I remember blue-green grass that smelled like lavender, sage, and myrrh, and the most beautiful quilts I had ever seen of The Milky Way Galaxy and the Eridanus Constellation. I remembered them specifically because Mama reminded me until the day she died about them, usually when she was doing my hair, having lunch with me after a long day of shopping (before the alcohol) or over a breakfast of ham, biscuits with red-eye gravy, and sweet coffee that I learned to drink at age five, after I discovered that I liked coffee more than Teacola Tea because I could put as much sugar in it as I wanted. Just about every house we visited while there had some form of the design of Eridanus on the quilts. Although patterns were distinctly different, the quilts carried the same theme of the galaxy and the Eridanus Constellation, and they kept me warm on a cold summer night.

Why would my father be interested in this?

At that time, my mother explained to me that Nana had told her the Milky Way Galaxy was the world we lived in, and that when our family members were fugitive slaves, they believed The Eridanus Constellation was heaven where a holy river rested that welcomed our family members when they died. But more importantly, The Eridanus Constellation led Sally Baptiste's family to the safety of Eva Creek Island during slavery, and well after that, led Jewel White to Jewel Park, New York. But the mention of Jewel White's name always irritated Mama.

Before Sally Baptiste reached her 90th birthday, she had described to Jewel White, her 78 year old daughter, what today would be called a "near death," experience. While Sally Baptiste lay unconscious in a segregated hospital from a heart attack, God showed her the holy river that resembled a string of jewels and told her that each jewel was infinite, beautiful, pure, and blessed. The river was in heaven where she would be going, but her child Jewel would see it on earth as well. And there would always be angels to help her along her journey. The river protected the family because God had blessed the water for us. Life lived there. She said God told her the river belonged to our family. She said God told her that every family on earth had earth, fire, air, or water that God had specifically blessed them with. Each element contained God's power, and every family in the world had inherited from God one of these precious elements that would bless and protect the family for generations infinitely. But the power had to be revealed to a family member by God. And to have it revealed by God, family members had to have pure, open hearts that would acknowledge God's power. Everyone had the power, but they had to seek it in the mansion of their heart until they found the power themselves.

Before Sally Baptiste died, she regained consciousness to tell her daughter Jewel about a vision that had haunted her even throughout childhood and well into adulthood. Somewhere in her soul she remembered the vision of this holy river, Eridanus, a constellation in the sky. She passed the vision on to Jewel, and Jewel passed it on to Nana. Nana passed it on to my mother Ruby Jewel Weaver. And Mama passed it on to me. As I remember now, where was my mother's quilt? Or Nana's quilt? Did they have more than one? Were they still in our old family home on Eva Creek Island? Did Daddy give Mama's quilt away after she died? Did Daddy have a quilt? Why did people who where not our family members have quilts with The Eridanus Constellation and Milky Way Galaxy sewn on them? Why didn't I have a quilt?

As I got older, I learned from history books that ancient people believed that the constellation, Eridanus, represented the waters of the first civilizations of the world, but that a Greek myth concerning a curious child named Phaeton had made the constellation famous!

So, why did most people on Eva Creek Island have quilts that resembled this holy river? At the time, my five-year old mind had never asked.

When I was eight, Mama explained over sweet coffee and biscuits fresh from her oven that Nana was a holy woman people came to for the laying on of hands. Even Nana's husband, John Weaver sent his patients to her when they wouldn't respond to medication. Wherever sickness rested in a person's body, Nana was called to lay hands on the body. The process of prayer and touch presented a spiritual blessing and healing to anyone who asked for her help. Jewel White and Sally Baptiste were also great believers in the laying on of hands and had each healed people this way.

When I was eight, I visited Nana's house in Bedford-Stuyvesant where she had moved to from Eva Creek Island. It was 1978, and the beautiful home on Stuyvesant Avenue had belonged to a Jewish couple who had sold it to Nana for a bargain back in 1970, the year I was born. I had a horrible cold and fever, and Nana laid hands on me. She gently touched my forehead, chest, and nose. She bathed me in water scented with oils of frankincense and myrrh, all the time praying in a language that I didn't understand then, but know now was Geechee. She took that further and went on into the Christian language of speaking in tongues. She then massaged my body with olive oil infused with lavender, all along praying as she touched each place. Afterwards, she served me a large bowl of gumbo with shrimp, sausage, chicken, and crab legs, which she topped off with a jelly jar filled with Teacola Tea.

As I remember, I never got another cold in my life after that. Not even a sniffle!

I remember Nana telling Mama after my healing that I should have received my "newborn blessing," my "five year old-blessing," and to prepare me for my "thirty-year old blessing." As far back as Sally Baptiste's birth, each child in my family had always received these three blessings. But neither Nana nor Mama ever explained what that meant, because a book my father wrote when I was born kept them from discussing many things about our family with me or with each other. So, why tell me anything at all? I had asked Mama over sweet coffee and sweet potato pie at age eight. She only smiled and told me with her eyes that she loved me.

"Dat a hut tuh Gawd, tuh not ruckuhnize all tree," Nana said in a strong Geechee accent as she watched Mama's eyes talk to me. Nana went further that day as she sat across the table from Mama and me.

Mama then told me, not above a whisper, that Nana also found freedom in the stars, so she made quilts and gave them away as gifts whenever she had a dream about freedom, and she took in children who couldn't be cared for by their own parents and gave them freedom. But that's as far as she would go that day.

I had never met anyone Nana had taken in. Mama mentioned that a baby quilt had been made for her. It was a quilt with a Jewish name that Nana showed me. Nana said that a Jewish woman by the name of Jurnee Miller had given it to her as a gift for my mother when Mama was born. I think Nana must have worked for the woman. Nana forced herself to stop talking to protect any other words from falling from her lips, but Mama seemed as though she had turned eight, right along with me as she waited for more words to fall from Nana's lips.

When Mama was telling me about the quilts in a kitchen scented with gumbo, Nana caught the words that fell out and whispered to me in her Gullah accent, "Dey b'puhwr in wu'ds. B'careful! Puhwr come nuh tote yah tuh de watuh. Lib' b' in de watuh. Dat be puhwr. Dey de blood b'holy ribbuh flectin' life. Creashun come from wu'ds. Creashun create puhwr. Creashun b'lib' in a holy ribbuh." Her large, hazel eyes would open wider, and she would hum softly a fragrant familiar spiritual about the blood of Jesus.

Nana would bless me with the invisible cross she made on my forehead whenever she stood in front of a child, and Mama would smile or frown at her depending on her mood or keep more of Nana's words from kissing me because when she talked like that she frightened us senseless.

Nana had pictures of all of her children. She kept lockets of their pictures. One she wore often was of Uncle Saul and his wife. Nana wore a gold, heart-shaped locket around her neck of a wedding picture of a dark man smiling along with a fair woman with dark hair. Mama told me it was her brother, Nana's son, Saul Weaver and his wife. She always said it like the words His Wife was the woman's name, because that's how Nana said it.

Mama told me that she never got to know her brother well. He died when she was seven. All she would ever say was that he was very nice to her. So when I asked Nana, the way an eight year old would, why she wore that locket more than the others, and why didn't she have one of Aunt Cecelia or Mama, she slapped my face. The silence lasted for the rest of that day. Privately, that night, when I asked Mama the same thing, she told me she didn't know either, and that she'd had her face slapped many times for asking the same thing. So I never asked again. And I never saw that locket.

I remember good food at Nana's house like fat corn cakes and powder soft biscuits with thick maple syrup and red-eye gravy, chicken n' dumplings, sweet potato pone with dark cane sugar, and Mama's coconut bread pudding that Nana teased her about. She said Mama made it the way buckrahs did. If Mama cooked a perfect meal, Nana said, "Dis up tuh de notch."

On Eva Creek Island, I remember Nana teaching me how to weave threads of sweet grass into a basket that I painted lavender and gave to Mama for Mother's Day. Gran'pa John spent an entire weekend trying to show me how to cast a net to catch mullet. When I caught a net-full, he celebrated by teaching me how to clean the fish. To this day, I have trouble eating mullet, although I love them if someone else cooks them.

Middle class and wealthy African American families settled quickly in Jewel Park after 1916 to plant their own seeds. The wealthy lived in Jewel Park's Silver Row. The middleclass lived throughout Jewel Park, and the poor lived on Crescent Boulevard. That's where I had lived with Mama, until her death. After that I lived in foster homes until age 21, and in every borough of New York City.

The people of Jewel Park named schools, businesses, parks, streets, boulevards, roads, and avenues after relatives. Daddy once told me when I was ten, doing a report on Jewel Park's history, that some of the names could be traced back to Sierra Leone, Liberia, Angola, and Native American nations.

Today, Jewel Park is a thriving suburb in upstate New York, and sometimes called a village, but it is still predominantly African American. Like homes in Jewel Park, many businesses had been passed down from one generation to the next after families settled here mainly from Eva Creek Island, and then from other parts of New York and the United States. Jewel Park is never to be confused with Jewel Avenue that runs through Queens or the town of Jewell in upstate New York that rests on the shores of the Oneida Lake, where Native American cemeteries kiss it, as well as Lake Erie, the last stop for fugitive slaves before reaching Canada, as native folks will tell you.

Colorful rows of unattached one-family brownstones lined my block on Dandelion Street. Carefully planted trees and gardens provided the background for brownstone steps and their adjacent windows. On Jacobson Avenue, five blocks from my home, cobblestone streets were filled with African American owned businesses like Janet's Geechee Supermarket, Brown Sugar Bodies, The Flower Blossom Soul Food Diner, and The Caramel Café, still famous for its chicken and waffles and caramel flavored coffee. We didn't have one franchise and we were proud of it.

Teacola Tea and sweet potato pie from Valerie brought the photographs back and took me through a fitful sleep.

Chapter Seven

I ushered Blue into the living room.

He was dressed casually in a sweater I had recently given him for his birthday. He was impeccably groomed with flecks of gray in his hair and a neatly trimmed beard.

I met Blue in graduate school. We were both studying to be teachers. Four years older than me, his interest was teaching music. Mine was English. Like me, he graduated with a masters degree in education, but after a year of teaching, he went back to school for a business degree, got it, and opened up his own nightclub in Jewel Park, The Blue Zephyr "A nightclub serving fine African American cuisine, live music, and a soulful atmosphere."

His ginger kisses from a gingerbread cookie he was still munching on dropped onto my forehead, eyelids, cheeks, and lips before he asked, "You okay?"

My breath, laced with whiskey and peppermint, reached him before my words did, "I'm fine," I said, as I turned from his embrace to walk into the kitchen.

I had two and a half hours to get dressed and be at work.

"Blue, what are you doing here?" I asked. A wave of pain moved from my forehead to the top of my shoulders. I listened for his answer from the kitchen as I got two Advil tablets from the bathroom cabinet, and then returned to the kitchen. I washed the pills down with a glass of water.

"Blue?" I called him again.

His smile was kind. It calmed me as we settled in the kitchen. He reached for my shoulders with his ginger fingers that were sprinkled with cookie crumbs, and then he touched my arms. He pulled me closer to him and seemed to whisper because that's really how he spoke, "You been drinking?"

"I'm fine. I fell asleep right after the funeral, that's all."

"Yeah, with a few drinks, right? Baby, you gotta' cut that shit out! It's..." He looked at a watch I'd given him as a birthday present a year ago; the face was lined in barely visible sapphire gemstones embraced by a silver band, "...only 6:30!"

"I'm fine," I said again.

"No you're not," he said, as he focused his serious dark brown eyes on mine. His barely visible mustache and beard stroked my face the way wind touches a rose in a Southern country garden.

Two years ago, Blue met up with me at Jewel Park High School. It was Career Week, and Blue was one of the guest speakers for the senior classes. We went out for dessert and coffee one evening, and by midnight he had offered me comfort and hands gifted in the art of love.

He placed his coat on a kitchen chair and sat staring at me. He reached for an Earth, Wind and Fire CD that lay on my kitchen table. In the living room, he popped it into the player to drown out the sound of the radio in the bedroom. He then watched me walk into the bedroom to turn off the radio and quickly return to sit at the table with him.

He said, "I'm sorry I wasn't there for you. I am really sorry, Imani. I tried to get to you. I couldn't get to your limo. And when I saw Cayenne and Mark, nosy Valerie...well, you know, I don't like them, and they don't like me. Why didn't you call on my cell when you got the news? I found out about your father from Valerie. And that's only because I saw her in church that Sunday. I tried to call you, but you wouldn't answer your phone. I stopped by several times. You wouldn't answer the door." Blue glanced at my blinking answering machine messages and sighed.

"I know. And I appreciate your concern, Blue," I said.

When we were in graduate school back then, we became more than good friends, even though I was dating several men, and he was living with Linda Cree, who, after all these years, is still his common-law wife. His brothers, Rayne and Niger, manage Blue's club, while Linda runs the accounting department.

We were supplements to each other. He replaced my loneliness with fine cuisine, planetariums, street cafes, bookstores with intoxicating coffee, Broadway shows, and autumn nights filled with hot chocolate, cotton sheets, and warm blankets.

I eased his stressful business deals with hot oil massages, ardent ambrosia with chocolate dipped strawberries, matching lingerie that showed off thighs he thought were pretty, and summer nights on the beach because they were convenient and did not include major holidays.

Now I wanted to remind him about our deficiencies, specifically, the woman he was living with.

I had seen her several times, especially at The Blue Zephyr. She was a pretty, dark woman with big eyes and a cute shape. She dressed well, had a good personality, and was an easy going, smart 25 year old who owned a brownstone, but rented it to four tenants while she lived with Blue.

When she found out that Blue was seeing me, she actually put her hands in my face and laughed. "You really think my man is going to leave me for *you*?" She laughed some more and went to sit down right next to me. I didn't want to fight, and I wondered often if she, too, used concealer to hide any of Blue's handprints.

She blew cigarette smoke my way and sipped a Slow Gin Fizz. Of course, I stopped going to the club regularly, but whenever I saw her, she had a smirk when she looked my way. From then on, I invested a lot of time into proving her wrong, hoping I would get the last laugh!

"Why don't you take the day, Sweet? Don't you have some days?"

"I have to go to work, Blue. It'll take my mind off of..."

He interrupted with soft words, "Off of what? That your father died on your birthday? That your grandmother died a day before your birthday when you were only eleven? That your mother killed herself that day before your birthday? That your father's ex-wife wanted to kill you the day your mother died? And you don't even know why. That it was Christmas Eve each time? Now your father! Imani, you got to face this, somehow. You can't keep running from it! Sometimes I think your family was cursed or something! I have never known anyone to have so many close people die around their birthday or a holiday! Damn, baby!"

"So, when did you become a therapist? I didn't know you had a degree in psychology!" I said, thankful that the ibuprofen was taking effect.

"Sweet, all I'm saying is you need some rest. I watched you at the funeral. Pretending shit ain't there don't make it go away!"

"Thank you, doctor. But I have to get dressed. Have some coffee! I'll make you some."

"Seems to me like you need it more than I do!" He said.

I breathed deeply.

"So, what are you doing up so early, Blue?"

"You forgot?"

"Forgot what, Blue?"

"I'm off today, Sweet."

"So, what the hell are you doing up so early? And stop calling me Sweet. I told you I don't like it!" I had acquired the name from him because during our coffee house meetings, to him, I enjoyed having coffee with my sugar.

"Look, I have a meeting at ten. I'm starting an Open Mic Night for poets down at the club. I'm holding auditions today for the first set for next month. I just stopped by to check on you and see if you wanted to join me for breakfast or just talk. I didn't think you'd be going to work!"

The Blue Zephyr was a house his parents had passed on to him when he was only 18, because they wanted to teach him responsibility. Blue also owned the family brownstone next door to it that he shared with Linda.

Blue, as well as his two older brothers, Rayne and Niger, ran The Blue Zephyr like a first class business.

He actually started The Blue Zephyr in his basement by renting it out for parties, poetry evenings, and bohemian wedding receptions, while his parents moved into a condominium in Silver Row where they continued their lucrative real estate business. In my last year of foster care, at the invitation of his sister June, who was a student in my graduate class and a good friend, I attended a party in the brownstone basement that Blue's family owned.

"So, where's your wife?"

Blue smiled. "At her office," he said.

"Her firm handles most of the accounting in Jewel Park now, thanks to her father, right?" I asked.

"Yeah, Cree Associates. They're the best. She's even been doing some business with Dr. Lance's wife, Winnie," he told me. Linda had recently taken the position of vice president, the youngest accountant ever in the firm's history.

"So why are you living with someone who's not even your wife, that you cheat on, after all these years?"

"Oh, come on, Sweet. Who's being the therapist now? We've been over this so many times. You know the answer to that already. Either you want to keep seeing me or you don't. Tell me now," he whispered.

"Answer my question." I said.

"You know how complicated it is."

"How? It's your house, not hers. You don't have any children. You don't even go out together. What's complicated?"

"So, you got a lot of paperwork, I see," Blue said, as he looked at the pile of folders in the bag I'd packed for school.

"Yes," I said. "I hate when you do this. You didn't answer my questions."

"Oh, come on, you can't be serious! Don't you have three days for grieving, at least?"

"I'm tired of grieving. I just want to get back to work."

He glanced at his watch. "Well, you can still join me for breakfast. I'll give you a ride."

"No, not today. I just don't feel up to it. But I could use a ride to work, okay?" I had to say it a second time.

"Yeah, it's okay, Imani." He painted a kiss on my lips with his fingers. "Sweet, you don't look too good. You sure you okay?"

"Look, I'm okay. I'm just tired. I went to bed late."

"Why are you drinking at 6:30 in the morning? What's that all about?"

"Look Blue, what I do is my business. I don't have to explain a thing to you. So would you please move out of the damn way, and let me get dressed!"

"Fine!" He walked closer to me, and whispered. "You have a problem. And it's not going to disappear. Didn't your mother drink? It killed her, didn't it? Sometimes, you are such a stupid bitch!"

I avoided his eyes, and could not slap him, so I pretended not to hear him. I learned that when you touch a scar gently, it doesn't really hurt.

"Have some breakfast, Blue. I'll be back."

"What you got in here to eat, Imani?"

"Everything," I told him. "Help yourself."

"Okay," Blue said, as he came after me, wrapped his arms around my waist, and kissed me on the back of my neck.

"See you in an hour," I told him as I pulled away from him and watched him walk to the kitchen.

He made coffee, and searched inside the refrigerator until he found sweet potato pie to fulfill the hunger in his six feet, two-inch frame.

I headed down the hallway to the bathroom for a shower.

Tears. I didn't even know why I was crying. "Damn it! Girl, get yourself together," I mumbled several times until I heard Blue raise his voice slightly to ask, "What did you say, Sweet?"

"Nothing," I yelled.

Chapter Eight

Jewel Park High School, a huge geometric circle, was covered in neat graffiti drawings of children in a playground having fun.

I hauled my bag of books, paper, my daily planner, journal and folders over my shoulder as I painted a kiss with my fingers across Blue's lips and closed the door to his blue-green Honda, still hung up on our deficiencies.

Space Goddess One was seated at her desk waiting for her next coffee break. The switchboard lights were busily blinking as I passed her in the main office. Ella Samuels was finishing the first bite of her bacon, egg, and cheese on a buttered roll as I said good morning to her. She gave me the "Shit on you," look and took a sip of her coffee. As the school receptionist, Ella spent most of her time telling people to kiss her 62-year old ass.

Occasionally, a call did get through, especially if they wanted to speak to the principal, Mr. Eldridge Dennison, a 50-year old, handsome black man who didn't take shit from anyone. Like any great corporation, it was wise to learn the culture! You did well at Jewel Park High School, affectionately called, "The Jewel," if you were a fast learner.

Doo Doo Breath said good morning to me. I inhaled the smell of rotten eggs as I said, "Good morning, Mr. Barnes." Peter was the assistant principal for the English Department and my immediate supervisor.

I moved my time card and returned it to the IN slot to indicate I was present. He did the same. More bad air hit my face as I tried to hold my breath and not eat his words as he said, "Imani, I heard about what happened to your father. I'm sorry."

"Thank you, Mr. Barnes," I said, turning my head to get some fresh air as I walked to the elevators with him. I was very happy to be appointed and tenured after ten years of teaching because this kept him away from me! Mr. Barnes and I got off at the fifth floor. He went to his office. I went to my classroom which I made sure was on the opposite side of the English office.

I took a deep breath. I reached for my cell phone because this was usually the time I called Blue.

I kept wiping the tears away as I checked homework, and I didn't notice Bless Brown watching through the door's glass partition.

Bless and I were finished, but I still hoped we could remain civil to each other. She opened the locked door with her master key. Every staff member at Jewel Park High School had one.

The sight of her forced me to create a fabulously fake smile. The water in my eyes disappeared as I greeted her with a pleasant, "Hello, Bless." But as I looked at her, I thought of her husband, Mark Brown.

Mark was always there on late nights. Sometimes Bless stayed later at most functions and often ordered Mark to see that I got home safely. I always did. Those nights, my love life triggered a lot of interest from him because I never seemed to have a serious relationship that lasted more than a few weeks.

Our first kiss began in his car. The fourth one led to the comfort of my bed after Thanksgiving 1998, when another order came from Bless for Mark to see that I got home safely.

We lived fifteen minutes by car away from each other in Jewel Park, but it took Mark three hours to get home that night. I never knew which fabulous fake he told Bless, but after that we saw each other once a week, usually after midnight, when his medical rounds as a pediatrician ended at the Jewel Park Medical Center, until the night I received the shower of champagne.

Mark had made it clear on the night of my birthday last year that it was over. The sting of his words, "I will never be all that you need. Not even your father could do that!" scarred me.

I had slapped him and pushed those words into the cave in my soul to live with the darkness. Whenever they surfaced I took to following him after I finished work. He got a restraining order to keep me away from him. Fear of becoming my mother forced me to stay away.

A few days after the Thanksgiving holiday of this year, Mark began speaking, using small words, then sentences, and sometimes a paragraph. He was no longer bitter, only cautious. Bless had stopped speaking to me a week after the shower of champagne she gave me. I had lost my sister/friend that I had known since age 14. Now, it was difficult to avoid her because we were both English teachers who worked in the same English department at "The Jewel."

"Why?" She had asked after viewing a picture of a passionate kiss between her husband and me that her eight year old daughter had innocently taken in 1998 that Christmas Eve. Bless had slapped me to her living room floor during a birthday party she had planned especially for me. A second time she asked, "Why?" as I threw my empty glass against her living room wall, barely missing a guest. Mark had given her a beautiful girl. Mark had filled the hole that had been left open when she became a foster child. Mark had given her a beautiful four-story brownstone, status, and his name, which sounded much better than Bless McCourt. She became Bless Brown just for Mark. And one passionate kiss with secrets behind it had taken all of that away.

Now, a year later, I did not know the answer. We had been foster sisters, had shared the same weight, clothes, styles, and jobs, we had been best friends until the champagne. And she still wanted me dead!

The sisterhood was now officially over. Bless shrunk from a size 18 to 12. I went from a size 16 to 20. Bless got rid of the perm and donned soft brown African locks to match the color of her skin. I got rid of a Gheri curl, and returned to wearing other people's hair. Bless began taking a serious interest in self-help books and bitterness. I began taking a serious interest in Early Times Old Style Kentucky Whiskey. I guess that's why I tolerated the gentle kisses mixed with backhand slaps so well with Blue Greene.

Bless' marriage remained more successful than ever.

Bless' voice brought me back from a far away place.

She was curt. "Imani, I have the final exam schedule. Here is a copy of it. Please add whatever comments you would like included in the exam, and put it in my box. I'll be typing the exam for the English 2 classes. Mr. Barnes would like the exam typed by the end of the week. Therefore, I need your comments by the end of the day. Thank you."

I kept smiling because she moved so quickly that I didn't have time to respond to her coldness, her remarks or the very stylish suit with matching, high heel boots she wore. I had to get up from my desk to take the papers from her because she wouldn't enter the room. She had said few words to me during the past year.

"Damn!" I said, as she walked quickly down the hall.

She twirled toward me like a dancer. "Excuse me?" She said. Then, "I see you've been talking to Cayenne and Valerie. They keep calling us a family. They keep calling my house talking some shit about how you need to be consoled! How we need to become *friends* again! Fuck you! I'm glad your father died! He was a sneaky bastard! And you take right after him!" Bless' laughter filled the hallway. Then she said, in a much calmer voice, "Stay the fuck away from me, bitch!"

Holding back tears, I whispered, "We have to talk, Bless. This has to stop. I just want to talk. Please! I made a mistake. I'm sorry. We never got a chance to talk about this. My father is gone. You still have Mark. Damn it! I never got a chance to explain. It's been a year, Bless. Shit!"

She walked toward me and entered my room again, slamming the door. I felt her breath touch my face. "The picture is still clear in my mind, bitch! I see that shit every day in my mind. Your lips on my man's! You fucked my husband! Not once. Not twice. I don't even know how many times. How could you do that?" She moved closer and grabbed me with one hand around my throat. She talked slowly, "If I could kill you, I'd do it! I hate you!" She spit in my face.

The fight was on.

I grabbed her arm and slammed her head against the chalkboard. She kicked me in my stomach and got a good handful of my hair. She yanked as hard as she could, and I fell to the floor, in time to look up to see a chair headed toward me. I rolled under my desk as the chair crashed into the wall. I rolled from my desk to a nearby wall, and Bless kicked me in my stomach. My head throbbed, and I felt nauseous as pain slowly touched every part of my body.

At this time, two security officers that neither of us had noticed were in the room. Each guard held on to a part of us as a crowd watched through the window. I lay on the floor with a rip in my blood-stained blouse where one of Bless' sharp two-inch heels had left a mark on my left side. She regained her composure, and I sat down at my desk to fix my clothes. She raised her right manicured hand and straightened her middle finger as though it was an exclamation point that shouted at me. She continued her dance as the sound of her high-heeled boots echoed down the hall past the silent crowd. A security guard trailed behind her. I watched her hand descend on her hips as she finished her pivot and continued toward her classroom, which was on the other side of the building.

Chapter Nine

Advil became a good friend as I listened to Principal Dennison. Bless sat across from me at the other end of the oblong conference table in his office. Two security officers, Larry Smith and Octane Johnson, stood by staring out of the window.

Mr. Dennison spoke first. "What the hell is wrong with you two assholes? It's nine-thirty in the fucking morning and I have to deal with this shit! Two of my best teachers! Beating the hell out of each other? Now I have to report this shit to the Board? Somebody, tell me, what the hell is going on?"

We both remained silent.

"So, we got Dumb and Deaf here today?" Mr. Dennison asked as Bless and I watched him take turns glaring at us. I could see Larry Smith smiling as he stared out of the window. His phone number was still in my coat pocket from before the Christmas break. He had called almost everyday, even after my father's death, but I had not returned his calls. He was definitely the wrong person to be in the room with us!

"Okay, this here is what I'm going to do. I want a report on my desk by the end of the day explaining what happened. I don't want either one of you back in the classroom or in this building until this shit is straightened out! I got two computers right over here. Bless, you can use that one! Imani, you use that one. Type the shit! Put it on my desk by three today. I can't stand the superintendent and bad press. A copy will be in each of your files tomorrow morning with my recommendations. If anyone of you files a grievance with the U.F.T. rep—who's on his way down here—I don't know where the hell he is—but, there'll be a hearing. You want that Deaf and Dumb?"

"I spoke, "Due to my father's death, Mr. Dennison, I really don't want to go through a hearing. I would like to settle this today. I enjoy my work here a lot."

"Really? Mrs. Brown? Whatchu' want?"

"Mr. Dennison, with all due respect, sir, this personal situation between Imani and my husband has really affected me over the past year. I like my job here. I feel she should transfer. She caused serious problems in my marriage. Seeing her everyday is a problem."

"Then, why don't you transfer, Mrs. Brown?"

"Me? For what? I didn't do anything."

"Witnesses tell me that you attacked Ms. Henderson by grabbing her by the damn throat! These two officers saw you. You spit in her face. Now, I'm not taking sides, but *you* started this shit today?"

"You know what, just forget it. I'll leave. I'll get my shit today. My husband is a doctor. He takes good care of me. Since the bitch is screwing half the school anyway, probably you too, Mr. Dennison, I'll leave! Fuck you all." Bless gathered her Fendi handbag and left, slamming the door behind her.

"Cool with me. Shit!" Mr. Dennison said. He buzzed his secretary, Alicia Honey, and continued talking, "Honey, in about five minutes, step in here. I need you to take a letter. It's for the superintendent's office." Mrs. Honey peeped into the office and smiled.

"Whatchu' smiling for? Damn! Did anybody like that bitch?" Mr. Dennison asked after Bless slammed the door to the main entrance of Mr. Dennison's office. Everyone remained silent. He continued, "Ms. Henderson, I'm real sorry about your father's death. You need to get your shit together, though. You a good woman, done a lot of good things here and in the Jewel Park community, but you got to get a grip on your private life. Stop bringing the shit to work. We all got shit to deal with. But you can't bring the shit to work! Type the report. I'll put it in your file. Talk to the U.F.T. rep! I don't want to deal with this shit anymore! Take the rest of the day. I'll get the word from the superintendent and the rep, and turn you on to it tomorrow with a call. By the way, thanks a lot for that letterhead! It's a nice color for my office. My secretary thanks you as well. Too bad, about your Pops. Look, come back on Monday, Imani. I'll deal with Bless. She's one angry woman! Personally, she's been like that long before this thing with you and her husband. Get some rest, understand?"

"Yes sir, thank you." I said.

After I typed my report detailing the events of the morning, I gave it to Mr. Dennison's secretary. Larry Smith escorted me to my classroom to gather my items and go home.

Larry moved so close to me I could smell spearmint. "Imani, you still ain't give me no answer about dinner. You know, maybe some dessert? I'm still waitin'!"

"Mr. Smith, this is not the time or the place," I whispered, trying to sound as professional as possible as I placed papers from my desk into my bag. I remembered how I felt when I went out with him on my birthday three years ago. He had invited me out, but I ended up paying the bill at a very fine restaurant. But that wasn't enough for me. I then slept with him that night.

The last time I had gone out with him had been the first week in December, to the B.B. King Bar and Grill Nightclub in Manhattan. I paid for dinner that night too. But we did not have sex for dessert. Blue was what I craved now.

I found Larry Smith cute, but tacky. I didn't like him that much, from his dirty fingernails right up to his funky armpits. But he had a nice body.

As I exited the very quiet building at only ten in the morning, Larry turned to me and winked, then whispered, "Don't forget my request, Ms. Henderson."

Chapter Ten

Photograph: *Age 5, I was running away from Mama. She had the straightening comb. She wanted to do my hair. The hair gel wasn't working because of the humidity. I had what she called, "The frizzies." I was under her bed hiding. She saw my foot. She dragged me from the bed across the floor with her 135-pound body.*

She had the ironing cord, which she had taken the time to cut from an old iron. The cord was blue. She slapped my behind. I was stunned. She then sat on me. She put my hands behind my back and tied Daddy's belt around them. She tied my feet together. She taught me not to yell. If I screamed, she slapped me again.

Mama dragged me to the kitchen chair for the second time in my life where I remained for four hours, tied up with the ironing cord and Daddy's belt. I wanted a Gheri curl, but didn't get one. She heated the iron comb on the stove. The green Dax pomade was on the kitchen counter next to two towels, a comb, scissors, a bottle of olive oil, essential oils of lavender, ylang ylang, and rosewood, and two-dozen pink, medium-sized, foam curlers. It was a Saturday, and I was going to church Sunday. I had to look pretty. No Gullah/Geechee words!

Mama put on music, B.B. King's, "How Blue Can You Get?" as she sipped whiskey from an orange juice glass. I remember the apartment we lived in on Crescent Boulevard being cold, although we had heat, and the landlord was Greta Johnson. We lived in her brick house. At the time, I resented that Daddy lived in a beautiful brownstone with another woman while we lived in a two-bedroom apartment on the other side of town in a less than beautiful place.

Mama oiled my scalp carefully with olive oil, slid Dax on the ends, and whispered, "I love you, baby. I don't want those people thinking I don't take good care of you! And I don't want you to ever speak that Geechee talk like your Daddy. When I was your age I spoke it, and people made fun of me when I left Eva Creek Island. They said I sounded ignorant. Well, I don't want anyone to ever call my baby ignorant! Your Daddy speaks it to show people that it's a language that you should be proud of and our heritage. But all people do is look at him like he's crazy and then make him say the whole thing over in English! I stopped speaking that way the day you were born. You don't come from ignorant people, remember that!" She sipped whiskey. I hunched up my shoulders because I heard the iron comb being lifted from the hot burner on the stove. It sizzled when it fried my hair. I didn't move until Mama said so. After four hours, she untied the blue ironing cord and Daddy's belt, and promised never to use it again.

And she didn't. She never pressed my hair again. She had been so drunk. But deep inside her soul, I think she felt bad about what she did. She learned to create box braids scented with olive oil and essential oils of my choice. My hair became soft and grew past my shoulders like hers, as she dressed it in colorful ribbons or barrettes. But I hid it in extensions after she died. And Daddy had hidden his language way before he died. Now I craved Gullah/Geechee words and my own box braids dancing freely with a soft breeze.

The doorbell rang. I heard Daddy's voice.

"Daddy?" I whispered.

The phone was ringing, not the doorbell.

Fear.

Music. It was on the radio.

The announcer recited the temperature and time while the music was playing, "How blue Can You Get?" by B.B. King. It was 6:30 A.M.

I breathed deeply. I pulled myself together by the third ring and tried to push the memories of quilts, gumbo, sweet coffee, the last time Mama did my hair, and Gullah/Geechee words away from my mind.

I smelled lavender.

I slowly reached for the phone by my bed.

"Hello," I said.

Nothing.

"Hello," I repeated.

Nothing.

"Hello."

The doorbell was ringing.

"Damn it, girl, you've got to get yourself together!" I mumbled my affirmation as I rushed into the bathroom to rinse my mouth with mouthwash, and I realized the smell of lavender came from my own braids, hidden by extensions. The doorbell rang again.

I had stayed up until two in the morning avoiding the phone and doorbell watching television until my headache left. I had fifteen messages on my answering machine, and I hadn't read my email since my father's death. After the tea, I had resorted to the assistance of Jack Daniel's, which was not as good as my favorite whiskey. I hadn't been to the store in a week.

"Just a minute," I said as I reached for my slippers and robe. I dragged myself from the bedroom's small bathroom to answer the door with the scents of peppermint and lavender.

"Blue!" I said, as I opened the door and felt ice on my face as I remembered his words, particularly, stupid and bitch. But he had a dozen roses, Richart Chocolates, and food.

"You and Bless had it out, huh?" He wore designer jeans and a tee shirt.

"How did you find out? I've only been home for about three or four hours."

"Nosy-ass Valerie! Bless called her. They're over at the church. I stopped by the café to get some chicken and waffles for us. How could you get into a fight with her, Imani?"

"She spit in my face and grabbed me by the neck!"

""Damn!" Blue hugged me and kissed my neck. "Are you hungry?" He asked.

"Yes," I said, as he continued kissing my neck. His lips traveled to my breasts and his hands massaged the black and blue mark where Bless had kicked me.

"Damn, baby!" He said feeling the bruise. He kissed that too, as he unbuttoned my bathrobe and massaged my body with his tongue. "I love that body butter, baby. It's delicious. You taste like chocolate," he said. I let him taste my thighs, and waited for him to taste more, but the doorbell rang.

"Damn!" he said. I dragged myself from the couch and put my bathrobe back on to answer the door. Cayenne and Valerie were standing there smiling, but each smile faded when they saw Blue enter the hallway from the living room.

"What's up, brother?" Blue asked Cayenne as he smiled at Valerie.

Avoiding Blue completely, Cayenne smiled at me. "Hey, Jewel, how you feel?"

"I'm fine," I told him.

Valerie walked in with another piece of pie. I smiled.

"Yes, you are. That's a pretty robe, Jewel. I like that!" Cayenne said.

"I bought it for her," Blue said, quietly. "It's silk."

"I heard about you and Bless," Cayenne said. "I'm going to meet a client, Jewel. I'll talk to you later, alright?"

"Okay, Cayenne. Later then," I told him as he hugged me. I watched him walk across the street to his car and drive away.

"We're busy right now, Valerie. What's the matter?" Blue asked, staring at the window, avoiding Valerie's gaze.

"The last time I checked, I didn't recall seeing your name on the front door or anywhere else in this house," Valerie told him.

"It doesn't matter. We're busy. What do you want?" Blue asked, looking out of the window.

"Valerie," I said, "Maybe we can talk tomorrow over coffee. I really enjoyed the tea and sweet potato pie. It was delicious. But, we'll get a chance to talk. Bless quit. I didn't. But, everything is going to be alright. I'm not filing a grievance; somehow, everything will be okay."

"Okay, girl," Valerie said, as she glared at Blue for a second, and then ran her fingers through my box braids. She hugged me and said, "If you need anything, like the police, just call." She whispered, but said the word, police, loudly.

Valerie and I shared a smile. "I will, Valerie. Thanks."

I watched her enter her home through the basement where soft jazz could be heard. I ignored the feeling of uneasiness creeping into my stomach as I tasted dark chocolate filled with the flavor of coffee liquor.

"Now, where were we?" Blue asked, as he loosened the belt to my bathrobe and slipped his warm fingers between my thighs.

As the chocolate melted on my tongue, I told him, "Right there."

Chapter Eleven

Brown Sugar Bodies was having a sale. The thirty-minute walk home from Jewel Park High School in the afternoon's cold, cloudy weather helped me to think. I had walked around all day with dark circles under my eyes from lack of sleep, peppermint breath, violet eye shadow on one eyelid, no lipstick, blush or foundation, and a one-inch run in my pantyhose; yet no one except an annoying student had noticed. I just wanted to go home, have a drink, put on some beautiful music by the gifted musician, Maxwell whom I adored, and get under the covers alone.

Larry Smith, the security officer at the school had left his home phone number, instead of the one on his cell phone, on a piece of paper in my mailbox. I felt the paper as I put my hands in my coat pocket. I crumbled the paper with my fingers as I walked past the building's main entrance looking for a garbage can that I didn't find, so I placed the crumpled paper back into my coat pocket.

I took the exit on the left side of the school that led to Jacobs Street and Robinson Boulevard. Robinson Boulevard intersected Dandelion Street and created a clear path home through the downtown area of shops, cafes, and businesses. I passed several of the homes on Benjamin Row, eight blocks from my middleclass neighborhood.

The brownstone steps had been rebuilt to sit on the side of the building of Brown Sugar Bodies to make room for a charming cinnamon brown porch. The porch wore two elegant quilts draped across it that were dancing in the wind. They were just like the ones I had seen on Eva Creek Island when I was five. I had been born in Jewel Park, New York, but like most people I knew, no one seemed to care much about them, or even the stories that went along with them.

I took a deep breath and collected my thoughts of the memory of them as I now took some time and studied their designs. One was consumed by The Milky Way Galaxy surrounded by glittering stars against a background of navy blue, with colors of the rainbow. The other had an outline of Eridanus, a constellation of stars that resembled a very long, winding river. This quilt was trimmed in earth colors of brown, green, and blue ranging from light to dark copies of these colors.

I had seen quilts like this in Nana's house in a wide range of designs when I visited Eva Creek Island for my Uncle Savior's funeral when I was five and at her brownstone home in Bedford-Stuyvesant when I was eight. I had come across information about quilts when I was in college doing research about the Underground Railroad.

Nana's quilts were similar in style to these, with the same galaxy and constellation, but they had different patterns and colors. It was as if someone had decided to make only one type of quilt, which I always thought was impossible. Nana's quilts were old and frayed, and their sole purpose was to keep us warm, not become historical artifacts. How did Ms. Melinda get these? I wondered. How did the church get them? Were they donated? Did someone buy them? Were they just collector's items?

"Hello, Ms. Melinda," I said as I entered the heavily perfumed shop. It smelled of vanilla and cinnamon.

"Hey, girl! Nice to see you."

"Nice to see you too, Ms. Melinda. How's your family? I asked.

"Very well, thank you."

"I saw you at the funeral. Ms. Melinda. Thank you for coming."

"Was a lovely way you sent him off. Lovely! Any of his other family come?"

"Other family?" I asked, as I went through the shop with a white basket selecting items I wanted to buy. The shop was not crowded due to the Christmas holiday being over and the late afternoon time. Mrs. Benson was known to the neighborhood as Ms. Melinda. She was 62, but you really couldn't tell, unless she told you. I remember a recent holiday tourist guessing her age to be about 48! She was flattered, but thought the tourist had gone too far. She had not one pimple, wrinkle or scar. She attributed her good looks and health to an organic diet of fruits, vegetables, and fish. In a feisty, unapologetic way, she joked that the only meat she had ever tasted had been her husband's. The first time I heard her say that, her great grandson, Ralph Jr., had to pick me up off the floor.

She was born in Harlem. Her husband had been born in Jewel Park, and when he passed on, she sold the real estate business and moved to Jewel Park to open an "aromatherapy salon" as she called it, "where African American folks could beautify their minds, spirits, and bodies." That was thirty years ago according to my father who had visited the shop only once, but knew the Benson family from writing business articles about them.

I don't remember my father ever buying anything from her shop, but I never heard her say anything bad about him. He liked to buy his oils of frankincense, myrrh, and the spicier ones from the brothers on the streets of Harlem. He called Ms. Melinda crazy because he felt her prices were "Ridick'lus!" I agreed. But it had been a long time since I had bought a lot of things from her shop. I loved to browse, and every now and then purchase lip balm or a bar of soap, but I wasn't a frequent customer.

"My family?" I asked her again.

"Why, yes. I believe so. I saw Mrs. Henderson. I apologize. Meant to say, Mrs. Taylor. She's Mrs. Taylor now. Been that for a while.

And I saw your father's brother, whose name I forget. But handsome as the devil!"

"My father's brother?" I asked.

"Of course, love. He was at the funeral. Didn't you see him, a tall, gorgeous man, about seven years younger than your father? You didn't see him?"

I couldn't speak. I smiled instead.

Ms. Melinda continued, "Well, at least I think that was your father's brother. He from South Carolina or so. They were all together, Mrs. Taylor, that fine young fella' she marry, Leroy, and your father's brother. Met that fine thing, years ago, in a Harlem nightclub! Was way too young for me, though, but hell, nowadays people don't even bat an eye when they see a fine young thing with a older woman! Hell, I would've went after him if I wasn't married, happily, I might add! You didn't see Mrs. Taylor at the funeral? Had on a fine fur!"

"Yes, Ms. Melinda. I did see her at the funeral. I didn't see my uncle, though. Did you say other family?"

"Why yes. Oh, well, I mean Mrs. Taylor. I just reckon he had other family, so as you not all alone. No child need to be alone in the world! I know you not no child, but you know what I mean."

"Yes, Ms. Melinda, I understand. You know, this may be surprising to you, but I didn't know that my father had any brothers or sisters."

"Well, my Lord! How could you not know that, child?" Ms. Melinda asked.

Her question left me wondering what else she knew about me, even though I didn't know her that well.

I smiled again as I watched Ms. Melinda stare at me as if I had two heads. She gave me the impression that she believed that I knew my family well. To avoid being turned into a Martian by her gaze, I let her believe that I did.

Ms. Melinda continued, "Mrs. Taylor lookin' mighty good these days. Said she saw you. Spoke to her just the other day. Came in here for some rose water, lavender oil, and some brown sugar rub. Said she needed something soothing."

"She came here?"

"Yep. Seemed to be in a hurry. Still got that loud maroon BMW. Mercy, Lord! Her nice looking, young fella' were with her. Believe it were Leroy Taylor, that boy she marry after she up and left your father. Leroy Taylor father own all them supermarkets down South in Georgia and South Carolina, Taylor Associates, I believe. Matter of fact, they just opened one up here in Jewel Park two weeks ago. Store got more collard greens and chicken than I seen in a lifetime. Got chittlin's too! Lots! The Taylor family so rich, they palms never itch! Ain't that a prune to capture? The other fella look just like your father. Well no need to ponder the thought. Autumn said she were going to stop by to see you again, though."

"Really?" I asked. I had never met Leroy Taylor, but I knew that he was much younger than my father. I had no idea who she was talking about concerning the "Tall, gorgeous man." I had no idea Leroy's family owned a chain of supermarkets or were even that well off. First there was the divorce from Daddy, and then Leroy just seemed to appear on Autumn's arm. I had never seen any relatives from Daddy's family. Daddy seemed to have a dislike for Leroy the same way Autumn had a dislike for Mama. Just the mention of Leroy's name would make Daddy put you out of his house for the evening. I guess seeing Autumn with a younger man hurt Daddy's ego!

"Yep. You ain't seen her?" Miss Melinda asked.

"No, Ma'am. Not since the funeral," I told her. I didn't even know if Autumn was still teaching math. Did she still live near Starrett City in a condominium in Brooklyn? What did she want? I wondered. All I could think of was Autumn's anger at me for not calling her to tell her about Daddy's passing.

"Well, how you holdin' up these days, Imani?"

"Just fine, thank you."

"That's good to hear. Ain't seen you in months. About five, I recall! You seem to show up when I ain't here, girl! You put on some weight too. You goin' way out in Manhattan to shop like your father did? Well, now! Well, I got everything they got, and then some!" She laughed loudly, and went on, "What can I do for you today, love?"

I bought some Chamomile Ginger soap for Valerie, a large bottle of Clove Love Foot Lotion for Cayenne, and Ylang Ylang Hair Oil for myself. I knew that Valerie's daughter loved the lip gloss Brown Sugar Bodies sold, so I bought some for her also.

Ms. Melinda quickly tapped the computerized cash register with her brown fingers as I took each item from my basket and placed it onto the counter.

"Anything else, love?"

"No, Ma'am."

"That'll be $72.50," she said as her son Oscar Benson, the third, who had been in the stock room came out to pack my items in a brown shopping bag with the logo of a gingerbread girl holding a basket of lavender flowers painted on it. Oscar smiled hello as I adjusted my eyes to the cash register's total and slowly counted the cash I didn't want to pay. His son Ralph peeped out of the stock room and waved my way. I waved back at both of them.

"Thank you, Ma'am. Have a nice evening," I said, as I paid Ms. Melinda.

"You too, love. I'm so glad you came by. Us folks needs to support each other. Don't be a stranger, now! Stay warm. Look like a storm coming. They said we 'bout to get a foot by tomorrow morning. A foot! Mercy, Lord!"

"I'll stay warm. I won't be a stranger. You stay warm, too, Ms. Melinda. Good evening. Oh, Ms. Melinda?"

"Yes, love?"

"Where'd you get those quilts?"

"The quilts on the porch, love?"

"Yes, Ma'am."

"Oh, them things sure is old. They belonged to my husband, Oscar. He was friends with your father's brother. Not good friends though. More like acquaintances. That's really why I remembers him.

They just played cards together once in a while. He didn't care for your father much, though. Thought he was too siditty! I think them quilts was in Oscar's family, date back, I guess, to about slavery times, maybe a little after that. I don't reckon seeing them until way after we were married though, and that was back around 1967. One day I was cleaning out the attic and I just found them."

"I see. They're very pretty," I said.

"Yep, sure is. Got to tell you though, I can't sell 'em. Oscar, my husband, made me promise not to. He was deep into art back then. Now Oscar the third is a collector. They used to be out there all year 'round. It's amazing no one ain't took 'em yet. But I brings 'em in nowadays. They pretty worn. I got another one downstairs. Oscar said it was made by a Jewish woman your Nana Zola Jewel knew. They calls theirs…Oh, I can't pronounce the name, but it start with a P. Got goose feathers in it. That too been here since 1967. Leave that outside and don't know what's bound to happen to them feathers! Sort of like a down coat. But it's a quilt made like a blanket with pretty designs. Can't sell that either, love. Was a gift, you know. But can you imagine though, the ones out there could be from slavery times, and not one torn rag nowhere? Oscar the third, my little art historian, used to say they was blessed or something, just like them country folk say. You know them country folk talk funny. They sure is bewitchin' folks! I keep them quilts in the basement now. I put 'en out just for the holidays, you know? The ones on that porch only been out there two or three days this year. I was about to bring them in just when you come in. Ain't that funny? Even Autumn been askin' to buy 'em. Strange, huh?"

"Yes." I said again. She smiled. I continued, "Well, Ms. Melinda, are any of Oscar's other relatives living? I really would like to know where he got those quilts from."

"He got a lot of folks down near Savannah. But they young ones. Nieces, nephews, cousins, and the like. Don't reckon' they know too much 'bout no quilts. You can talk to my little art historian, Oscar the third, maybe he can help you."

"That's fine."

"I'll ask around though, love. Seem like somebody should know something," she said.

"Yes, Ms. Melinda. Thank you. If you find out anything, would you please call me?" I asked her, as I scribbled my phone number and email address on a yellow, sticky piece of paper and handed it to her. I told her, "I've seen them before in my grandmother's house down south. My people were from Savannah too, but on the island."

"That so, Imani?"

"Yes, Ma'am. An island called Eva Creek."

"I remember hearing about that. By some river with some strange sounding name start with an O?"

"That's right. The Okefenoke Swamp? I asked her.

"No. That's not it," Ms. Melinda said.

"The Ogeechee River?" I asked her.

Yep. I think so. I think that's it. But his family not from no island. They from Savannah, Georgia."

"I see."

"Love, you sure inquisitive, today!"

"Yes, Ms. Melinda. I'm just curious."

"I reckon you is." She said.

"One more thing, Ma'am."

"Yes, love?"

"You ever heard of something called an Orphan Train?"

"No, don't believe I have." Ms. Melinda said, thoughtfully.

"Well, you have a very nice evening, Ma'am."

"You too, love."

She waved as she turned me in to a Martian.

I didn't want to look like a fool asking her to tell me who my family is. So I smiled at her, puzzled. I could just hear her: "Child, don't you know who your people be? Why you don't know that?"

This was a woman who treated her own family reunions like religious holidays. Like many people, she had probably heard stories about my father and my mother's family, but unfortunately, like me, could not find enough information about us to put an entire puzzle together.

Autumn Brook Taylor was back in town looking for me? Each time I thought of her, I thought of terror. She hated me so much. Why? She had hated me all my life. She knew my father's brother? God, what else did she know? And she hated my mother more. I was ready to know the answer now because like her, I too was wrapped in hate and the only thing I loved right now was a taste of Early Times Old Style Kentucky Whiskey to help me understand:

Why did my mother kill herself?

Why did Autumn hate her?

Why does Autumn hate me? Why is she looking for me? She knows where I live. She wanted to buy a quilt from Ms. Melinda? Why?

"What happened to my family?" I whispered to myself.

Chapter Twelve

Snowflakes peeked through my living room windows and clung to them until their watery bodies dropped to the ground and formed ice. I had dreamed for twelve hours, uninterrupted, of things I now could not remember. It had been such a long time since I had had a good night's sleep.

I decided to take the day off.

I phoned the school office to let them know that I wouldn't be in, and that I was taking a personal day. After speaking with space Goddess One, Ella Samuels, who smacked and sipped something, she connected me to Space Goddess Two, Gertrude Ramsey, a retired gym teacher who worked unsalaried and was responsible for obtaining substitute teachers to cover regular teacher's classes. I gave Gertrude my schedule and hung up the phone with my mind absorbed on quilts.

There was a dusting of snow on the ground. But that was just a tease. More was on the way for the night. I checked to see that I had my cell phone to call Blue in case the weather became audacious enough to shut down a city's transportation. Blue had an old powerful station wagon and a jeep he used for in-climate weather. The last thing I wanted to do was take the Jewel Park Cross-town Bus, which was a forty-five minute ride to the elegant Silver Row neighborhood that stretched across Jewel Park's other side of town where the really wealthy folks lived. Out of fear, I never learned to drive, and I was sorry.

I walked two blocks toward the Jewel Park Cross-town Bus on Dandelion Street and Lincoln Boulevard. Before the cold forced me to utter a curse word for the bus, it came, and I rode leisurely for a half an hour watching my neighborhood change from a middleclass one to one of wealth and privilege. This bus didn't pass through Crescent Boulevard where the Red Light District was along with all the folks who lived there and had illegal gigs on the side.

Crescent Boulevard traveled down the neighborhood I knew best, but had avoided after Mama's death. I had lived there with her on Crescent Boulevard and Turner Avenue in a pretty, two-bedroom apartment while Daddy lived on Dandelion Street with Autumn in a brownstone I was taken from at age eleven, and before that a brownstone in Silver Row with Autumn. I was still resentful.

I needed to do some cleaning and see how much of him I could capture through old mail, answering machine messages and any paperwork he left unattended, but I wasn't going to spend the night there in a snow storm!

Clara Rogers now owned his Silver Row brownstone, but she was 70. How would she be able to manage his three story home, even though it was paid for? I had met her years ago. She had answered the phones at Jewel Park High School while he worked there, but she had left nearly ten years ago, just about the time I had started teaching there, because her hearing was bad. Valerie told me she was at the funeral. If something happened to this woman, the apartment was to go to her son. I had never met him. Why?

During the week before the funeral, I had spent a lot of my time at the bank assessing Daddy's accounts.

Daddy had obtained a doctorate in African Studies from the prestigious Jewel Park School of Research, published a half a dozen books, traveled extensively, and had a hobby in genealogy. Although the most fascinating thing about him is that he lacked self-knowledge or refused to share it. He knew how to obtain complete computer searches on Mama's relatives and his friends, and knew Mama's history better than she did, but not until I became emancipated from the foster care system at the age of 21, did I know that my father never searched for himself.

Why? At the time, while Daddy taught history at age 23, he also worked as a freelance writer for *The Jewel Park News*, an award-winning newspaper, where Autumn, who was also 23, worked as an editor after she quit her teaching job as a math teacher at a school in Silver Row. Had Mama worked in Silver Row also? Why hadn't Mama ever mentioned Daddy's brother?

Daddy had interviewed Nana for an article about growing up on Eva Creek Island. The news article later became an essay in a book Daddy wrote about my family.

Mama told me that from the time that book was published when I was born, people started keeping a distance from my parents, and as I got older, even from me. Although Daddy was from South Carolina, no one knew which part of South Carolina he was from or where he lived before he settled in Jewel Park, not even Mama. She never talked about her life on Eva Creek Island.

Daddy's notes and the photographs of my childhood seemed to be carrying me to my family as well as to a language I had buried.

At the House of Angelic Souls Funeral Home, which Dr. Lance's 23 year-old son, Deacon Andre Clarke owned, I had to fill out so many forms that I got dizzy. To my surprise, I found out a lot about how Daddy handled his finances!

Daddy's bankbook contained close to $25,000 in savings. The cash value of his mutual fund was $900,000. His Tax Deferred Annuity offered to pay $300,000. His individual Retirement Account contained $40,000, and death benefits for $25,000 covered all funeral costs, leaving me several thousand dollars left over from it. I added his mutual fund, T.D.A., and Roth I.R.A. account to my own mutual fund, T.D.A., and Roth I.R.A. accounts that my father had set up for me when I had turned 21. I added the money from his checking and savings accounts to my own; he had opened them for me when I was 13 and whenever I got paid, I continued to keep them afloat. The house in Silver Row was valued at $400,000, very cheap compared to the other homes there, and was paid for.

He had no debt because he only had one credit card that he never used. He paid all bills on time! Money was not something daddy played with! He took care of money as though it were a child.

Why had Daddy left a house that was paid for to someone he worked with, instead of me? Or even Autumn? Who was this Clara woman and why didn't she speak to me at the funeral? And what did Autumn want? Why hasn't she come to the house?

At Goldtower Park, the bus turned, but did not enter the park. It was the last stop. A few nannies got off of the bus with me. They probably thought I was one also. I passed Denver Street and surveyed the quaint cafes, restaurants, gourmet shops and boutiques that kept me company as I walked to Silver Row Boulevard. I exited Tower Lane and took a short cut through the bridge that connected Butterfly Lake to Silver Street where my father's house was along with a row of four others on a quiet block. Four inches of the powdery stuff was now on the ground. It was 12:30 in the afternoon, and I got myself two slices of pepperoni pizza from the shop on the corner. I walked down to Lake Avenue past more shops and restaurants, including one of my favorite Indian restaurants that served great Roti. I passed Carson's Hospital, and I inhaled the intense smell of good coffee and bread from the Tatum and Greene Bookstore on the next corner. Blue's brother Rayne owned it along with a cousin. I turned down Lake Avenue and walked past The Jerusalem Temple Baptist Church at the corner. I came to my father's brownstone in the middle of the block.

I had seen Clara a week before my father's death, when I had stopped by his house to drop off a fruit basket for him because he had told me he wasn't feeling well, even then. Clara had been sweeping the hall floor when I had stopped by his house. She had waved and smiled, but I was in a hurry and had not really spoken to her. Daddy had been asleep. I had quickly dropped off the basket in his living room with a note about Sunday dinner, and left. Clara seemed distracted, but filled the house with deep Southern singing and the smell of biscuits with maple syrup.

After walking up several steps, with my father's keys, I opened the front door to the smell of garlic and fried fish. I passed the first floor apartment my father had occupied and the second floor apartment he used as an office to follow the delectable aroma of good cooking to the third floor and knocked on the door.

The stunning brother who answered took good care of himself.

Chapter Thirteen

"Imani Henderson?" He asked.

"Yes," I managed to say, surprised.

"Yeah. I know you! Saw you at Matthew Henderson's funeral. Knew it was a matter of time before I met you. You're lovely, baby. Come on in. And this is really something, because I'm not usually home on Friday's. How you doin?" He spoke in a subtle Southern accent as he extended his arms to embrace me.

"Fine," I said, still puzzled. *How did I miss him at the funeral?* I thought. I tried to speak and turn around and leave.

But he spoke in a reassuring manner that put me at ease in my father's house. "I'm Carmel," he said in a voice that was calm and tender. He continued, "Come on in. I just started a late lunch. I took the day off because of the storm that's coming—I didn't want to get stuck at work—and I had a taste for some fried whiting, grits, okra, and tomatoes. I'm just finishing up some biscuits."

He led me into the apartment with his arm still around my waist and wiped his other hand on a light brown apron he wore over a sleeveless white tee shirt, a pair of black jogging pants and designer sneakers. It seemed as though a sculptor had carved the shape of his body into well-defined curves.

"Would you like something to eat?"

His apron read, Eva's Creek.

Interested now in the stunning brother's dark brown eyes, smooth, brown-sugared skin, teeth lovelier than Blue's, and a name on an apron of an African slave woman who had married a Creek chief and formed an island that protected my ancestors, still puzzled, I said, "Yes. Are you a new tenant?"

He gave me a smile filled with charm.

"No," he said. "I'm Clara's son."

"Clara. Oh, yes. She used to work at Jewel Park High School?" I was really asking a question. But it sounded more like a statement to him. "I only met her once," I told him.

"Yeah, she was the receptionist there. That was long ago, though. I was in college."

"Really?" I said.

"Have a seat. Make yourself comfortable." He set the table with fine dishes and linen.

I hesitated, as I set the pizza on the table.

"Everything smells so delicious," I said as I rested my coat and pocketbook on the back of the chair.

"Thanks. Let me put that in the refrigerator for you. Pizza ain't got nothing on this!"

Charm filled the room again.

I smiled with him and noticed on the dining room wall a family picture of him with another man whose arms were wrapped around Clara Rogers' waist.

Carmel looked younger in the picture, maybe 20.

"Imani, are you planning to move to Silver Row? You could stay in one of these apartments and probably work out of the other one like your father did," Carmel said, placing the food on a large serving platter, and then onto the kitchen table.

"No, of course not. I just came to clean up my father's place and get the apartment in order. Since the building's paid for, I guess I might use his apartment as a weekend retreat, that's if Clara doesn't mind. I don't know anything about real estate, and I certainly wouldn't mind having you as a neighbor! And I'm glad it's paid for."

"Thank you," Carmel said, as he went on. "I was hoping that was possible. I love this building. And, yeah, about the whole real estate thing, I feel you. But you know, you really should think about renting this place out to tenants. This place could bring in a lot of money. Three floors. In a brownstone! In Silver Row! You should really think about it. My mother wants nothing to do with that. Neither do I. I just don't have the time. You should really think about renting it, since you own it."

"I will," I said as I tasted his words, "...you own it." The house was Clara's. I had no documentation that proved that I owned the house in Silver Row. I told him, "I don't own this. Clara does. You do, if she doesn't want the responsibility. That's what I thought my father wanted."

"No, Imani. I do not own this. A year ago, my mother signed over all rights of ownership back to your father. The house is paid for, and in your name. And another thing, some lady named Autumn wanted you to have a box. It's in the living room. It's not that big, but it seems to be filled with paper, mail, letters, I guess. I tried to give them to Autumn via UPS, but she sent it back to me with a note explaining that it belongs to you! She came by here about a week before your father died. They had some kind of heated argument, but I came in on the end of it. Matthew didn't even recognize me. It took him about an hour before he realized who I was. They were polite when they heard me enter the house—they were in the hallway—and helped me with my luggage. After we eat, you could, maybe take a look at that box. This is your house. And, by the way, I would love to remain here as your tenant! Butter?" Carmel asked.

"Yes. Thank you. Anything that was sent to Autumn—I'll tell you about her later—can certainly wait!" I said as I watched him butter the biscuits. He brewed some coffee.

I panned the room and got a telephoto shot of the L-shaped apartment and the backyard below as I glanced at the family photo of him with Clara, and I guess, her husband. Two children were in the background. Four bookcases lined the living room's back wall.

My father's apartment was shaped the exact same way, except that it led to a backyard paved with cement.

Carmel's apartment had a worldly theme, even though most of the furniture was contemporary. From the African baskets made with palmetto leaves that they still made in Sierra Leone and on Eva Creek Island that rested on the kitchen countertops and dining tables, to the Kente rugs that covered the parquet floors in the dining room and matched the Victorian living room tables and chairs, the six and a half-room apartment had an authenticity that sheltered the warmth and style of a home that was well loved.

"How did you learn to cook like this, brother?" I asked. "My mother cooked like this," I told him, still waiting for his answer.

"Yeah?" He asked. His answer was a smile.

I hesitated again after taking a sip of coffee, and then asked, "Carmel, how did your mother come to know my father?"

He said, "I really don't know. See, I was raised in Savannah, Georgia. I went to Morehouse in Atlanta, though, where I got my bachelor of arts degree in business administration, then I went on to The Art Institute of Atlanta, Georgia and got a bachelor of science degree in culinary arts management, and then I moved to Brooklyn when I was 25, but only stayed for six months. I did some traveling for a few years, got a good job as a chef in Atlanta, and had my own apartment there until recently. I also think you should know that Clara is my foster mother. I never knew my real parents. All I know is what she told me. She took me in when I was a baby and managed to keep me from being passed around like some animal. Actually, it was her husband who found me on the steps of a hospital where he worked as a radiologist. They raised me from infancy and a whole lot of other children too," he said as he pointed quickly to the dining room pictures of the children I had noticed in the picture with Clara and the man. He continued, "I want to start my own family—a wife and kids, you know?"

"Yes, I understand. Seems like you and I have the same problem, Carmel. You mean to tell me you don't know anything about my father, and you've been living here for nearly ten years?"

"I haven't been living here for ten years. I just moved here from Atlanta two weeks ago! I plan to stay here for a while, though. My mother shipped my stuff up here and had the whole apartment redone. Your father hadn't painted the apartments or done any work on the house. It was nice, but it needed a lot of work. I'm still decorating. I just put in a new boiler and I have to redo the windows. It gets very drafty in here. But I've only been actually living here for two weeks."

"Two weeks?" I asked.

"Yeah. I thought you knew. See, when Matthew passed away, my mother called me. She was very sad. She raised him, you know. He was long gone off to college by the time Clara took me in. So I guess you could call your father, my foster brother."

"What?" I said, shocked. My heart began doing the 50-yard dash. I asked, "My father, Matthew Henderson, was a foster child?"

"Well, yeah, Imani. You didn't know that?"

"Hell, no!"

"Damn. I'm so sorry, honey. I thought…"

"Carmel, my father kept so many secrets. I found out a few days ago that he had a brother who looks just like him, but he's seven years younger than him, which would make him 45. And he was buried wearing a gold wedding band. I don't know who it belonged to. He wasn't married! Do you know anything about his brother?"

Yeah. Charles Henderson. He's in town, you know. He was at your father's funeral. You didn't see him?" Carmel gave me the same Martian look Mrs. Benson had given me.

"No," I said. "I don't know any of my father's relatives. Why didn't Autumn introduce me to him? I saw her, but she was already in her car."

Carmel calmly said, "Hey, Imani. I don't know. At the funeral, since you didn't know me, I felt you needed your space, and I felt there would be another time for us to meet. Mama and I came back here. We tried to call you, but the line was busy or when we did get through the answering machine was so full, we couldn't leave a message. So, we just waited for a better time. Your Uncle Charles is seven years older than me, and seven years younger than your father. Matthew moved out of Clara's house when he was 14 because he got accepted to college at that age! I was a baby at that time. So, I grew up knowing Charles, but not really making a connection that Matthew and Charles were biological brothers. It wasn't until after I left home that I figured things out. No one actually sat me down and told me anything. I never asked why. I just know Matthew didn't get along with Johnny, my foster father, Clara's husband, but Charles did. When I moved to New York for those six months, I lived with Charles in a nice house in Bedford-Stuyvesant, Brooklyn. Charles was never home, so I rarely saw him. After I went back down South, Charles moved in with his girlfriend somewhere in Rego Park, Queens. I saw him at Matthew's funeral, but he seemed to be in a hurry and pretended like he didn't see Mama or me. He was alone, and I don't remember him being with Autumn. I would have remembered seeing her. It hurt Mama that he didn't speak to her. I grew up with Charles for seven years. He was cool. A real ladies man. But he never liked the attention, and although I was very young. I remember Charles as being a very shy kid, extremely shy. Unlike your father, Charles would visit Clara around the holidays, but would never spend the night. She was really hurt when he didn't speak to us."

"Do you have any pictures of him, Carmel?"

"No. He and your father never liked to take pictures. I don't have any pictures of either of them. Clara didn't talk much about either of them. They had the same last name and looked so much alike. Whenever Mama did mention them, she seemed hurt, like it was hard for her to talk about them. Like me, no relatives ever came around to visit them. Anyway, we were a family, not a biological one, but a family. Neither of them ever came back to visit her or Johnny after they turned 18. That hurt her a lot. All the kids she took in always returned annually just to say, "Thank you." So I guess I could call myself your uncle, right?"

I smiled.

There was that charm again. He continued, "My mother lives on Eva Creek Island now in the same house she raised me in. After the funeral she packed her stuff and moved back down there. That's where she's from, you know."

He was eloquent and self-assured. I found myself staring at him as he talked following every curve the sculptor had created. Men like him didn't even look my way. Blue was an exception.

"Carmel, my father frequently had nightmares about someone being murdered in 1901. But he wasn't born until 1947. Did your mother ever talk about that or my father's family?" I asked.

"Not that I know of. I mean, yes, she talked about Matthew and Charles, but usually only if someone mentioned their names first. She bragged about all of her children and affectionately called us her ocean of jewels." He paused. "Imani, tell me about Autumn. The first time I saw her was at Matthew's funeral, and then she came by the restaurant yesterday."

"Autumn?"

"Yeah. Mama never liked her, but never explained why. When your father married her, I was nine, but I didn't go to the wedding. I just know that I remember Mama talking about Matthew marrying some woman named Autumn that she didn't like. At the funeral Clara pointed out to me that Autumn was Matthew's ex-wife. Then it seemed like Mama let hatred ooze out of her body. It was very clear to me that she didn't like Autumn. Well, Autumn came to my job yesterday and asked for my mother. I told her what I told you, that she was in Georgia. She said some nasty things about your father, handed me a box addressed to her, but she said it was yours. I told her that I didn't know you. She said she knew me, and my mother well, and that she wanted me to leave it in Matthew's apartment. I wondered why she just couldn't go over there herself and drop it off at the door. I thought maybe she had a key. Or why didn't she go to your house? I can't believe he's dead. She left the box on the counter, and stormed out of the restaurant." Carmel finished his coffee and poured himself another cup.

I savored the buttery grits and shrugged. Then I said, "Tell me about the restaurant you own." And I pointed toward his apron that now rested on the kitchen chair next to him. "What do you know about Eva Creek Island? And what did Autumn say to you?" I asked.

"She didn't say anything to me. I grew up there. I knew of your family, but we lived on the other side, near the Okefenokee Swamp." Carmel said.

"Really? We were closer to the Ogeechee River. It led to a lake that my grandmother, Nana Zola Jewel used to baptize people in a long time ago!" I told him.

"Yeah? At one time, my mother knew your mother and grandmother, I think. They spoke that Geechee talk that I never learned because I didn't want those buckrahs to think I was illiterate. Damn! It's my first language and I grew up being ashamed to speak it! So did Clara and Johnny. Your father spoke it though. So did Charles. My mother was friendly with your grandmother because they went to the same church. Autumn did look familiar, but I couldn't place her face." He said, as he added a teaspoon of sugar to his coffee. He continued, "After she left the box, she stormed out of the restaurant mumbling curse words and called your father a lot of names."

I shook my head. "Where did you get the apron?" I asked, adding seven tablespoons of sugar to my coffee.

He stared at me for a moment and then smiled.

"It's my mother's," he said. "She passed this restaurant and this house on to me, but I told her the deed should be in your name. I still don't understand the house. Why she really doesn't want it. I understand why your father would leave her a house, guilt, maybe. This is a beautiful place to live. And I've never owned a house. But she's had it for nearly ten years. She just wouldn't live here with your father. It wasn't even until last month that she stayed here for the first time. She loves Eva Creek Island. Some real estate firm offered her three million dollars for the house on Eva Creek Island and the land surrounding it! I told her to take the money, but she wouldn't. The restaurant, she had for…" He paused as he searched for the memory, then, "She's had it since 1983, and won't sell that either. She owns a portion of it, but I believe that at the end of this month, it will belong to you also. Your father was a very shrewd man. It seems like he really trusted you to take care of his property, all of it!"

I stared at Carmel's eyes.

Chapter Fourteen

"Carmel, my father was very secretive about his life. See, I was a foster child too. My father could have taken care of me, but he didn't want to because his wife didn't like me. I feel numb thinking about that. Most people in Jewel Park moved here from Eva Creek and knew him, but like you knew him, mysteriously. When he filed for custody of me, the courts ruled that it was in my best interest that I be raised by my mother because my father traveled a lot, and the judge felt there was too much tension between Autumn and my mother for me to be raised in Daddy's home. Whatever happened before I was born really affected the court's decision to place me with my mother, instead. Then after my mother's death, I went to a group home. Daddy's wife at the time was Autumn Brook Taylor. My mother was Ruby Jewel Weaver. They hated each other. I don't know why. My mother was a model and a math teacher, and she owned a restaurant in Jewel Park, but I never got to know her. And I don't know what happened to the restaurant Mama owned. I know Greta Johnson, Mama's landlord and neighbor before she died, stopped renting her apartment out after my mother's death. Greta turned my mother's apartment into an office. I know that my Nana had a house in Bedford-Stuyvesant, Brooklyn between 1970 and 1982; that's probably the house you stayed at. After her death, I don't know what happened to it. I know my mother owned a restaurant in Jewel Park because when I was about eight or nine, I would go there and sit on a stool in a kitchen and watch her cook right along with the other cooks that she had hired." I paused for a minute, then continued, "The home in Bed-Stuy is not boarded up, but every time I go there, no one is ever home. The next-door neighbor is an elderly woman who can barely see, therefore, she never opens her door! The other neighbor travels a lot and is never home. I think someone comes by once a month to get the mail, but I never have met them."

He smiled and said, "You know, I bet you know more about your mother than you think you do! I lived in Bed-Stuy for those six months I was in New York. That was back in 1989. There were two tenants living there, plus me. I paid my rent to your father. He owned the house. It's probably still in his name. You should check that out, Imani."

"I will," I told him as I went on, trying to dig up images of my mother. "Autumn was looking for me too. But she knows where I live in Jewel Park, but won't come by the house. Why couldn't she send this box or package or come by with this Charles Henderson or officially introduce me to Leroy Taylor? Damn it! What the hell is her problem? Carmel, is the box large?"

"No. It's small. It's in the living room, if you want to see it, I can…" He motioned toward the adjoining room.

"I'll get it when I'm ready to leave," I said, afraid of what might be in it. Afraid of what I could remember about Mama. Then I said, "Autumn came to the funeral and spat at me when I saw her. I don't understand why she would be so nasty to you. Carmel, did you ever read my father's book, *The Children of Eva Creek Island?*"

"No, but I've heard about it. My mother had a copy of it, but I never knew what happened to it. It was published around 1970 or '71. I remember seeing a copy of it. I was really young, though, but there was a lot of excitement down South about it. It had a picture of a quilt on the cover, real nice, you know? Mama didn't like the book very much. I know that!"

"Well, I was born in 1970. So whatever was so horrible about it definitely happened either when I was born or before. How old are you, Carmel?"

"Thirty-eight. And you?"

"Twenty-nine."

"Damn! So you were fostered, Imani?"

"Yeah. Eight different homes. At 21 they emancipated me, and I was lucky, I guess. Autumn and my father divorced that same year, and he gave me the house on Dandelion Street and moved here."

"Damn, baby!" He placed his hand over mine at the table. I still sipped coffee, but I really wanted a drink. He said, "Well, I manage The Eva Creek Soul Food Restaurant in Jewel Park, and you officially will own it next month. It serves soul food. Damn, what did your father or mother ever tell you about your self, your family or Jewel Park, Imani?"

I shrugged and sipped coffee, embarrassed that I could not answer him. Carmel continued, "That's the real danger of being a foster child, Imani. Not knowing your history. During slavery, many fugitives created new families because they couldn't find the old ones. You see all the problems we're having in our community because of that! He sighed as if someone had hit him hard in the stomach, then he continued, "Eva Creek was a family restaurant, owned by my mother, her sister, and brother. Mama's the only one left. They called her Mama Clara back then. She's deaf, but I'll email her for you. She likes the Internet, and is on it all day. If you want, I'll ask her to email you. Is that okay with you?"

"That's fine, Carmel. Since my father's death, I haven't had time to use my computer at all. I must have about a hundred emails!"

He smiled. "You can add my address to that list. My mother had the restaurant completely renovated. I'm just the manager, but I love to cook, so most of the time, you'll see me in the kitchen. It's on Lindsay Street, off Park."

"I think that's where my mother's restaurant was. Is there a club called Catfish across the street?"

"Yeah. It used to be called Catfish; now it's a coffee shop."

"That's my mother's restaurant! I don't know if I should cry or hug you," I said. He smiled, squeezed my hand, and kissed my cheek.

"Do you use Rogers as your last name too?" I asked.

"Yeah. When I was about ten, my foster father..." He pointed to the picture of himself with Clara and the man I noticed earlier. Carmel continued, "...her husband that is, Johnny Rogers, died. Your father never changed his name to Rogers. I guess he knew he was a Henderson. So did Charles. When my mother took in children, siblings came along together, but your father came first, and then Charles just appeared. I know I was just one, but my mother talked about your father often when he was in college. He was only 14, you know, when he went to college." I nodded, as Carmel continued, "If Clara and Johnny didn't talk about him so much, I wouldn't even have known that Matthew or Charles lived there. We knew nothing about the Henderson family.

"Clara and Johnny took good care of me. They gave me everything I desired, needed, wanted. Anything. They even gave me the peace of not knowing why I was abandoned. There's a peace that comes with not knowing, Imani."

"Yes, Carmel. But sometimes that peace can turn into hopelessness. I never had peace. It's like an empty void. Not knowing. It's like a space filled with air. Anything can come in and fill that air, even dirt, the void never leaves. You understand what I'm saying?"

"Damn, baby. I really do." He finished his fish and was now working on the grits. He asked, "So, I hear you teach."

"Where did you hear that?"

"Your friend, Valerie, I met her at the funeral. She told me. I didn't really tell her who I was, but she knows my name."

Ms. Nosy, I thought.

"The biscuits are fantastic, Carmel," I said as I took another from the platter and poured syrup over it.

"Thanks. Help yourself. Got the recipe from Clara. Mama can throw down in the kitchen. That's how she made her living, you know?"

"Really?"

"She cooked for the church just about every night. They paid her, well, I might add. Johnny cooked too. But Clara cooked for the church, a Baptist one. Don't remember the name, because I wouldn't go. I developed a relationship with God that didn't involve going out of the house on Sunday, especially in the winter! But Clara kept that church well-endowed. Sometimes I think people just went because they knew they could get a good dinner after service. Even buckrahs from other counties came to eat!"

He went on talking about his foster mother, sipping coffee, something we had in common, especially with the sugar. "Clara played down her looks though. She had been an actress in her early teens and twenties and had even worked for a while as a dancer at The Cotton Club. But she said her looks caused her a lot of pain, and she gave up show business."

"My mother too. She was very fair," I told him. I asked, "Carmel, have you ever heard of something called an Orphan Train?"

"Yeah. When I was in college, I read something about that. From like 1850 to the middle early 1900s a lot of children, mostly poor, homeless, abused white immigrants from the big cities like New York for example, whose parents and relatives were so poor that they handed their children over to this reverend, a minister named Charles Loring Brace. He was affiliated with The Children's Aid Society. Well, he arranged a kind of foster care system where children were literally put on trains headed toward the Midwest and South to be placed in good homes with families, mostly farmers, to escape the slums of the cities. Years later, they found that a lot of these children who had been placed out had been severely abused. But a lot of kids also found great homes. And you know something, even some of those children helped out with the Underground Railroad? It wasn't until after 1930 that the government implemented laws that protected children from things like hard labor and a foster care system that didn't have checks and balances. What's interesting though is that our children, African American children, were just taken in by other African American families at that time. It was like, you saw a kid who was homeless, and you just took him in. Sometimes the whole family. No questions asked. You raised them like your own. There was no state or government agency or official to intervene. There were a lot of African American communities who did that back then, even right here in New York. They even had their own orphanages, like the one in Weeksville. Today Weeksville is known as Bedford-Stuyvesant, but back in 1838, a black man named James Weeks founded it, as a settlement of free African Americans. Sort of the same way Jewel Park, New York was."

I sipped coffee, and then spoke again. "I remember Nana lived near a run down mansion. It's a bed and breakfast now. But Nana's house was on that same block."

"Well, I don't remember a bed and breakfast or a mansion, Imani. There was a very large house on the block, but I just thought the people who lived there had old money! I haven't been back there. But if you want, maybe we can take a ride and see if we can find out who owns your Nana's house now."

"I'd love to do that, Carmel."

"Anytime you're ready." Carmel continued, "Before the riots of the Sixties, Bedford and Stuyvesant were two separate communities. Bedford was where the black folks lived. And Stuyvesant was where the white folks lived. Both sections embraced middle class families. There's a lot of history about that community on the Internet. You should look it up."

"Carmel, how did you find out about this train thin, this Orphan Train thing? My father was doing some kind of research about it before he died." I watched tears form in his eyes, but he quickly brought a smile to his face and sipped coffee when he noticed my gaze.

"I had a good political science teacher in college, a brother," he said. "Jewel Park, Weeksville, and even Eva Creek Island are merely representatives of America. You know how many small towns in New York alone that we've never heard of? It's like that all over America. Beautiful, vibrant towns, filled with loving families, of which some of them, unfortunately, can't get pass skin color or just terrible family secrets. You understand where I'm coming from, baby."

"Yes. I hear you, brother."

"Imani, personally, I think even more has to be done. We came out good, baby, you and me. But there are so many kids out there lost. Just lost; so lost that it breaks your heart. Damn!"

"Yeah, I know," I said. "And then there are the ones like us who grow up," I told him, and I whispered, "with scars people never see." I saw his glance as I wrote my email address and phone number for him.

I leaned back in his kitchen chair sipping rich coffee and watched snowflakes fight to hold onto Carmel's windowpanes and float into the air before they fell to the ground to form a river of ice.

Chapter Fifteen

In my father's house were many rooms that I hoped would be crowded with ancient papers, words, and photographs. The deep sweetness of indigo ink filled the basement air. A spirit of patchouli-scented breath followed me from the basement to the first floor. A window in the living room had been cracked open to invite the wind to eat fragrances of ginger, cinnamon, myrrh, and clove as it touched contemporary art, chairs of velvet, four matching bookcases that doubled as wall units; two of which held a 32-inch Sony flat screen television accompanied by a video cassette recorder he had rarely used; two smooth leather couches in clove brown, a rocking chair, glass tables so clean they reflected sunlight prisms. Ginger-colored shutters with wide opened eyes that I knew Daddy often shut. Leather slippers that I wore more than he did, although they fell off my feet whenever I walked in them. An old television stand that served as a resting place for new books, magazines, and newspapers, and a cherry wood dining table. All this led to a wide horseshoe-shaped kitchen, holding dead flowers in a large glass vase.

The wind turned the apartment into an icebox that had been unplugged for several hours as it traveled throughout half-decorated rooms that stared at old paint, two bathrooms, two bedrooms, and a kitchen with me.

Where did the flowers come from?

Heat screamed from an electric radiator where a nonworking fireplace once danced. The patchouli scented breath made me shiver, and I jumped at the sound of a knock on the door.

I stood in the silence of fear, slowly pacing from one room to the next, not sure where to begin. I jumped again at the second knock.

"Imani?"

"Yes," I whispered.

"It's Carmel. You okay? You seen the snow? You think you can make it back home? Imani?"

I looked at my watch. It was three in the afternoon.

I told Carmel it was okay to come in. I had left the door unlocked. He turned on the light in the living room.

"Yes," I whispered again.

"Oh, baby," he said, as he saw my face and hugged me. Then, "You think you can handle this alone?"

"Yes," I whispered.

Dark brown eyes studied my hazel ones and I shivered as patchouli breath kissed my back.

"It's the window," Carmel said, as he slammed it shut.

"Maybe some medicinal tea might help, even though we've gone through a pot of coffee! I have some Valerian herbal tea. It's very good for headaches and sleeping. It's just as good as Valium."

"Yes. I'll give it a shot," I told him as the word Valium flew out of the cave of my soul. I kept repeating the word in my mind until the memory rose of my mother taking Valium on the last night she lived. "Thank you," I said.

"Are you going to stay over? It looks bad out there," he said, glancing out of the living room window. "I could set up the guest room for you. I don't know how you'd feel about staying down here, you know?"

"The guest room would be fine Carmel, okay?"

"That's cool."

We walked past the dead flowers and into Daddy's kitchen where I had placed about fifty folded boxes against the dining room wall after the funeral, and then I had searched hard for Daddy's brandy. Instead, I found a half empty bottle of *Chanel No. 5* perfume in a dresser drawer in his bedroom next to his size 44 boxers, tee shirts and socks, all white.

I finished gathering sweaters, pajamas, underwear, and clove-scented incense from the last dresser drawer and started working on the two Victorian desks that rested on each side of the dresser. The king size bed kept getting in the way. I gathered papers from that desk to save for the shredder if they weren't important. I kept trying to imagine Daddy with his girlfriends in the king size bed. After he and Autumn divorced, he had had a parade of women around him, I guess to make Autumn jealous. It didn't work though, because she loved Leroy Taylor.

The large eight-ounce mug of tea smelled like old socks.

"So, what you got there?" He asked.

"I don't know. My mother used to wear this fragrance." I held up the bottle and sprayed some of the sweet perfume so that he could smell it.

"Nice," he said. "This is going to take a long time," he added as he surveyed the room and then folded his arms across his chest. Clothes were still hanging in the closet. Shoes were scattered on the closet floor along with belts, books, and papers. I had planned to pack those items and turn them over to the Salvation Army. And I hadn't even looked at the rest of the house.

"Smells good," was all that Carmel said as he inhaled the scent for a second time.

I sipped more tea before putting the cup down.

"What could that be about? Why would he keep a bottle of perfume that my mother wore?" I whispered. "Mama's been dead since 1982!"

He smiled, and then said, "Strange. You need to talk to somebody who knew him well." He gazed at the beautiful bottle of perfume, and then the snow through the bedroom window that faced the backyard. The wind slammed it into the windowpanes. "I know," I said. "I think it's time I found Autumn. Only sixteen people signed the guest book at the funeral. There were at least one hundred people there."

"Carmel said, "Talk to Autumn."

We smiled.

I placed the half empty bottle of perfume in my bag. "Has anyone been in here since my father's death, besides me?" I asked.

"No. No one, except for my mother. She was probably the last one in here. I think she left everything the way it was. She didn't like coming down here when he was alive! Said he gave her the creeps sometimes because he was always so quiet. And when you talked to him, all you got were one word answers, rarely a complete sentence."

Carmel sipped ginger ale. "Clara straightened the place up before she left. Left you some flowers. I meant to throw them out after they died. Sorry. She cleaned out the refrigerator. Stuff like that. No one else could get in here, but me. And the last time I was down here was when your father and Autumn were here."

"I see." I glanced at the papers. There really weren't that many, but it was just enough to annoy someone who wanted to quickly get out of a house that death had touched.

"What happened to the bills that kept arriving after his death?" I asked.

"I don't know. Maybe my mother placed them on one of the end tables in the living room. I'll look." He finished his soda and went briefly into the living room. He came back with phone, gas, and electric bills for Daddy's apartment for the first week in January. He handed them to me, and I placed them with the papers that could be shredded.

"Nothing else?" I asked.

"No, nothing," Then he said, "I guess after you go through everything, you might find other stuff. Take a look at that box he sent to Autumn before you leave, Imani. I'll sit with you if you want. My mother left the basement neat. Maybe you might find something down there or in his office." He said.

"I hope so," I said, as I tasted the honey at the bottom of the mug. "Maybe by tomorrow afternoon the streets will be partially cleared, since it's a Saturday, and I'll be able to get the bus back home."

"If the roads are not bad, I'll drive you," he said. Then, "I have to work tomorrow, anyway."

"Thank you. I'm going to spend some time down here. I'll be okay."

"That's cool. When you're ready to come up just push on the door. It'll be open. I have some calls to make, but you'll hear the television. You could watch a movie or something, if you like. I'll get that room together for you. I'll put the box on the kitchen table. Want some more tea or something to nibble on?"

"No, I'm fine," I said.

"Yes, indeed, you are! Very fine." He said. He left me sitting on the bed with my eyes crossed at him. I really wanted that pizza I'd bought earlier in the day.

I checked the messages on my cell phone. There was only one from Blue. He had text messaged me with: "Where are you???"

Anger returned, mixed with confusion.

Chapter Sixteen

Carmel had never been married. He had no children. He was seeing a woman in Jewel Park named Zalia. I didn't get that much information from him because his telephone was a constant interruption.

I found no more bills or papers.

The box remained on the kitchen table where Carmel had placed it.

"Let me help you with that, Imani," he said, as I tried to remove the tape from around the corners of the box. He got a knife and opened the box.

As I peeped in, I saw only black and white photographs. They reminded me of the time when my father and I went to dinner in New York City at the South Street Seaport. A tourist had taken our picture. I wanted to see a book that Daddy was holding. He wouldn't even let me touch it or see the title. I had brought a box of pictures of him, me, and Mama that I carried often in my journal. At that time I was about 18 and thinner, and I had them with me in Mama's jewelry box to talk to Daddy about them. But we never got a chance to talk about anything. We argued about Autumn and I left him sitting on a bench staring at the water as I went home alone.

"Look at the date, Imani."

"The date's been scratched out," I said. Autumn must have had to sign for this. I don't see a date anywhere."

He picked up one photograph that was practically yellow. "Who's this?"

"I don't know. I don't know who any of these people are, Carmel."

There were fifteen pictures of people I had never seen before and five pictures of people I knew because I had copies of them as well. There was one letter that was so old I could barely see the ink on it.

Carmel glanced inside the box and then I placed everything carefully back. The pictures had to have been taken before 1950, at least. And all seemed to be at various family gatherings. "What am I supposed to do with this?" I asked as I resealed the box with tape.

"Whatever you do, don't throw them out, Imani. They have to mean something. Maybe they were people your father knew. Maybe your mother's friends. Maybe people Autumn met a long time ago. You really have to talk to her, Imani. Why would she send something like this to you unless she knew the meaning? Why?"

I smiled with Carmel as I placed the box on a chair with my bag in the guest room.

"I'm really tired, Carmel. I think I'm just going to turn in for the evening." I wanted to think and look for memories I had buried.

He smiled. "It's only nine o'clock!"

"I know. I haven't been getting a lot of sleep lately," I said. I gently closed the bedroom door and listened to Carmel turn the television down and answer his pager.

Tea fed me uninterrupted sleep for twelve hours.

I awakened to the sound of a weather report and the smell of scrambled eggs, sausage, toast, and coffee. And I savored it.

I placed the pictures I had avoided for years back into my bag, but I left the ones in the box alone.

Carmel knocked on the door.

"You hungry?"

"Yes," I said as he opened it. He was gorgeous in denim and a sweatshirt, and he smelled of *Michael Kors* cologne.

"You know that place in Bed-Stuy, where I stayed when I visited New York, there was a framed painting on the wall. Whoever lived there was deeply into astronomy. There was some kind of constellation on a quilt that also hung on the wall near that picture that resembled a river."

I said, "Cayenne, when I was a child my mother told me that Nana Zola Jewel hated Jewel Park and refused to live here. Eridanus is the name of a constellation. It's a holy river. In Greek mythology it's the river that Phaeton was thrown into by Zeus, the father of all gods of Greek mythology. As a teenager, Phaeton wanted to prove to his friends that he was the son of the sun god Apollo because they had teased him and called him a mortal, which was an insult. After having a long talk with Apollo, Phaeton discovered that indeed he was Apollo's son. Phaeton asked his father Apollo if he could ride his chariot across the sky. Apollo thought Phaeton was too inexperienced to control the horses that carried the sun across the sky, but Apollo let him ride the chariot anyway to prove his love for his son and to keep his promise to him that he would let him ride the chariot. As Phaeton was riding the chariot across the sky, he almost destroyed the earth. To keep him from further destruction, Zeus, Phaeton's grandfather, struck him with a thunderbolt, and Phaeton fell into Eridanus.

"But my family believed Eridanus was created at the same time the world was, and that it existed among the world's first civilizations. They believed it was the constellation that led them from slavery to the freedom of Eva Creek Island and then to Jewel Park, New York. Everyone in my family has a quilt with The Eridanus Constellation on it, except me, I guess. Nana Zola Jewel once told me that on a good night, you could actually see the constellation of Eridanus from October to December anywhere in the world."

Carmel remained quiet and seemed to be in deep thought.

"I would like to find out who owns Nana's house. This is so overwhelming, Carmel."

Carmel nodded.

Carmel hugged me. He smelled so good. "It's okay," he whispered. He repeated it as he gently wiped my face with soft fingers.

We talked and watched snow form ice on windowpanes in the kitchen.

Chapter Seventeen

Carmel's jeep moved smoothly through the snow as it made its way quietly to my house.

He hesitated, then said, "Come on down to the restaurant sometime. If you like, I'll send you over a complimentary meal."

I thanked him and took his business card. He had written his home number and email address on the back as well, along with the words "Uncle Carmel."

""Stay warm, Imani." I waved and smiled. He watched me step over a mountain of snow and go inside carrying the box that Autumn should have opened. Then he drove away, avoiding ice.

* * * *

The answering machine was blinking again. As I went to hear my messages the phone rang. I poured myself some whiskey.

"Yes?" I said, answering the phone.

"Girl, who was that?"

"Oh, God! Valerie?" I sipped slowly from a glass meant for eight ounces of juice. I dropped three ice cubes into the warming liquid.

"Yeah, girl! Preach to me, now!" She must have been staring out of the window when Carmel's car pulled up to my house.

"Valerie, it was Carmel."

"God is something else, girl!" Valerie said.

"Carmel's a culinary chef. He owns The Eva Creek Soul Food Restaurant. He's the manager, but prefers to cook."

"Oh, yeah? I bet he cooks really well too!"

"Yes!" I said, without elaborating.

The warm liquid from the glass gave me feelings.

"Why don't you come on over? You think you gonna' make it to the conference?"

"What?"

"The women's conference over at the church?"

"They didn't cancel it? It's terrible out there."

"You know they not gonna' cancel that! They moved back the time. It's not starting until six. That'll be going on until about midnight. You should really come, girl. It's about the divine woman in us. You know, the goddess. I'm going! Why don't you come on? We can go together and have a girl's night out. You need to go out and have some fun. Cayenne told me after the funeral that you think you really ain't got no one. Well, girlfriend, you got me! Come on out with me tonight, Imani. And, girl, I heard from the grapevine that Cayenne's girlfriend, Angela, is a lesbian!"

"Valerie, please! How did you find out?"

"Ask Cayenne! Come hang out with me and we'll talk then." Valerie said.

"I'll see."

"Well, let me know, Imani, by about four, 'cause I got some things to do around here, okay?"

"Yes. Valerie. I'll call you by then. Later, girl!"

"Later." I hung up and called Blue.

A woman's voice, harsh from lack of sleep, answered, "Yeah?"

I hesitated and had decided to hang up after five seconds, when she said, "Blue ain't here, bitch."

I heard the slam of the receiver in my ear.

I sipped slower.

As I glanced out of the window, I saw Joy, Valerie's 12-year old daughter, shoveling snow with four of her friends. She was repaying me for the lip balm from Brown Sugar Bodies. They were having fun.

I sipped from my glass and listened to my phone ring. I listened to Cayenne's message.

"Hello, Jewel. We haven't talked since the funeral, and since you won't return my calls or even step outside to ring my bell, I decided to keep trying. I really have to talk to you about something. Jewel, look, you have to knock down that wall you put up with everyone, especially me. I just want you to know that I love you. I didn't expect you to be home, but I'll be back. You want to come over tomorrow for coffee so we can talk? There's a lot of stuff that we've never talked about. And I just want to talk."

I remembered the way he looked right though me with those beautiful eyes.

When his message ended, I tried to focus on an infomercial about Pilates, but it dulled me to a fitful sleep with the help of Mr. Daniel's.

I awoke at 10:30 P.M. to gunshots that came from a television movie, and what seemed to be a tension headache. I dialed Blue's number.

"Hello. You've reached the Greene residence. We cannot come to the phone at this time. Please leave a message and we'll return your call as soon as possible. Please wait for the tone." After I pressed the dial tone button, I nestled the receiver between my neck and ear as I used the remote to change the channel. The ice had melted in the Jack Daniel's but I swallowed the rest of it in the glass. I reached into my bag and let my fingers touch a piece of crumpled paper. I pulled it out of the bag and dialed the number on it.

Larry was on his way over.

I took a deep breath; poured some more Jack Daniel's and sipped slowly—hoping to get to the store soon to get my favorite whiskey.

By 11:30 P.M., I had showered and scented myself with the perfume I found at my father's house. The doorbell rang. I rinsed with mouthwash and answered the door, leaving my empty glass on the kitchen counter.

"Blue?"

My heart began doing the 50-yard dash.

"Blue. I tried to..." Cold lips touched mine immediately. The coldness of his lips also touched my neck and shoulders.

"Delicious," he said, as he pulled me toward the living room after locking the front door."

I breathed slowly, and even slower as I talked, "Blue, I tried to call you, but Linda..."

"Yeah, I know. She told me you called."

"I didn't leave my name, Blue."

"Well, it had to be you," he said. "She knows that."

"Yes, but I thought you had forgotten. There's so much going on tonight with the conference and..."

"Yeah. I saw Val, Angela, and Winnie. They stopped by. Still there. They had a nice program going on at the church. I thought you would have been there. I'm really glad to see you." He hugged me just as the doorbell rang. The 50-yard dash continued again in my heart.

I walked slowly to the door. "Yes?"

"It's Larry."

"Oh, God," I whispered.

He rang the bell again.

"Imani, who is it?" Blue asked from the living room.

"An old friend," I told him.

I opened the door slowly.

"God, you look good!" Larry said loudly. "You smell good. Probably taste good." He pursed his lips to kiss me, but I moved back to open the door wider. Larry handed me a large bag of Chinese food. "Got some good stuff I know you like. Some vegetable fried rice. Chicken with snow peas. Egg rolls. Chicken wings. Some chicken dumplings. Wonton soup. I think they put in some extra wontons.

Let me get to the bathroom. I forgot the hot sauce though, but I guess you can make up for that! Oh, and I got these just in case!" He held up a small box of Lifestyle Condoms that he shoved back into his coat pocket. He gave me a boyish grin and marched right past me taking off his down jacket, gloves, hat, and scarf, and headed toward the bathroom.

I ran after him, but Blue greeted him in the hallway next to the dining room. They both fell silent as I slowly walked toward them. "Blue. This is my colleague, Larry Smith. He works at The Jewel. Larry, this is Blue. He owns the Blue Zephyr." This was not the first time they had met and the look on each face indicated that they remembered.

I saw Blue glance at his watch. "It's 11:30, brother. What's up? Something going on I missed?" Blue looked at me with questioning eyes.

"Hey, brother. Ain't no harm done. We just friends, "Larry said. "Just stopped by on a Saturday night to see how the sister was doing, that's all. Ain't no harm."

"I see you brought food. Got enough for me, Imani?" Blue said, his anger rising. "It's 11:30 in the fuckin' night!"

"I can explain," I said, thinking of a fabulous fake.

"Look man, I don't need this shit. I was in my nice warm bed, getting ready to go to sleep. I don't need this," Larry said as he put his jacket on. He snatched the bag of food and walked out. I followed him to the door. Before I could close the door completely behind him, he looked at me and said coldly, See you next week." Then he whispered, "Ho," and turned and walked to his car, an old station wagon. He got in, threw the food in the back seat, and slammed the door. He drove down the block, slowly avoiding ice.

"Explain," Blue said. He stood close to me.

"I don't have to explain anything to you. I'm a grown woman."

"You're drunk again!" He whispered.

"I'm not drunk."

"You said you could explain. Well, do it."

"I don't have to explain anything to you," I said again.

He backed me into the wall and his peppermint breath was in my face. He asked quietly, "Did you do the brother again?"

"You're hurting me, Blue. Get off of me."

I really thought I saw the moon, then stars, then the Parquet floor. Blue stood over me and then lifted his arms to the ceiling like he was in a church getting ready to testify. He hesitated before he spoke, "Damn! I'm sorry." He reached down to pull me up. He kept repeating how sorry he was. He hugged me and whispered another apology. He kissed my face where his fist had showed me the moon and the stars, but I was afraid to speak. He was shaking as he held me in his arms. "Let's sit down," he said.

He took my hands to help me off the floor and walked me to the couch. His arms were around me.

"What the hell was going on here, tonight?" He asked.

I whispered as I tasted blood in my mouth. My vision was blurry as I said, "You don't have the right to ask me that."

"I'm sorry," he said. "That's the brother I remember from a while back that you were screwing. Seeing him really upset me. Look, Sweet, what do you want from me?"

"I want you to leave her. I want to know that I can reach you when I need you. I want you to not go off in the middle of the night just to be with her. I need you to love me."

Blue wiped my face with a napkin.

"Linda and I have an agreement," he said. "For business purposes, we have agreed to work and live together."

"What for? Make me understand that, Blue. She has her own house that she can live in. But she's living in your house. You own your own business. She gets an income from her four tenants, plus, she's a vice president of her father's accounting firm. What is it that I'm missing?"

"We do a lot of business together. We work well together. People know us as a team. She's the best accountant I've ever had. We don't sleep together anymore. She does her thing. I do mine. It's going to take us a while to work out our future living arrangements. She would have to move a tenant out of her house to move back in. She would lose a good thousand dollars in rent a month if she did that. It wouldn't be right to make her go through that kind of hardship."

"She could raise the rent, Blue. There are a lot of things she could do."

"I promise you, we just need more time. That's all I'm asking. Tonight, I just acted like any other man. I know what that brother was up to."

The kisses began slowly and then became adventurous as they traveled through my mountains, hills, and valleys. They were delicious and I was forgiving.

I sipped whiskey. I played Maxwell's "Whenever, Wherever, Whatever," on the CD player, while Blue finished showering. I got strawberries from the refrigerator and heavy cream that I whipped with powdered sugar and Grand Marnier. I soaked the strawberries in Grand Marnier and brown sugar and placed them in two wine glasses topped with whipped cream.

I listened to Maxwell's words and sipped whiskey with ice.

Would someone ever care about me like that? Love me like that? Want to be with me like that? Give me his breath If I wanted it? I needed it. Not even my father had done that.

I played the song over and over again. As the alcohol killed the beautiful, lavender butterflies that had fallen in love with Maxwell's music in my stomach, I replaced them with strawberries that I licked and sucked with whipped cream.

When Blue finished showering, we ate strawberries to delicious music, but some of the lavender butterflies had survived, and they were now hiding behind the oak trees in my soul.

The next morning Blue enjoyed his favorite gingerbread waffles. Only one of them swam in maple syrup. They were sweet and crisp and kissed with reserved strawberry juice left from the whipped cream and Grand Marnier.

I had forgiven him.

Chapter Eighteen

I woke up with pain that I could not push back into the cave. Tears visited as I remembered stars falling with me on a Parquet floor. It was one in the afternoon. For brunch I sipped an eight-ounce glass of Jack Daniel's.

"Get it together, girl," I told myself. In the bathroom, I found the Advil and took two pills.

The doorbell rang. The Advil was working well.

"Damn! What happened, baby?" Cayenne asked. He hugged me and I took a deep breath.

"Blue!"

"Why didn't you call the police?" Cayenne asked. "Or me?"

"I was scared and embarrassed. He was angry because I had another friend from my job here. Larry Smith," I said.

Cayenne seemed to search for something inside of me. He asked, "Why did you invite Larry over? He's like a big kid."

"I don't know. And Blue is not married."

'He's married, Jewel. Call it common-law or anything you want. He's been living with her for years. Didn't he know her when she was a teenager?"

"I think so."

"What makes you think you can come between that?"

"I wasn't trying to come between them."

"Then what were you trying to do?"

"I don't know."

"You know. That's an easy thing to say, 'I don't know.' Most people do know. My brother was married to the love of his life, Bless, your best friend. Your main girl. And you slept with him! You had a relationship with him. Why? Please don't say that you don't know."

He sipped tea and nibbled on one of the strawberry croissants he had brought with him. I had never talked about my affair with Mark to him. I was surprised. He continued, "You know everything. You know everything because it's in here." He put his hands over his heart. "Everything you need to know is right here, in this place. That's where the kingdom of God is. Right there!" He pointed at my left breast. I smiled. "You have to go to the kingdom, baby."

"Cayenne. Not today." I said. Those eyes were looking through me again.

"When?" He asked. He took my hands and kissed them. Then he stared at me with profound interest and said, "That wall is so thick you can't even reach the kingdom of heaven. It's within, baby. You know what you keep doing? Sabotaging yourself."

"Let it go," I said. "I have. We talked last night. We're going to work it out."

"Jewel, you're not even listening to me. Listen to me, Jewel. Don't say anything until I'm finished. Okay?"

I nodded in agreement.

"You should consider getting some help."

"Help? You mean like a psychiatrist. Don't dress it up by telling me I need to 'see someone' or a 'counselor' or 'be in therapy!' That shit is for buckrahs. We don't do that! And there's nothing wrong with me. I'm still grieving, I guess."

"You interrupted me," he said. "Winnie is a pastor. She has a ministry for women dealing with the kind of issues you're dealing with. They offer counseling and support. I think if you talk to her, she could really help you. I talked to Bless too. She also needs some help. She's become a very bitter and angry woman. Cold. I personally think that the two of you need to really sit down and talk. You two never talked, not even to Mark, I think. You think you were the only one he cheated with? The list is as long as my arm. And you know, the crazy thing about it is that he still does it, only now, it's with women that few people know. I talk to him all the time about it. He smiles like it's a joke. Like it's cool to break your wife's heart with her best friend. And bitterness is deep.

"You know, Jewel, I don't even remember the last time I heard your precious laughter or even saw your smile; I mean really saw you show off those pretty teeth. You need to cut out that drinking. You have changed so much since graduate school. It's like you're a different person. I don't even know you anymore. Yet, I know that you are still here. Right there." He pointed to my heart. He said, "No brother can do for you what you won't do for yourself."

He touched a spot that I didn't even know was showing. Anger filled me as its breath crawled out of the cave of my soul. "You know you have a lot of nerve, Cayenne. Men like you always think you're better than everybody else. You try to pretend that everything's fine all the time. You never acknowledge the rumor that your own mother was a prostitute and a drug addict—heroin I believe. You never talk about your father, some businessman that you don't even know. Your own mother didn't know who your father was. You never talk about that. Ever! Now you want to give me advice about my feelings. My drama. My issues. My need for 'counseling.' Please!"

Cayenne finished his tea and poured himself another cup, replacing the old tea bag, never taking his eyes off of me. Eyes so deep and brown they reminded me of amethyst.

He spoke slowly and softly, "My mother was a prostitute. I met her nearly four years ago in a hospital in Long Island, with the help of your father. The H.I.V. ward."

"What?" I asked, now sorry that my tongue had become a sword. He had never mentioned this to me. I had always believed that both he and Mark had never known either of their biological parents. Now, here he was telling me that he knew his mother and where she was. I had hurt him and it showed in his voice and in his eyes.

"She's H.I.V. positive. And she was a prostitute. She couldn't tell me who my father was. I was born healthy; she called my health God's miracle. Me too." He whispered into the tea that he drank like warm water this time.

I stared at him for a moment, and I would not speak.

He rose and placed the empty cup in the sink with the plate that held the croissant. There was still a box of them left. He had brought chocolate, strawberry, and fruit filled ones.

"Enjoy your Sunday, Imani." He walked slowly down the hall, got his coat, and left.

"Cayenne, wait!" I ran after him, got my coat and bag, and followed him to the place he rented in Valerie's house. He stood in the doorway of his apartment staring at me. There was water in his eyes. "I'm sorry," I whispered.

He continued to stare, but tears streaked his face. I put my arms around him, but he would not respond. I held on and we went inside. The house was quiet. Valerie's family was not home.

"I'm sorry, Cayenne," I repeated.

Silence.

"Cayenne?"

"She looked so terrible. I was able to reach her from the files of an old address that one of my former social workers who happened to know your father, had. She had been homeless for years and had been living in a shelter. She didn't even know who I was. She has dementia, now. I don't have any other biological sisters or brothers. I've been visiting her once a week for four years. I take her some food, gifts, clothes. Stuff like that. She has a picture of herself when she was my age. She was beautiful. She worked as a paralegal. She started partying hard, hanging with the wrong crowd, and getting high on the weekends. The job went. Then she got desperate, and gave up. I don't even know when her birthday is. So I celebrate my birthday with her every

November 26th. I visit her three times a week. She doesn't even know who I am now," he repeated.

"I'm sorry," I whispered. "Maybe I can go with you the next time you visit her? You've been visiting her for four years, and you never told me?"

"That's right," he said. Mark doesn't even know. Not even Bless or Valerie, and I'd appreciate it if you didn't tell them. I'd like to do that in my own time. I'd like you to meet her, my mother. Her name is Nia."

"That's pretty. In Swahili that mean's purpose. It's also one of the principles of Kwanzaa."

Cayenne placed his keys on a tinted glass kitchen table surrounded by matching chairs in bronze trimming. He had expensive, contemporary furniture that complemented fine art on pastel walls, mellow lighting, and an entertainment system that made me feel as if I was in a musician's studio. I hadn't been in his two-bedroom apartment in a long time. His laptop computer light blinked; he noticed and turned it off.

He lit a cedar wood and rosewood candle, turned on his stereo and a mellow trumpet on a Miles Davis CD made love to a subwoofer turned down to level one.

"You never talk about yourself, Cayenne. Everything always seems to be fine with you. I guess that's why I said what I said,"

"You said what you said to hurt me."

There was that stare again. I focused on the topaz carpeting on the living room floor. The music was gentle now. So was his voice.

"You heard me?"

"Yes," I said, keeping my eyes on the thick carpet that I had so often buried my feet in.

"Did you want to hurt me?" He asked.

"No."

"So, why did you say what you said?"

"I don't know." We said it together and this forced me to glance at him. Those eyes.

He smiled.

He spoke slower. "Consider what I said, Jewel. Get some counseling. Winnie is the one to see. How do I know? Dr. Lance helped me a lot. You know he has a doctorate in family therapy as well as ministry."

"I didn't know that," I said.

"He has a private practice. I don't think he counsels anymore, but he has a good staff that's affiliated with the church. It's private and confidential. He's been like a father to me. I owe him a lot. See, Jesus took me in his arms and held me. He became my mother, father, sister, and brother. That anger and hatred I carried as a teenager and young adult are all gone. Thank God I never killed or hurt anyone, because God knows five or ten years ago, I could have been in prison. I got so low one time that I wanted to die. And I happened to be in the gym at the church working out next to Dr. Lance, and he asked me what was wrong. I cursed him out and told him to mind his business. He knew a lot about me. Mark uses sex and women when frustrated. I used sex and women. Went to a lot of strip clubs too. That became my thing every weekend, until recently when Mark went with me. I watched what he did with one woman. The brother was embarrassing! I fight to never go back. I used work. And just like you, when I was feeling when I didn't want to feel, I had a sharp tongue that I could kill you with. I hid behind my education. If I couldn't intellectualize my feelings, then I didn't have them. I was so angry with my mother I wanted to hurt somebody bad. Five years ago, Dr. Lance showed me the kingdom within, and Jesus saved my life. I gave all that hatred and anger to Him. That manipulation. Is that the side of me you want to see? It's still there, dormant, you know. I just have to stop praying. Is that the side of me you've been wondering about all these years? Is that the side you've been looking for? The side of me you think I should show? Doing this lady; doing that lady; just out there, unprotected? Knowing my mother's situation? I was crazy! Well Jewel, if you think that, then you're worse off than I ever was.

Break down that wall, baby. You have a beautiful kingdom inside of you where a goddess lives."

I smiled and then asked him, "Angela went to the conference yesterday and laid some heavy stuff on you, didn't she? Is that what you wanted to talk to me about?"

"No," he said, "I'll tell you all about Angela later. I wanted to talk to you about your father. But that's for later. A long time ago, I went to the God in me. You should have gone to that conference. I heard it was hot. But what I wanted to talk to you about is deeper. Closer. It's about your father."

"What?"

"Later. I'll talk about that stuff later," Then he said, "Yeah, Valerie told me the conference was good."

"I'm not in to stuff like that, Cayenne. I resent the people at that church. My family was a part of that church. And those people pretended we were invisible. They hated my mother. I don't know what they thought of my father, except they were distant toward him. They didn't like me very much. The pastors didn't seem to care. Winnie and Dr. Lance were the only ones who ever were kind to me. I was an active member in that church, Cayenne. Where were they when I needed them? How do you deal with not knowing your family, Cayenne? Your people? I was so lonely. For once, I would just like to have an aunt or an uncle or a cousin to go to for a holiday and sit down and have dinner with them and talk and laugh and play cards and eat barbecue and remember when and smile over photo albums and eat sweet potato pie. Just once I would like to do that. But that is never going to happen, because I have to accept the fact that I don't have a family. And that shit hurts. You know, Cayenne, if all that pain that's buried inside of me came out..." My eyes examined the carpeting again.

"That's a beginning. See, I never knew you felt like that. 'Cause every time I see *you* and ask *you* how you're doing, you say, 'Fine!' So I guess we have a bit of the same problem, right Jewel."

I fixed my blurry eyes on the carpeting. "You know, Cayenne, I appreciate your kindness and your love, and your concern. But I don't need any counseling."

Cayenne sat on the sofa facing me.

His pause brought uncomfortable silence to the room. Finally he whispered, "You want to pray with me?"

"What?" I asked, almost embarrassed. I looked at him as if he was crazy.

"Pray with me, baby," he said.

"Pray with you? I'm not praying with you! I don't feel comfortable doing that, Cayenne."

"Give me your hands."

He kissed them like he used to when I was 14 and he was 19.

"Cayenne, this is so stupid. I do not want to pray with you."

"Just try it, Jewel. It doesn't hurt. I promise."

"I'm not getting counseling. So I hope you don't include that in your prayer!" I told him as I let his fingers embrace mine.

He smiled, closed his eyes and bowed his head. I followed as I listened to Miles Davis' trumpet whispering "Jean Pierre," and Cayenne, whispering, "Dear God, thank you for this time you've given me with my sister, Jewel. Thank you for this day, Lord. Thank you for blessing my life and giving it flavor. I don't come to you today for my needs. I come to you today for my sister, Jewel. Dear God, hold her in your arms the way you held me, and rock her gently in your bosom while filling her with your love. Oh, God, take away the pain, confusion, hurt, fear, anger, hatred, frustration, and any block that keeps her from joy, happiness, peace and your flow. Oh, God, I call on you today to bless her life. Teach her to find you Lord in all of your glory and beauty. Dear God, show her the jewels of her heart and the family of her soul. Dear God, show her the goddess. Let this be the beginning of a new day. Remove the block. Remove the wall. Knock it down, Lord, and build her up. In Jesus' name I pray, so be it. Amen."

Miles Davis was still on. Cayenne wrapped his arms around me as "Jean Pierre" softly disappeared and the uncomfortable silence entered the room again, for a moment. Then "Back Seat Betty" filled the room with laughter. Miles Davis played on until "Fast Track" ended.

Chapter Nineteen

Valerie and Redd were home. From Cayenne's first floor apartment, we heard footsteps above us. They had company. She must have heard the trumpet.

"Hey, Cayenne? You home? Valerie yelled.

"Yeah, Valerie. Jewel's here." He smiled, as he looked my way. I stood there smiling back as I went through his fantastic CD collection. He loved jazz and favored John Coltrane the most. He put on Coltrane's "Giant Steps" CD. The saxophone hushed me.

"Hey girl, how you doin?" Valerie shouted. She was on her way down.

"Who smells so good?" Valerie peeped into Cayenne's apartment holding two buckets of fried chicken.

"It's the candle, Valerie," Cayenne said. "Cedar wood and rosewood."

"Want something to eat? We got chicken," Valerie said.

"That's cool with me," Cayenne said. "But I can't right now. I was supposed to be gone an hour ago. Save me some, okay?" He hugged Valerie as she smiled.

"Cayenne, Bless is upstairs with Mark. He told me to tell you that she fixed her computer, so you might as well relax—you don't have to go over to her house after all. She came by to talk to my husband though, about the mutual funds, T.D.A., and I.R.A. he set up for her.

"Yeah? I need to talk to Redd too about that. I'm glad I don't have to go out. I'm really tired." Cayenne said. He sat on the couch.

"You!" Valerie said. "I'm pissed at you!" She continued, pointing at me.

I sighed. "Valerie, I just couldn't," I told her.

"Yeah, I see. What the hell happened to your eye?"

"Nothing, really. I had a little accident, that's all," I said, embarrassed.

"Yeah. With somebody's fist, right?"

She frowned at me as I searched for a fabulous fake.

Those eyes. Cayenne hugged Valerie and ran upstairs with the food.

Valerie said, "They're playing Scrabble. It's like old times, girl. Come on up and get some food. Don't worry about Bless. We about to send her home! She treats that beautiful little girl of hers like dirt. Seem like all the joy has left her. She's ice cold. Ain't never seen Bless like this! I hope things work out! Look, Imani I know you been drinking a lot. I know Blue puts his hands on you. We know. Anyway, Cayenne is helping Bless put together a demo tape for her music career, and he's teaching her how to use her zip drive. And my little Mocha is recovering from the flu. so Mark is checking up on her. Come upstairs girl, and let's just be a family again. We love you. You know, Carmel received an email this afternoon from his mother, that lady, Clara. He said it's important. He was ringing your bell like a maniac, so we asked him over here to wait for you. He couldn't wait. Said he had to get to the restaurant for a staff meeting. He gave me this envelope to give you from his mother. I know you're glad it's sealed shut! Lord knows, I wish I could have opened it!"

I stared at the envelope, and then ripped it open to only find a paragraph of writing. Disappointed, I told Valerie that I would talk to everyone at another time, and I left her standing there remembering my bruised face as I returned to my brownstone.

Chapter Twenty

"That's right Miss. No. I'm not a resident. Yes. I'm a neighbor. My name is Cayenne Brown. That's correct."

"Cayenne?"

"Yeah, Valerie?"

"She opened her eyes."

Valerie was in the kitchen adjusting the Venetian blinds that led to my backyard. She lifted me by the arm from the kitchen chair and walked with me to my bedroom as Cayenne remained on his cell phone talking to a nine, one, one operator. Mark grabbed me by my waist to help her. I gave him a "Shit on you" look, but I don't think he noticed or cared. After all, it was over.

Cayenne continued talking to the operator as he followed us to the bedroom. "Miss? Yes. She seems to be awake now. Yes. Please send an ambulance." He placed the phone on a hook that was hanging on his jogging pants.

"Shit!" What happened, man?" Mark asked them.

"I don't know, Mark. She must've been like this since last night. Did they fix the door?" Cayenne asked him.

"No. It's still hanging off the hinges. Some men are working on it. What happened?" Mark asked.

Cayenne told him, "Well, we smelled smoke. Valerie smelled it first. She was getting ready to run over to The Temple of Faith Church to help set up a banquet she was catering later in the day. She came down to my apartment, and when she realized that it wasn't me or our neighbor on the other side, we headed next door to Jewel's house. We kept calling her name and banging on the door. No answer. We heard the teakettle whistling. And then we smelled smoke. We called the fire department. We found her passed out against the kitchen table, ready to fall right off the kitchen chair. The fire department just left. The teakettle was burning. Another couple of minutes, it would have exploded, and we would have been looking at an entirely different situation. Thanks for coming, man."

I felt Valerie pat my face with a cold, damp cloth, as she helped me get into bed with my clothes on and pull the covers over me. She told me, "We're your family, Imani. You gotta' get some help." She whispered, and then she turned to Cayenne to say, "She must have read that note that Carmel gave her yesterday about all that strange shit her father was investigating about her mother's family. It must have upset her."

Then, no one said a thing. I waited. Nothing. I wanted to tell them that I didn't care anymore. I wanted to tell them how Jack Daniels helped me forget.

"How is she?" Valerie asked Mark. Words remained stuck in my throat. I wanted to tell her how much my head hurt, but I closed my eyes. No one seemed to notice.

Mark told Valerie, "I don't know. She doesn't look well."

"You think she's okay?" Cayenne asked.

Mark said, "Seems so now, but she was definitely drinking. You can smell it all over the house. You saw the empty bottle on the kitchen table, right?"

"Yeah, damn!" Cayenne said.

"A liter bottle of Jack Daniel's?" Mark said.

"Shit! You think she drank it in one sitting? It looks like she finished it, Cayenne!"

"Maybe, I don't know, man. You think she did?" Cayenne asked him. Valerie finished wiping my face with what felt like a cloth filled with ice water. She then went in to the hallway near the living room. Someone was at the door.

"Naw. Maybe she did it over a period of time. I think the whole bottle in one day would have killed her, Cayenne. Plus, we found a packet of sleeping pills. But it looks like she only took two of them. How long she been drinking? You know?" Mark asked Cayenne.

"No, Mark. The first time I saw her drinking hard liquor was the day she got the news of her father's death. She used to take a little something every now and then on the weekends, but damn, she must have been drinking a lot over the past year. I never seen no Jack Daniel's. She had some whiskey on the day her father died. But I thought that was his. And that bottle was nearly empty. Wine. Brandy in her tea like her father, most of the time, coffee though, maybe a Pina Colada at The Blue Zephyr, but Jack Daniels? Never seen that, man!"

I slowly opened my eyes to catch Mark staring.

"Well, let's see if she can talk, now that her eyes are open, Cayenne."

I kept seeing shadows. I was feeling them touching me. I was trying to tell them to stop. Someone's fingers were in my hair. I found some words and asked quietly, "What the hell's going on?" I kept asking them. No one would answer me.

"Her eyes are open, now. Thanks for coming, Mark. Can you take a look at her?" Cayenne asked.

"Yeah, sure," Mark said.

Why are they looking at me like that? "Leave me alone." I said.

"Imani?" Mark asked.

I whispered, "Stop touching me. Go away. My head. It really hurts. Why is it so cold in here? It's freezing in here."

"Imani?" He repeated.

"What time is it? I have to go to work."

"Imani? Can you see my fingers?" Mark asked. He went on. "Look at my fingers. Keep following them," he said. Up. Down. Left. Right. Little circles. Big circles. All that did was make my head hurt more.

"Imani? Where are you now? Can you tell me that?" Mark asked, continuously waving his hands in my face.

"I don't know. Home?"

"Where are you now, Imani?"

"Home?"

"What's today's date?" Mark asked.

"My head hurts. I can't remember. It's January, I think."

"What time of day is it?" Mark continued.

"Turn on the lights. It's dark in here."

"The lights are on, Imani."

"All of them?"

"Yes."

"It's night?"

"It's 6:30 in the morning, Imani," Mark said. He placed his fingers around my wrist. Was he trying to hold my hands? I held his hands, but he kept grabbing my wrist. I grabbed his hand.

I told him, "I'm sorry."

"It's okay, Imani. I understand. It's alright. It's going to be okay. Imani? Did you drink the whole bottle of Jack Daniel's?"

"I'm sorry. I just wanted to…"

"It's okay. The ambulance is here. We're going to take you to the hospital. We want to make sure you don't have any DTs, Delirium Tremens or withdrawal symptoms. We want to check your brain's chemical balance, your liver, and give you a complete physical. Anyway, from what I've read about alcoholism, DTs don't show up for at least six to 48 hours and sometimes they can show up after you've stopped drinking for up to a week. They're very dangerous. And we know you've been drinking a lot, Imani."

"No. I haven't. I'm sorry. I don't want to go to the hospital, Mark. I'm sorry." I kept repeating it.

"It's okay. We're going to take good care of you. What's the last thing you remember, Imani?" Mark asked with ice following his voice.

"I was sleeping. A whistling sound. It kept whistling.'

"She's incoherent," Mark said as he turned to Valerie and Cayenne.

I told them, "I am not incoherent, damn it! I was just so tired. I took two sleeping pills. Then I had a drink or two. Maybe more. Then I just wanted some coffee. All I had was instant. So I had to boil water. But I fell asleep. It was so late. Like four or five in the morning. I know what DTs are, Mark. I don't have that kind of drinking problem!"

Mark smiled, the sarcastic way he always did when he wanted to make you feel like you had two horns on your head. He asked me, "So, tell me, Imani, what kind of drinking problem you *think* you have?"

"Go to hell, Mark."

"Hush, baby. It's okay," Cayenne said. He kissed my forehead.

Then he smiled with those eyes.

Two emergency medical technicians were in my bedroom. They were whispering to Mark, who told them that he was a pediatrician. I felt someone hold my arm and wrap what felt like a thick rubber band around it. I was scared to move.

"Please try not to move, Miss," one of the technicians shouted. He put something to my mouth and told me to take a deep breath.

I did.

"Zero point two oh," the other technician said. He continued talking. He counted to three. They moved me to a cold bed.

"No," I told them. "Stop."

"It's okay, Jewel. Valerie's here. And I'm here. Winnie's on her way with her daughter, Dr. Clarke. They're going to meet us." Cayenne said.

"Where? Why?" I asked Cayenne.

"At the hospital, Jewel."

"No. Stop. I don't want to go to the damn hospital. I just need some aspirin. My head really hurts. Please stop."

A door slammed.

Chapter Twenty-One

"Thank you, God. You are so worthy to be praised. We bless your holy name."

Winnie was whispering. Cayenne, Valerie, Mark, and Lateesha joined in, chanting the same prayer of blessing.

News footage from the 1963 March on Washington of Dr. Martin Luther King, Jr. giving his famous "I Have a Dream" speech on the television could be heard in the background.

I opened my eyes to face a television set of Dr. Martin Luther King, Jr., eloquently speaking to a crowd of more than 25,000 believers as a news correspondent interrupted him to remind viewers of what they missed on a sweltering August day in 1963, and that the dream still lives on thirty-seven years later in a holiday honoring him.

The prayerful whispering stopped while the news stayed on. Lateesha Clarke, a psychiatrist and director of the church's Clarke Center for Holistic Health and Healing placed her hands over mine and stood over me staring at me, as I made sure my sheets were pulled entirely over my body up to my neck. They had undressed me completely while I had been sleeping.

"How are you, sister Imani?"

"Fine," I told her. I tried to avoid her emerald eyes that reflected the sunlight. It danced into the room and brought on a new headache for me.

I must have been squinting because she asked, "Would you like me to close the blinds?"

"Yes," I whispered. My throat was sore.

"I haven't seen you in such a long time, Imani. I didn't even know you still lived in Jewel Park. I just moved back from Manhattan to run the center myself. I attended your father's funeral, but on that day, I had an emergency and had to return to the city. I'm sorry."

Her voice was soothing. I thought of velvet smoothness and was reminded of Bless.

I said, "You look really young."

"You mean, for a doctor," Dr. Clarke said with a smile that accentuated great teeth and a heart-shaped face the color of brown sugar. A hint of blue green was on her lower lids and a soft color of aqua, so soft you almost missed it, played over her eyelids. Black brown African locks with cowrie shells near her waist hung gracefully over a navy blue suit with a mini skirt. She wore flat shoes and antique earrings with a matching bracelet. She was Dr. Lance's 26-year old daughter from the first marriage.

"Where am I?" I finally asked her.

"Washington Avenue Medical Center."

"Damn it." I said with a sigh.

"You want to tell me what happened?"

I wanted to say, "Hell no!" Instead, I accepted her warmth and said, "I almost set the house on fire."

"Really?" Her eyes wanted more information.

"You already know what happened," I told her, embarrassed. I guessed that Valerie, Cayenne, or Mark had filled her in.

She told me, "I heard about what happened, but I'd like to hear your view."

"I don't really know what happened. The last thing I remember is that it was about four thirty or five in the morning and I wanted some instant coffee. I put the teapot on filled with water, and I rested on my kitchen table. The next thing I know, I'm being carried into the bedroom by Mark and Valerie, and then there're two E.M.T. people standing over me, counting."

"Do you know what they were counting?"

"No," I told her.

"Your blood alcohol concentration level. It was the equivalent of a person who had consumed approximately twelve drinks in one hour! We also found a small dosage of sleeping pills in your system. You know, you could have killed yourself or worse, drifted into a comatose state? You want to tell me what you think about that?"

I laughed nervously. She had to be wrong about that. I didn't feel drunk, just sleepy. I didn't remember how many drinks I'd had last night, but I had been drinking throughout the night. I wanted to forget a lot of things after I read the letter Carmel had given me from Clara. Plus, the bottle was only half full. I had had ice in the glass! How much damage could two damn sleeping pills do? My mother did it all the time.

I breathed deeply, trying to forget that. I just know that photographs were visiting my mind that I couldn't handle seeing.

Dr. Lateesha patted my hands. "It's okay, Imani. It's alright. We're waiting for the doctor before you are released. But, we'd like to talk to you first. Is there anyone you'd like us to call or be here with you when we talk to the doctor? If you want, I'll leave and let just you and the doctor talk." She smoothed her skirt and she sat down on the chair next to my bed.

"No," I told her as I thought of Blue. I then changed my mind and said, "You can stay. Can Cayenne stay?" I saw his eyes and his smile from across the room. He was staring at me as Valerie, Winnie and Mark were quietly leaving the room. Cayenne came over to my bed as the doctor walked in, a very handsome black man I recognized immediately.

"Hello, everyone. I'm Dr. Lawrence Clarke. How are you, Imani?" Lateesha greeted her 28-year old brother with a smile. He had been at my father's funeral. He played the saxophone with the band that worked at The Blue Zephyr. He was softly scented with inviting cologne. He too wore his hair in African locks, short, neat, and tightly curled.

I felt nauseous.

"Fine," I told him.

"That's good, Imani. I'm glad you're fine, because you could have gone into a coma. Sleeping pills too? God must have something special planned for you, sister. You're still here! Do you want to die?"

"What?" I asked him, surprised at his question, and an attitude I mistook for arrogance.

"I asked you if you wanted to die."

"No. Of course not," I told him.

"Do you plan on having children?"

I laughed as I said, "Not anytime soon."

"Well, if you keep drinking, Imani, you will die. And your hopes of starting a family will be that, just hopes. Alcoholism is devastating. What I just want you to understand, Imani, is your future is so beautiful. You have so much to offer. I've seen how well you work with the children at The Jewel. I know how much you love them. You have a lot of talent. Don't you ever reflect on your achievements? You've overcome so much. I know that you received several awards for your work with children in Jewel Park, even recognition by the president of the United States at a White House dinner your father bragged about years ago. I remember you being very active at our community center when you were younger. You were a good leader, organizing fashion shows, bringing together mentoring programs for teens, helping our church set up a job fair for college students when you didn't even live in Jewel Park. I remember, because I participated. You may have a year or two on me, but I remember you. Don't you ever reflect on that, sister?"

It seemed to me that my achievements had not mattered, and I would never be able to live up to the genius of my father, so why talk about it or remember? My achievements were buried. I nodded.

Dr. Lawrence went on, "I don't want to see you or another black person die of this disease. Alcoholism, drug abuse, and addictions are all caused by secrets. It seems to me that you're in the beginning stages of alcohol dependency. That's where Dr. Lateesha comes in. You can receive outpatient counseling at our holistic health center that Dr. Lateesha runs, with an emphasis on holistic healing. You can be treated. But you have to want to be treated. I'm going to ask you a few questions, and we'll start from there. Okay?" He now smiled.

"Fine," I said.

He grabbed a yellow, legal size notepad and took a pen from the breast pocket of his white overcoat. After asking me several questions about my health and drinking habits, he wrote an essay as I watched him turn to the next page on the yellow pad. There was uncomfortable silence in the room.

"Okay, Imani. That's enough for now. I'm going to set you up with a therapist at the center. You can make an appointment after you get dressed. I recommend you lose some weight also. I think you have clinical depression. A healthier diet would help your depression. Exercise. A positive environment. Dr. Lateesha will talk about all of that. Also, I'd like to see you in a month for a physical to see how you're progressing. You should get annual checkups, and you should also make a G.Y.N. appointment. You shouldn't let things like that go by. The last time you had any kind of physical was six years ago. At your age, you really should get annual checkups. I can't stress how important that is, Imani. You're slightly anemic, so I'm recommending some iron pills. You don't need a prescription, but an over the counter iron pill would be great, like Slow Fe. You should take one iron pill a day with a vitamin supplement. Your cholesterol is high, 248. I'd like you to get it down to under 200. Your blood pressure is also high. There are a lot of options, Imani. Do you have any questions?"

"No," I said.

Dr. Lawrence said, "You can get dressed now, Imani. Make an appointment with Dr. Lateesha for a therapist with the Clarke Center, and she'll take it from there." Dr. Lawrence had filled three pages on the yellow pad with information about me. He put the pad in a folder the hospital had already started for me and wished everyone in the room a good day. He exited when his name was called over the hospital's speaker system.

Cayenne asked, "You want to join me for dinner, later? We can talk and just chill, okay?"

"Dinner?" I asked, and then I smiled.

"Yes, dinner."

"Well, I don't want no damn salad," I said.

"Now, that's the Jewel I know." Cayenne smiled.

Chapter Twenty-Two

The weather had created ten inches of snow for the people of Jewel Park to struggle with and had kept many patrons away for the week from the Eva Creek Soul Food Restaurant. I dodged work again for three days, and I had not been out of the house since I had gotten home from the hospital. Principal Dennison had found a way to keep me out of trouble since Bless had resigned from her teaching job. And I wasn't sure how much longer I planned to work there either.

I still had not returned any of the messages Blue had left on the phone and the last thing I wanted to do was go out, but Cayenne was persistent with gifts of silky body lotions. Soup, salad, and sandwiches came from Valerie, and my favorite coconut cake came from the church's restaurant that Valerie and Redd owned, The Prayerful Café Corner. So I dressed well. I was comfortable, and the cold and slush-filled streets didn't affect me.

I ordered smothered fried chicken, white rice, collard greens, coconut cake (four layers), and coffee with cream that I desperately tried to drink with only three sugars. The attempt failed, and I ended up adding eight or nine teaspoons in my coffee. Cayenne's eyes followed each teaspoon and then focused on me after he finished a plate of grilled mullet, red rice, and collard greens.

"This is fantastic," I said. I watched him stare me down as I drank my coffee slowly to avoid any beverage with Mr. Boston, Mr. Daniel's or Early Times Old Style Kentucky Whiskey.

"Yes, Jewel, it is," Cayenne told me as he waved to several of his clients sitting at a table nearby.

The décor of the restaurant was like the food, warm and satisfying. The restaurant reminded me of a cozy, large living room in a brownstone.

"Is everything alright?" a familiar voice asked. I looked up into the eyes of Carmel. He smiled and shook Cayenne's hand, and then kissed my cheek.

He and Carmel spoke for a while about business. Carmel then informed me that I had to attend a staff meeting because I owned the restaurant, something my father had worked out with Clara before he died.

"Enjoy," Carmel said, as his girlfriend Zalia walked up and embraced him with a short kiss on the lips. She waved to us afterward as Carmel said, "I'll check ya'll later." He looked at Zalia and turned back to us, "I have a serious meal of my own that needs some special attention. Enjoy yourselves." He smiled.

"I didn't know that brother managed this place. I've seen him quite a few times at the Blue Zephyr," Cayenne said.

I told him all about the meal Carmel shared with me at my father's house.

"He's Clara's son?" Cayenne asked. He said, "I remember Clara."

I told Cayenne, "Well, she emailed me something. It's just a paragraph telling me to talk to Autumn with a message at the end that sounded like some kind of warning, 'Before it's too late!' She thinks Autumn is my aunt. If that's so, then my mother and Autumn are sisters. But what made him marry Autumn instead of my mother? In the email, Clara wished me well and invited me down to her home on Eva Creek Island where she now lives."

Cayenne placed his chin in his hand and rested his elbow on the table. I stared at his manicured fingers. He leaned back in the chair and continued to sip tea. A minute passed before he asked quietly, "How do you feel, Jewel?"

"Fine."

He smiled with those eyes and leaned closer.

"Did you get to talk to Dr. Lateesha?"

"Yes. I have an appointment with her tomorrow."

"That's good, Jewel."

I sighed. Dr. Lateesha's card was on its way to a garbage dump along with the appointment time, and I was definitely not going back to Dr. Lawrence. I had already planned what I would say to Dr. Lateesha if she called. I sipped coffee.

Cayenne smiled and the lavender butterflies I felt whenever I heard Maxwell's music reappeared, new ones, and I remembered being named Beautiful the day I was born.

Chapter Twenty-Three

The Early Times Old Style Kentucky Whiskey was smooth and easy as I slowly sipped it from an orange juice glass filled with ice. I filled the room with Maxwell's Urban Hang Suite CD. After spending an hour looking in the Jewel Park phone book, I found a Silver Row address for an Autumn C. Taylor and a phone number. I wrote only the address down and placed it in my journal.

I called in sick on a rainy Friday. Space Goddess One was not surprised and offered to share the information with Space Goddess Two who I did not have to speak to.

The alcohol made me forget to put the answering machine on, so when I answered the phone, I expected it to be Blue because I had promised to call him back.

"Good morning, Imani," Dr. Lateesha said pleasantly.

I could not think of a fabulous fake, and I could not hang up, so I said, "Good morning, doctor." I forced my mouth to move correctly. I feigned innocence in my forgetfulness about the appointment I should have kept an hour ago. I kept thinking, *Shit, shit, shit, shit, shit* as I spoke.

"Imani, you had an appointment with me today at 8 A.M. Why are you still home? Was there a problem?"

Shit, shit, shit, shit, shit, I kept thinking as I said, "Yes, doctor, I'm not feeling well. I think I have a really bad cold. I apologize for not calling. Can I reschedule for next week?"

"No. Why don't you call me when you're not drunk. Do you think you can remember that, Imani?"

"Doctor, I am not drunk! As a matter of fact, I took the day off just for the appointment, but I took some cold medicine and slept through the morning. I'm very sorry."

"Yes. So am I, Imani. Would you like to come in this afternoon or evening, perhaps? I have two openings: one is for four-thirty and another is for seven. We also have emergency appointments until midnight. I'll be here until then also. What would you like to do?"

"Well, Dr. Lateesha, I'm not feeling that great, and I really would like to reschedule for next week."

"What exactly is wrong, Imani? I may be able to help."

"Well, I have a cold, and probably a fever and I think I ate something that didn't agree with me. And I'm not drunk, doctor. I really resent your comment."

"Okay. What day do you think you can come in next week, Imani?"

"Friday evening, around 7 P.M."

"We only have a four-thirty opening, next Friday. Can you make that?"

"No. I have another commitment. What about the week after that?"

Dr. Lateesha breathed heavily and said, "Why don't we do this? Come on in this evening, around seven. Get some sleep, and I'll come pick you up. How's that?"

Shit, shit, shit, shit, shit "That sounds fine, doctor. I'll see you at seven," I told her.

"This evening, Imani."

"Yes, I'll be ready."

"We do a complimentary consultation, but we don't usually pick people up. So, this will not happen again. If, for some reason, you miss this appointment, I will not contact you again, Imani. It will be up to you to reschedule. I hope that you reschedule with the Clarke Center. If you're not comfortable here, there are other places I would refer you to or you could find help on your own through your healthcare provider. Are we clear on this?"

"Yes. That's fine, doctor. I'll be ready. Thank you so much."

"Now, you're at 1630 Dandelion Street?"

"Yes. That's off of Robinson Boulevard?"

"Okay, Imani. I'll see you at seven. Get some rest."

"Thank you, Dr. Lateesha. I will."

"Damn it," I whispered after I hung up the phone. Blue had left several messages on my machine and had left one message telling me he would stop by tonight around seven, and I hadn't spoken with him since we argued. I fell asleep as I forgot all about Blue.

*   *   *   *

"Being sober all the time, would definitely help you put the pieces of your life together, Imani. Though out of fairness, concern, and a conflict of interest, I cannot be your doctor."

Dr. Lateesha's office at the Clarke Center was small, but decorated with awards and achievements along with beautiful Kente cloth that accented the walls. Her desk was filled with pictures of her gorgeous husband and daughter in various family poses.

I had spent forty-five minutes telling her about my puzzle, and fifteen minutes filling out a questionnaire with the same questions Dr. Lawrence had asked me at the hospital, but I became vague when she asked about my personal life, my relationship during childhood with my parents, the different homes, relationships with men, relationships, period.

After she kept getting one word answers from me, she said, "I'm beginning to understand. Imani, the information you tell me is confidential, and I will never repeat it to anyone. It's the law. The questionnaire you filled out is also confidential. That stays in my file and is not shared with anyone. We are very professional here. I want you to know though, my brother and I both knew about your mother's drinking because she tried to quit. She really did. As children we saw her here often. She knew my mother Gladys before my mother died from alcohol abuse. But my brother and I only knew your mother through her fashion magazines. Like your father, your mother was a very private person. She would never attend the sessions or the AA meetings she was referred to. She stopped going to church." Dr. Lateesha sighed as she watched me.

She continued, "I'm referring you to Dr. Renee Alton. She's here at the center on Monday's, Wednesdays, and Fridays. You can reschedule an appointment now or call tomorrow. Also, we have an AA chapter that meets here every Friday and Saturday at 7 P.M. That's included in your treatment. You must also attend Sunday services regularly, and join a church ministry. Once a week prayer meeting is also a requirement. I understand you are still a church member. That is a requirement if you decide to participate in our complete healing process. All you have to do is go. When you attend the chapter meetings for Alcoholics Anonymous, you'll get a buddy—that's someone you can talk to and support you through tough times. You'll also get a prayer partner, a spiritual guide to pray with. Are you ready to make these kinds of commitments, Imani?"

"No, Dr. Lateesha. Honestly, I'm just not ready." I told her truthfully, after an hour of what I felt was a waste of time. And then there was the problem of paying $150 a week for telling my problems to a stranger. Even though I had the money, I didn't want to hand over a check for that much money just to talk to someone. My H.M.O covered the expense, but then my name and personal information would be accessible to any employer, insurance agent or just about anyone who needed to do a background check. Cayenne had told me that anyone could find out anything on the Internet if they paid the right price. I didn't want people knowing that I was under the care of a psychiatrist and going to AA meetings! There had to be another way to get help.

"Dr. Lateesha," I said, "I do need some help, but I'm not ready to do it this way. I have to do it my way."

"And what way is that, Imani?"

"I don't know. I just don't know."

"Look, sister. You're on, what I call, Easy Street now. You can function. This is the period where you can make a choice. But it's a thin line. You've developed what I call in my book, The Awareness Boundary. You know that you drink a lot, and that you have a problem, but the drinking has not left you incapacitated. You have the ability to stop at any time. This is what you tell yourself. And for a while, that's true, but under stress, you start again. And this is a cycle. Until one day, you set the house on fire. Or you oversleep for an important meeting. Or you get fired. Or something tragic, beyond your control happens, and you dip into what I call The Void. This is the place where I believe your mother was. This dark place where you feel you'll never see any light. No one can help you. You're all alone. That's when the alcohol takes you to a place of numbness. You need more each day, until you wake up one day and can't remember why you smell or why there's blood all over you because you've had your period for three days and didn't realize it or on a different day, you can't get home because you don't have any money to get home because someone robbed you while you were sleeping on a filthy sidewalk and the place between your thighs is uncomfortable because you've had sex and you can't remember with whom. This is what you don't see in the movies that glamorize alcohol use. The last stage is disease, insanity, death or all three. Sister, whatever you do, realize now, that this is the best time for you to get help. Are we clear?"

"Yes doctor," I told her.

Chapter Twenty-four

Lavender from my freshly braided hair whispered to me as I passed rows of fresh cut grass, some even peeping through cement, where dirty ice had formed from thirty-degree weather. I was shaking so badly that I draped the scarf that was around my neck over my head, as I glanced at the Autumn C. Taylor, Silver Row address I had written down, looking carefully at the numbers of each house until I found the one I needed that matched the one on the paper. It was the same neighborhood my father lived in; she was only two blocks from his house.

I rang the doorbell deeply hidden in front of the clutches of a brick house where a softly painted brown porch rested against plants. They barely breathed in six colorful terra cotta pots that leaned against a warm living room window behind the brick walls of the brown stones of the house. I took a deep breath and stopped to put a piece of peppermint candy in my mouth. Three cups of coffee instead of whiskey, and the memory of Dr. Lateesha's words had left me so anxious that I breathed in more air to calm myself.

Leroy Taylor answered the door quickly, wearing gray boxers and a scent that reminded me of patchouli. The only picture I'd seen of him was one that had fallen out of Autumn's wallet years ago after her divorce from my father when I had seen her at Dee Dee's Deli in Jewel Park. The picture of him I had carried around with the other nine was a younger version of him. In the deli, Autumn had not spoken to me when I had stood right behind her and she was showing Leroy's picture to a cashier she knew while at the same time making sure I had gotten a good glimpse of him as well. I remembered they shared a joke about the endurance younger men offered to women her age. He was ten years younger than she.

"Imani? Can I help you?" I stepped back against the cold wind as I stared at how beautiful he was up close, and I remembered the mocha chocolate man with slanted eyes in a plaid shirt on a fishing boat with my father, and a beautiful Southern accent. I stepped back again and took in the size of his body and its exquisite strength. Closely cropped, tight curls of gray framed his eloquent face.

"It's cold as hell out here, Imani. Good to finally meet you. I'm Leroy Taylor. You Matthew's daughter, right?"

"Yes," I told him.

"Whatchu want, gal?"

I quickly said, "Mrs. Autumn C. Taylor? I'd like to speak with her. Is she home?"

"I think she been expectin' you. Come on in, gal!" He said, hesitantly, not caring how much my eyes wandered around his tall, muscular frame or how the cold was torturing my body.

I took a deep breath as the sound of Patti Labelle's voice singing soulfully on an upstairs stereo greeted me. Like a ghost standing behind it, the door slowly opened as I saw the hand that had reached for a knife when I was eleven, pull it open and catch more coldness.

"Cece, she's here," Leroy said, as he winked at Autumn. Her head touched his shoulder. He bent down and kissed her gently on the cheek as he whispered, "Cece, I know you can handle this, love. Just take it slow. I'll be here for you." Leroy kissed Autumn again, this time on her lips.

In a sheer negligee barely covering her thighs, French manicured toenails and fingernails to match, flawless makeup and spiraling curls touching her shoulders, she resembled a curvaceous doll that had been dipped in mocha chocolate, and maybe a woman five or ten years older than me, rather than one that was 52 years of age.

"Hello, Imani. Come in." she said, seeming not to remember the decades we had shared avoiding each other. Autumn smiled as if she knew exactly why I was there.

I walked in and opened my coat, careful not to take it off as I took in the Southern drawl of an accent Autumn had spent a lifetime trying to get rid of, but couldn't, and the Gullah/Geechee words still returned.

Leroy sat in the kitchen facing us over a plate of baked salmon with some kind of white sauce, a baked potato, and steamed broccoli with a heavily buttered roll. The second time he glanced at us he took his plate and went up the spiraling black staircase to the bedroom where the music was coming from. The stereo clicked off and a television clicked on to the sound of a game show.

I watched the woman I had never really seen, noticed, or knew, walk quickly to the couch where a lavender bathrobe that matched her negligee was, letting the scent of *Coco Chanel* follow us. She put the robe on, along with matching slippers that were an inch high.

"Have a seat Imani. It's been a long time, hasn't it?" Autumn said.

My icy stare indicated that I did not want to stay long, but that if I had to, I would not get comfortable.

"Let me take your coat," Autumn said.

"No, thank you. That's okay." I told her.

Our hazel eyes became part of the conversation. More fear traveled through my body.

Her gaze made me change my mind; I removed my hat, coat, and scarf and placed them next to me on the soft leather couch. I glanced at the fireplace where the warmth in the room was coming from.

Matching oak end tables held aqua green lamps trimmed in lace. Two champagne glasses, half full, were on the rectangular green, glass coffee table.

The home was rich with ancient artifacts. An actual quilt that hung on the nearby wall with the constellation Eridanus graced the entire kitchen and living room area. Autumn pointed to the quilt with the constellation of Eridanus. "My mother made that for me when I was five. Isn't it beautiful?"

"Beautiful," I repeated without much enthusiasm, "But I want to talk to you."

"Waffuh?" Autumn asked again, calmly.

"I need to know some things about my parents that you may be able to help me with."

She showed me a mouth filled with perfect white teeth, and then more seriously asked, as if she had been waiting for me, "So where would you like to begin."

Her own icy stare was melting and this made me more uncomfortable. Autumn then said, "Why don't you start, Imani? Why didn't you call me when Matthew passed?"

I started to tell her that I didn't know, but I remembered Cayenne's laughter at the sound of those words, and because I didn't want to deal with any fabulous fakes anymore, I told her, "I was afraid to call you." I waited for her to ask, "Why?" But she didn't.

"That's ruckuhnizable," she said. Autumn continued, "Your father and I agreed that if he shoud pass away, I should contact you. Of course how could I? I have been so angry with your mother for your entire life. And it wasn't even her fault. To see to it that we did speak, he left you a note in his daily planner. I know this because the week before he died, I spoke with him about setting a date and time to meet with you. We wanted to talk to you together. But he died.

"After your father's passing, it has only been recently that I have begun the process of letting things go. Fuhtrue! Some things, I have saved for you, though." She said this with that wicked smile, and then continued. "I found myself getting sick at all of the memories. I started getting a cold every other month, and then headaches, insomnia, and stomach aches. Once I even thought I was pregnant! That was just riddik'lus! But once I let the bullshit go, well, things have been better. By the way, did you get the box of pictures?"

"Yes."

"Good." Autumn said. "I know you won't ruckuhnize any of them, but you should have them. You'll understand why later," she said.

I took a deep breath as I touched my Coach bag where the puzzle of my life was.

Autumn surprised me when she said, "Let's begin with the knife. Remember the knife?"

I breathed deeply as I met her eyes with fear. I whispered, "Yes."

Autumn continued, "And from then on, I learned to hate. But see, Imani, my hatred goes way back to red clay. Savannah, Georgia, red clay. And deep wounds."

Tears had formed in her eyes, and she took a sip from one of the glasses of champagne. "Would you like some?" Autumn asked.

I hesitated. "Do you have anything else?"

She pointed to the bar, a small room decorated with antique liquor bottles mounted to the walls behind the kitchen counter.

I mumbled, "Coffee please," and then I asked for sugar.

"Fine," Autumn said, as she went on. She laughed without smiling and went into the kitchen to put on a pot of coffee. "This is the best coffee in the world, It's Kona Coffee. I get it shipped to our supermarket, Taylor Associates, from Hawaii. I'm sure you'll find it up tuh de notch."

After she drank Leroy's glass of bubbly, she lifted a fancy bucket filled with three bottles of champagne nearly buried in ice, placed one bottle on the coffee table, uncorked it, and poured herself a glassful of champagne, the color of a pink rose.

Chapter Twenty-Five

I was waiting for curse words and spit and icy stares. But none came after the coffee or champagne.

"I'm sure Carmel or Clara has told you about Charles, your father's brother. Your father instructed them to." Autumn said.

I took a sip of the coffee and was careful with the sugar as I nodded. "I met Carmel, and he told me about Charles." I said. "I'll start with the knife. Why the knife, Autumn?" I asked.

"Fear is the worst kind of sin, Imani. Your mother ever bad mout' me?"

I smiled.

Autumn took in a deep breath after sipping champagne. She whispered, "I am your great aunt. Ruby was my niece. She was the daughter of my brother, Saul Weaver. He married a white woman named Jurnee Miller Stalworth who gave birth to your mother, Ruby. Jurnee's father murdered my five uncles by setting a fire to my grandmother's house in 1901. Nana Zola Jewel, my mother, tried to keep this a secret for her entire life because her mother, Jewel White, asked her to. The pain was too much. But your father discovered the truth and wrote about it in a book in 1970 called, *The Children of Eva Creek Island*. My brother Saul was brutally beaten by a Klansman for marrying Jurnee. Your father's father—Jackson Henderson, witnessed Saul's beating, and years later he was murdered. Your father spent his life trying to find out who murdered his father!

"There's a video cassette I made for you to help you understand what I'm about to tell you. I made the tape because I didn't think you and I would ever get a chance to talk. It waits for you on the Gullah Sea Island of Eva Creek in the house your mother and I grew up in. There you will also find the blessings you never received.

"Well, my parents, Nana Zola Jewel and John Weaver, had seven children. Nana Zola Jewel fostered Ruby as the eighth child. Saul was my brother. In 1936, Saul married a white woman named Jurnee Miller Stalworth. Six months after the marriage, she and Saul wrote a letter to my mother begging Mother Zola to help them find a new home because she was pregnant with Saul's child and living in a Baptist Church on Eva Creek Island where Clara Rogers worked. Saul and Jurnee had your mother Ruby in our house on Eva Creek Island in 1937, where they had lived for the last six months of Jurnee's pregnancy. After that day, Jewel White, my grandmother, never spoke to her daughter, Mother Zola again."

Autumn gave me time to understand why by finishing an entire glass of champagne before she continued talking. She kept pushing her curly hair away from her face. She poured herself another drink. I needed more than time. But I said, "You are my great aunt Cecelia Jewel, the one no one ever talked about! You know, my mother didn't like Jewel White! God, how Saul must have hurt them! His love was God's love." I said to her softly.

Autumn smiled, "Back then, though, there just wasn't that much love in the world, not for that! Not Jewel." She continued talking, "On the night Mother Zola died in 1982, your mother Ruby, your father Matthew, and I had been at the hospital with Mother Zola and there she told us the truth."

She continued, "That night Mother Zola told Ruby that a white woman was her real mother. Mother Zola told us the whole story. That woman's father was a murderer, and Saul knew it! And your father knew it, and wrote about it!

"Ruby always thought Saul was her brother. When he died, she was only seven. And then at age 45 Ruby finds out that the man she thought was her brother all those decades was really her father? The lie cut her deeply.

"That night in 1982, I told Mother Zola about the box I had stolen from her closet when I was 16. She was too weak to scream at me, so she whispered to all of us that there were pictures of Ruby's mother's family in that box and of Ruby's mother. Ruby became irate. The box never meant anything to me. But I knew that it was important somehow to Mother Zola because she had kept it a secret, hidden away in the back of her closet where she kept her money. She had bankrolls of the stuff!

"When I went in to her closet, I was really looking for money to travel and to spend in New York. I took only a portion of the money I found. I grew up hating her because of the way she treated me in comparison to the way she treated your mother Ruby. And I hated that John Weaver, my father, with his hazel eyes and fair skin, never acknowledged me as his daughter because of my darkness. He never believed that I was his child, although Mother Zola assured him that I was theirs all the time, going out of her way to show him the birth certificate and point out to him the similar features we shared regardless of our skin tones. She even got me to take a blood test right in front of John, who was a very well known doctor on Eva Greek Island. I was ten. My heart got broken that day, and I never forgot what my own father made me do just to prove that I was his. After that, I felt I didn't' belong to anyone.

"Ruby and all the others were treated sweetly, just because they were lighter. They had long hair and gray eyes. The only thing your mother and I had in common was our eye color. We had hazel eyes like John. I liked the color of my skin, but I hated the way they all made me feel about it, like I wasn't good enough. But Jewel White liked me! I was her favorite!

"The most devastating thing I remember about my skin color is that we went to a party at a friend's house as sisters. It was a 'bag party.' Elite black folks gave them, usually sorority and fraternity members. To get in you had to take a brown paper bag test. If your skin was darker than the brown paper bag, you couldn't get in. Well, your mother got in, and I didn't. I remember standing there as a sorority sister Ruby had pledged with made me stand next to the bag. I was just one shade darker than that damn bag. One shade! But the bitch stood there waving her finger in my face, laughing, explaining to me like I was some kind of stupid pet that I wasn't light enough! What really bothered me more, though, was that your mother left me all alone that night and stayed at that party most of the night dancing and having fun. It was her birthday, July 4, 1962, and she was a famous model by then. I was 15 and she was 25. All I could think about after that night was running away. And the following year, I did. By then she was already in Jewel Park, New York. So was your father.

"Well, in the hospital in 1982, Ruby cursed me out when she found out that all this time I had pictures of her biological mother. She felt that Mother Zola and I had known all along about that box of pictures and her real mother. But I didn't, and she didn't believe me. Ruby cursed me out and that sent Mother Zola into cardiac arrest instead of the diabetes. Ruby kept cursing at me, and then at Matthew. My God, how Ruby must have felt! We cursed back, all the while not noticing the flat line on the monitor. The nurses came running, and by the time we looked over at Mother Zola, she was gone. But tengk'Gawd, before I told her about the box, all four of us had talked.

"Imani, when I got home that night, I drank beer after beer because I could not comprehend Mother Zola's words. I was familiar with these words when I was fifteen, thanks to Clara Rogers, but I had buried them. Mother Zola had forced me to.

"Just the mention of Mother Zola's name and your mother's name sent me into a rage. By the time you arrived, I didn't care that you were eleven.

"At that time, your real uncle, your father's brother, Charles Henderson, was a tenant in Mother Zola's Bedford-Stuyvesant house. Your father owned that house. Matthew had planned to move to Bedford-Stuyvesant, but I didn't want to move there. So he contacted Charles and put the house in his name after Mother Zola's death because I didn't want it.

"When the book your father wrote was published, the entire family asked the publisher to stop its circulation, and they did, after about two months, because Mother Zola was going to sue the hell out of them. And I was the editor! But I was 23 and had not returned to Jewel Park after leaving at age 16. Mother Zola had no idea I was married to Matthew! Or that I had helped Matthew! She felt betrayed. I had never done any fact checking, because your father was a great journalist. And my God, how he must have felt after what he found out. He spent his whole life living in fear, and he kept a whole lot of things to himself.

"My brothers and sisters were close to each other and to Saul and Ruby. We were raised to believe that whatever an adult said was truth. Savior, the oldest, was my favorite. He kept my secret until the day he died. The night I ran away, he took me to the bus depot and made sure I was safe, but I never spoke to him or any of them after that night! Malika, Linda, Sally, Ruby, and Solomon. I was so lonely in Jewel Park, but I had to succeed! So I let my hatred make me forget them. Now they're all gone!"

Chapter Twenty-Six

I watched Autumn wipe tears from her face with a delicate napkin. She continued talking and sipping champagne. Leroy remained on the phone in an upstairs bedroom, very business-like.

"On that night, back in 1982, before she died, Mother Zola asked your father for forgiveness, and told your mother, me, and your father that everything in that book was the truth. But by that time, Matthew's reputation as a journalist was history. And Charles, bless him, had bought a house in Queens with a woman named Eden that he eventually married, but no one knew that either. It was 1982! Your father gave Charles Mother Zola's house! Charles still lives in Queens with his wife, but he rents the house to three tenants in Bedford-Stuyvesant. He was at Matthew's funeral though, but he left right away. He has built a stable life as a train conductor in New York City and wanted no part of Matthew's world. Eden is a nurse. They have three children: Juanita, Aisha, and Paul. They are your cousins, and they're all about your age.

"Your father and I divorced because he had never stopped loving your mother, and I hated him for that. I hated you more. Before he married me, he had planned to marry her; had a wedding ring and everything. He kept it hidden, though. But I found it buried way in the back of his underwear drawer, a gold wedding band. So for the funeral, I asked that he be buried in it. At least one man in the family is married in heaven to the woman he loves! Fuhtrue! That took a lot for me to do. But when I did it, I felt a burden was lifted. I finally gave him the love that he should have had. When I saw you I was angry though, 'cause you didn't call me like he wanted you to."

Autumn sighed as I heard Leroy read numbers loudly from a spreadsheet.

Autumn said, "A Klansman murdered five of Jewel White's six children. His name was James Stalworth. One of Jewel's children survived, my mother, Nana Zola Jewel. And her son grew up to marry James Stalworth's daughter!

"Your father discovered this in 1970 right before he was to marry your very pregnant mother, along with something even more horrifying about himself! He married me, instead.

"Back in 1901, Jewel White survived because she was in the kitchen with her daughter Nana Zola Jewel; they were the only ones awake. She, the child and her husband, Horizon White, Sr.—he was at work—survived. Clara Roger's mother saw the whole thing and passed the story on to Clara. Clara was the one who told us. But what she told us about your father was frightening too.

"Horizon White, Jr., Jewel White's oldest son, had gone to the mainland for groceries for Sunday dinner. It was such a familiar, simple thing to go to the grocery store in town, even on a Friday evening. A white woman about 20, a Miss Viola Stalworth, had noticed a beautiful gold watch Horizon wore around his neck and had asked him to show it to her. It was a birthday present Jewel had given to him because her mother had given it to her to pass on to the oldest child at age 30—it was a family tradition—to pass heirlooms on to the oldest child. Horizon Jr., showed it to Viola just as the woman's brother entered the grocery store. He saw them from behind and suspected Horizon to be kissing his sister! Back then, in 1901 that was a crime that usually led to murder for a black man to be kissing a white woman in Georgia.

"Viola's brother, James Stalworth, was also about Horizon's age, 30. Although there were witnesses to what was really going on, James became infuriated and threatened Horizon with death for touching his sister—who told the truth about the whole thing—but wasn't believed!

"It was never proven in a court of law that that man burned down Jewel White's family's house and killed her children in the middle of the night, but everyone in Eva Creek knew that the Klan did it and that Mr. Stalworth was the leader because he bragged about it. That's why even today folks on the Island don't let anyone on the Island unless they know you coming—you got to call first!!!

"Imani, that happened in 1901. Years later, in 1921, James Stalworth, who had led the Klan to the Island to murder Jewel's children, married Eleanor Lowell, a woman from a well-to-do white family in Georgia. James Stalworth was originally from Brooklyn, New York, but he visited family in Georgia frequently, just like he did in 1901. He had worked as a journalist in New York and had fallen in love with a young, Jewish girl named Judith. He was a Klansman and didn't even know Judith was Jewish! She was from a place in Europe named Oswiecim, Poland. It's now known as Auschwitz. Fuhtrue! As God is my judge, fuhtrue! Judith was born in 1902. Her parents moved to New York a year after she was born. Due to a sick relative in Poland, they moved back to Poland in 1903, but left Judith in the care of a relative living in Brooklyn's Crown Heights. Judith grew up in Brooklyn, and worked in a factory. When she met James Stalworth—the poor child was thirty years younger than James Stalworth—she fell in love with him and became pregnant with Jurnee in 1919. James Stalworth abandoned Judith and Jurnee and moved to Georgia where he did very well working on the family farm. Judith found out where James lived and arranged for Jurnee to live with James because she was very sick and was living in poverty. She put her on an Orphan Train and sent her to Georgia to live with James. But James didn't want Jurnee, although his wife Eleanor did. Now, an Orphan Train wasn't something folks talked about much back then. But it was a good thing for Jurnee, bittersweet! Fuhtrue! By the time Jurnee arrived in Georgia, Judith had died from pneumonia, and the relative that was to take care of Judith passed away a year before Jurnee was born. Judith's mother may have died in the Holocaust. Records show that Judith's mother was only 12 when Judith was born. Judith was nearly fifty during the time Poland was invaded by Hitler's soldiers. We couldn't find any records indicating what happened to Judith's father either. The names of Judith's parents were Gregory and Sabina Miller. They may have moved to Poland from another part of Europe.

"James and Eleanor raised Jurnee Miller to be an intelligent, educated woman."

All I could do was watch Autumn as my craving for coffee went away. I wanted an eight-ounce glass of Early Times Old Style Kentucky Whiskey.

She continued, "Last year in October, your father found out through Orphan Train records that Eleanor Lowell is alive and is living on Eva Creek Island. Your father had planned to visit her. There is a picture of her that she sent him, along with other photos that I sent to you in that box. If Eleanor Lowell can meet us, I'm sure she can identify some of those pictures in that box. The box originally belonged to Jurnee whose biological mother had probably sent it along with her on that Orphan Train. Jurnee left it with Mother Zola. Your father and I felt that it was our responsibility to see that you had the pictures.

"When your father and I had found the information we wanted—we've kept in touch all these years after our divorce—we were going to sit you down and tell you all about this. But he died.

"We never forgave Saul Weaver, my brother, for marrying Jurnee and we took it out on Ruby.

"Jurnee Miller Stalworth was shunned by James Stalworth's family. Mother Zola took her in pregnant with Ruby when no one else would. Mother Zola raised Ruby as if she was my sister. But on the day your mother Ruby was born, Jurnee died in childbirth. Mother Zola and her husband John Weaver were the only ones in the room with Jurnee when she gave birth. How did Jurnee die? She was a healthy, vibrant woman of 18. Talk flew after Jurnee's funeral. And folks started whispering that Mother Zola or John killed Jurnee or cut the baby from her so viciously that she bled to death. John was a doctor. Mother Zola was gifted in the old tradition of the laying on of hands. The accusations hurt Mother Zola and she just shut down. Wouldn't talk about Saul or Jurnee, and kept your mother Ruby so close to her that by the time Ruby could talk, she was calling Mother Zola, Mama.

"And here comes your father in 1970, opening up an old wound. I thought your father was just after money. He was really after the truth about how his own father died. What is even more startling is what he discovered about the circumstances of his own father's death!

"By March of last year, he had gathered enough information from the Internet to prove that Mother Zola and John had nothing to do with Jurnee's death in 1937, just so their souls could rest!

"In 1970, every day, he was in the library looking for somebody from Jurnee's family through archives. He spent his life trying to put a puzzle together. Eleanor wrote him a letter—That's also in the box I sent you—explaining that before Jurnee went in to labor, she had tried to convince her to live with Eleanor's mother, but James Stalworth had come home early and found Jurnee in the house. He was going to beat her with his bare hands! But she ran like hell to a boat that took her from the mainland to Mother Zola's house on Eva Creek Island. And Mother Zola took care of her well enough to see to it that at least Ruby survived. Had Jurnee not made it to that house, she surely would have died, the baby as well.

"Jurnee lived on the mainland, but spent summers on Eva Creek Island with church missionaries.

"Jurnee came back every summer as a missionary. By the time she turned 18 she had fallen in love with a black man, Saul Weaver, my brother, who worked as a youth leader at the Baptist church that Clara Rogers attended.

"My grandmother, Jewel White, began to take notice of this relationship. She had moved to Atlanta by then, but she kept in touch through family reunions and visits with Mother Zola. They were very close. But when Jewel got hold of the news that Saul was seeing Jurnee Miller Stalworth who was the daughter of the man that had murdered her five sons, she couldn't take it. She called a family meeting with Mother Zola and John. They vowed not to ever discuss what happened in 1901 publicly. But when Saul married Jurnee, my grandmother couldn't take it. When Jewel did visit us, she wouldn't even look at Ruby, let alone hold her. None of my brothers and sisters understood this. By the time I was born, Grandmother showered us with lots of love and affection, but left Ruby out. She never bought Ruby one present. Never hugged her. Never talked to her, not as I can recall. Never said a word; not even hello or goodbye when she came to visit. I remember Ruby trying to hug Grandmother once. But Grandmother shoved Ruby so hard to get her away from her that she fell on the floor. My God!"

Chapter Twenty-Seven

I couldn't drink or eat, although Autumn offered me dinner. Her words filled me more than food ever could. Autumn continued, "It was Christmas, you know, and Ruby was 20 and I was ten. Ruby just sat on the floor holding a bottle of *Chanel No. 5*, a present from Mother Zola, after being shoved by Grandmother. It was so heartbreaking to see that. Ruby didn't cry. Nothing! God! Well, we never saw Grandmother again after she shoved Ruby. It was like Jewel White just disappeared off the face of the earth."

Autumn said softly, "There were only seven of us, but Ruby was raised as the eighth. All of us went on to do good things. We became professionals and got good educations.

"This beautiful lady, Clara Rogers, Carmel's mother, was just exquisite. All the girls wanted to be like her, act like her, walk like her. She was an actress who worked with the best of them of her time. Men just went crazy over her. She worked at a Baptist church, cooked like a gourmet chef. One Sunday after church, all of our brothers and sisters, except Saul, all of us, including your mother, Ruby, filed into Clara's kitchen in her house. That was something we did once in a while. It was after Sunday dinner for her family. And Mother Zola was home waiting for us to eat her food instead of Clara's, with her own company from church. Clara's mother and mine were good friends up until that night.

"Your father was there too. Boy, we were so young! Five. But I don't think he paid attention to this story. A child is like a sponge, and that story was like mildew—just growing along with him—until he couldn't help but remember! He must've put the pieces together as an adult. Your mother was 15. But I remembered everything Clara said when she told us this story about five beautiful black children who were our blood relatives. She told us that Jackson Henderson, Matthew's father, had actually witnessed my brother Saul's beating. Two years later, Matthew witnessed the murder of his own father!

"Then he moved in with Clara—My God, Imani.

"His family was from South Carolina, but he had never been there or even met his own aunts and uncles and cousins. He had grown up on Eva Creek Island.

"He never called Clara mama, though. She was Miss Clara to him. He didn't tell me the truth until after I married him, and even then wouldn't talk about his family, especially when he found out who I really was. I don't know why Clara decided to tell us that story that day. Maybe, it was because we had all come to her house together, at the same time. That warm summer night Clara told us that she was going against Mother Zola's wishes. Your father never remembered this. I think he blocked it out."

Autumn paused for a moment; then the memory forced her to wipe tears from her face. The sun was gone for the night. Leroy was still on the phone, this time laughing about a ball game.

Autumn continued, "Their families lived just down the road from us. Clara's mother was there in 1901! She was 29. Clara wasn't born until 1930. That night Clara explained the story her mother told her when she was a child about how *her* mother had watched the Klan destroy Grandmother's house from the living room window from down the road with the lights off, and then Clara's mother had gone into the basement with her family, fearing her house would be next. Well, that one story that happened in 1901 was just enough for me! It was a rare thing for the Klan to show up on Eva Creek Island, but they did!

"But then she added a second story that happened in 1937. Fuhtrue! Clara told us how her mother had told her about Saul. The Klan didn't kill him, but sure came close to it! Saul had come back from the store with a bloody, mangled arm, and by the evening he had disappeared. A month later she heard news that Saul had taken a job as a janitor in a church run by a black man named Reverend Joseph Henry Scott Clarke who was married to a black woman named Camille. When they moved the church from Eva Creek Island to Jewel Park in 1937, Saul moved there with them. Saul was the family pharmacist, but he had only practiced with our father, John Weaver for two years.

"Saul had married Jurnee near the beginning of 1936, but when she died in 1937, he felt he had nothing to live for and took a job as a janitor at that church, and then he moved to Jewel Park. Mother Zola and John knew the truth.

"So Saul took a job as a janitor at The Temple of Faith Church and by 1944 he was dead.

"Clara told us a church member had said that he knew why Saul left Eva Creek in a hurry back in 1937. That church member was a man named Jackson Henderson, Matthew's father, your grandfather on your father's side.

"See, hell broke loose when Jurnee died after giving birth to your mother Ruby. Saul ran away that same day because somebody beat him nearly half to death with a tree branch. A week later he was in Jewel Park working as a janitor in Reverend Joseph Henry Scott Clarke's church.

"In 1943, Saul had mysteriously visited Mother Zola for Thanksgiving dinner, but left that night to return to Jewel Park. He had lied and told everyone he was working as a pharmacist in Jewel Park. But there had been a witness who knew Reverend Joseph Henry Scott

Clarke and who knew exactly how Saul had lost his arm. By 1944, Saul had dropped dead cleaning a church pew! Heart attack!

"In 1937, there was only one witness—your father's father, Jackson Henderson. Matthew had this nightmare where he would scream and moan, and beg for 'them' to stop. He'd wake up screaming about a man's arm falling off. And he'd be covered in sweat. But he'd never tell me anything else.

"Your father Matthew wasn't born until 1947. But in 1944, Matthew's father, who I never met, but I know his name was Jackson Henderson, was nearly 38 and knew Saul. Unlike his wife Eastlyn who was a member of the Baptist church Clara worked at, Jackson was a member of Reverend Clarke's church.

"Jackson Henderson saw what happened to Saul's arm. The attack on Saul took place in 1937 by a group of Klansmen who beat him with a tree branch, on the same day Jurnee died in childbirth! Fuhtrue! Somehow Saul found his way to John Weaver, who amputated the arm and sent him on the fastest train to New York with Reverend Joseph Henry Scott Clarke. They didn't kill Saul like they killed my uncles, but the similarities were the same.

"Jackson told only two people as many times as he could, Reverend Clarke and your father, Matthew. Only the reverend felt a story like that should only be told to Gawd! So I guess that's why his own children didn't know it.

"Not even Jackson's wife, Eastlyn Henderson knew the story. She died when Matthew was just seven from tuberculosis after giving birth to Charles. But Mother Zola knew. John never kept any secrets from her.

"Anyhow, Jackson made it sort of like a bed time story for Matthew and didn't stop telling it to him until Matthew ran away at age seven to the beautiful lady who lived down the road who served great coconut cake after church service, Clara Rogers. Seven years later, Charles was living there too. Before then, Charles lived with his grandmother on Eva Creek Island, and she died when Charles was 14.

Matthew's grandmother was like John Weaver when it came to skin color. Fuhtrue!

"Then the horror! In 1954, Matthew found his father in a ditch dead, with both arms missing. Saul's violent perpetrator had seen Jackson Henderson watching him beat Saul and had waited—until 1954 to get him! But Matthew always blamed himself. He felt if he had not run away from home, his father would never have been out late at night looking for him, especially if he knew that the beautiful lady with the delicious cake was looking after his son. Matthew saw his father's armless body and the murderer fleeing from the scene and kept it to himself until our wedding night when he woke up screaming at the top of his voice about murder. When the police found the body, Matthew pretended he didn't know anything about it. Can you imagine what that must have been like for a little seven year old child?

"He confided in me that the murder—a Klansman, wore a sheet. To this day, we don't know if that man is living or dead! This must've terrified Matthew because he never knew if the Klansmen who committed this crime had seen him!

"But he found his father with no arms, in a ditch in Georgia while he was out playing down a dirt road not far from his own home on Eva Creek Island that the family had moved to from South Carolina, and at age seven, he ran like hell to Clara Roger's house. That happened only the second night after he had run away! Lord, Jesus!

"I held that man like he was a baby, because that's the way he cried. On our wedding night! My God, Imani! People be surprised what children remember, and what they don't.

"I don't know what seeing that really did to your father, but he didn't tell me about it until our wedding night in 1970. So he wrote a book, hoping someone from Eva Creek would come forward and explain why Saul would marry a woman whose father had killed five of his uncles. He hoped that someone would also come forward with the name of the murderer of his father. Did someone know who had beaten Saul besides his father? But no one ever did come forward. We knew who had burned Grandmother Jewel's house down, but we didn't know who had beaten Saul. We didn't know who had killed Matthew's father. And Matthew spent his life trying to find the answers.

"This damn thing had haunted and frightened him. The woman he loved, Ruby, your mother was carrying his child, and he was too frightened to marry her after he found all this out. He married me, not knowing that I was related to Ruby and that Saul was my brother and Ruby's father! My God!

"In August of 1962, Matthew and your mother went off to college in Jewel Park. Ruby had been modeling and traveling throughout Europe and Mother Zola insisted that she go to college. So Ruby and Matthew ended up going to college in Jewel Park, and I continued high school in Georgia. I had already been angry with Ruby for just being light skinned, but when I found out she was dating Matthew while I had dated him at age 16, I couldn't believe it. And hate found its way into me when I eventually went to college in Jewel Park. Then I felt rage when he got engaged to her, all the time not remembering that he had met me at age five, then again when he came to speak at my high school in Georgia about The Civil Rights Movement! When I went to New York, that's how I found out they were dating each other.

"I had been with him before her. I followed her to college, but somehow they had hooked up, and I reminded her about the story Clara had told us. Either she pretended that she didn't remember, or she just really didn't remember.

"Saul had been beaten so badly by the Klan for marrying a white woman, that his pride wouldn't let him face the people on Eva Creek to tell the truth about his arm when he came back to visit the family that Thanksgiving in 1943. People hated him already for marrying Jurnee. The last thing he needed was to come home, tell what happened to his arm, and have people say 'I told you so!' He couldn't tell them the truth about what happened to him in a ditch on a cold, lonely night in Georgia. But John Weaver and Mother Zola and Jackson Henderson and a reverend knew and kept that a secret until years later when they read about it in Matthew's book.

"Well, Mother Zola found out what Clara told us!"

Chapter Twenty-Eight

"My God. We ran home to ask Mother Zola if it was true, and she told us Clara had lied. When we asked why she thought Clara would lie about something like that, Mother Zola told us she didn't know.

"But Mother Zola got a gun and was about to blow Clara straight to hell if the police hadn't come. By that time, Clara's mother had long passed away.

"We watched in terror, scared to death that Mother Zola was going to jail that night. Everyone on the Island heard about it the next morning. And no one ever talked about what happened in 1901, in 1936, in 1937, or in 1944 ever again, until 1970 when your father wrote that book.

"Matthew and I started dating seriously in 1969. He asked me to marry him. I turned him down in 1969. But when he asked again in 1970, shit, I married him! What woman wouldn't have? But he was strange, your father. Liked to keep to himself. No relatives ever visited us once. He never talked about his mother or father. I don't think he and Charles got along well. Charles is much lighter than him, enough to pass a brown paper bag test! But we had each other, and I guess that was enough for him.

"But, I used to look at those gorgeous eyes he had with those long eyelashes, and there'd be so much sadness behind them. Then I started finding things he had kept that Ruby had given him: scented letters, underwear, napkins from places they'd been. I got tired of that shit. He'd come home smelling like her perfume. That goddamn man! And hate, you know, consumes you. He never once stopped loving Ruby. Shit! One night we were in the throws of passion, understand? And he called out her name! And that's when hate wrapped me up in its arms. I hated your mother. I hated you. And I cried every day for the love Matthew gave your mother and you. I learned how to do a lot of things for that man. Things only God will ever know. And the rage I felt for the love I couldn't get from him, Imani, I passed on to your mother and then to you.

"We divorced because I was so filled with hatred that I feared I would kill your father, especially since those nightmares never went away, and he started working on a second book about Eva Creek. I think his father's murder haunted him most, especially the connected spookiness he felt toward our family, especially Saul.

"By then I had started seeing Leroy Taylor. He was rich and fine. He knew your father from Eva Creek Island and hated him. What made it worse is that they looked like they could be brothers. But they weren't. Leroy Taylor knows his family. His parents were light like mine. But the children came in all shades. Leroy's parents gave him lots of love. Leroy looked down on your father, so your father didn't like him. But Leroy treats me well, always has. So I saw a good thing, and married him. It was a second marriage for both of us.

"People thought your mother was, well, crazy. Twice when you were a child, your father told me that he suspected that your mother had tried to kill you. This really frightened him. Your mother would stand in the middle of the street holding your hand as cars passed, hoping to get hit with you right along with her. The night she died, the police found sleeping pills next to a glass of water on the night table next to the bed in your room. We think she left them there for you to take. The police found you sleeping and probably thought you were dead too. But you woke up and scared the hell out of them, not even knowing what had happened to your mother. They took you to the hospital for observation, and then you ended up at your father's house where I was.

"But you know, when your mother Ruby looked up at the sky, she was praying. She was talking to God! She did this often, especially at night down South when she looked for the stars.

"Mother Zola did this every night also, look up at the sky, and pray out loud.

"Your mother was a constant reminder of our family's pain and people just couldn't take it, Imani.

"Mother Zola valued life to such a degree that she believed God had created stars as pathways to heaven, and that once you died God took you to Eridanus and placed you in a holy river where you lived. As you lived there, you protected the ones who were still alive that you loved as your soul traveled from star to star on your way to meet God. Sort of like the way when people you love die and become angels that protect you. That lady in the bagel shop you always told your father about? She always sent you home with a treat; I believe she was an angel—maybe even Jurnee who came back in her form to protect your mother and you.

"When a child turned five in the family—Mother Zola believed this was the age a child began to understand the beauty of God—she gave that child a quilt with the constellation of Eridanus to protect the child throughout life. Anyone who was a member of Mother Zola's family got one. Sort of like the way babies are christened when they are born to keep any evil from entering them. Grandmother Jewel did it, and her Mother did it too—all the way back to our beginning. Even Judith had some kind of quilt that Eleanor found when she arrived with a reverend on an Orphan Train in Georgia. Eleanor passed that quilt on to Jurnee who passed it on to Ruby.

"Well, Mother Zola christened all her babies on the day they were born with holy oil she made with frankincense and myrrh, and then again at age five, with a quilt. Of course, she didn't christen Ruby's mother, but she christened Ruby and you. But you never received your second blessing—a quilt, because when Mother Zola saw you on Eva Creek Island, Ruby wouldn't let her touch you. Ruby and Mother Zola were very close, but when Ruby turned 25, they began to grow apart. So by the time you went down to Eva Creek for your Uncle Savior's funeral, Ruby kept you far away from Mother Zola, because over the years Ruby found Mother Zola frightening. Your mother talked about that to your father a lot.

"Mother Zola's quilts were never sold, but passed on to an ocean of jewels. We have never sold a single quilt, except for Ruby. The ones who have passed on left theirs for their children. We keep them for protection. If Mother Zola were alive today, she would say you suffered so much in life because you never received your blessings.

"There are three blessings, you know, that each member of our family receives. The third one is the laying on of hands at age 30. You'll be 30 this year. That's what your father was waiting for. He wanted to finish his second book about the family, and he wanted you to receive the third blessing. From me. I never received my third blessing either. But I had to be right, get myself together, get all the evil out of my system, and get right with God, like the church folks say. Get right.

"Your mother Ruby suffered because she threw all of her stuff away when she turned 30! Your father told me that! She sold her quilt for a damn bottle of whiskey to Mary Benson's husband, Oscar the second. His son, Oscar the third is an art dealer and he works part time at Brown Sugar Bodies. That quilt was to be passed on to you. And on Ruby's 30th birthday, she was on a modeling assignment in Italy, and would not return to Eva Creek for her blessings. She had a nervous breakdown that year over there, right around her birthday. The modeling agency she worked for fired her because each assignment they sent her on, she was drunk! Evil had found a place to live in her soul. She stopped drinking when she got pregnant with you, but kept right on after you were born.

"But Mother Zola continued to pray for our family. And that night in 1982 when I wanted to…" Autumn took my hands and held them. "When I wanted to hurt you, Mother Zola grabbed my arm, Ruby's arm, and your father's. She spoke in tongues, holding all three of us close to her. I know you don't know much about that, but it's a language only God understands. But Mother Zola also had the gift of interpretation, and she instructed your mother first, and then me, and even your father to help you receive your blessings on her behalf.

"I was so angry. I had to get right with God. We all had to. That is the extent of Mother Zola's love and protection. She had so much love that she took in a white woman pregnant with her grandchild; a white woman whose father had murdered her brothers, a white woman who had married her son, and she cared for this woman and helped her through birth and death; and carried it with her until she could no longer bear it. Most people today would still not understand that! I know I wouldn't have done it! She was determined not to carry it with her in death. And she told us. This was her way of restoring the honor of those named Jewel after it had been tainted by so much evil. I expected your mother to follow Mother Zola's instructions, but she didn't. She killed herself three hours after leaving the hospital. But Mother Zola knew what I didn't. She knew what your father didn't. That night, Ruby was changed forever. She drank herself to death by drowning in a poisoned river of alcohol. She gave her life away.

"So it was left up to me and your father to carry out Mother Zola's instructions. Well, it's left up to me now. And I had to get right with God, first.

"Why do you think you're here on this cold beautiful day, Imani? Mother Zola has reached heaven, right here in your heart." Autumn pointed to my heart, and continued, "You are the last link to the jewels of our family, Imani."

I wanted to digest more of her words as the lavender butterflies danced in my stomach, and my heart did the 50-yard dash. I waited for her to continue.

"So why did I change my name?" The butterflies traveled to my heart and rested there. Autumn said. "Savor these words first. You need to taste them because I've fed them to you so fast. Taste them, Jewel. Your blessings are waiting inside of you, but Mother Zola instructed me that night in 1982 to show you where they are.

"Mother Zola gave me a holy name, Cecelia. It means celestial or heavenly. When I was born, Imani, she told me I reminded her of a heavenly Jewel—Cecelia Jewel Weaver—that's my name. But in all my years up until the time I married your father I didn't feel like a jewel or heavenly. I felt like autumn because I was turning cold and I was falling like leaves near a brook. So I changed my name to Autumn Brook. It was self-esteem, self-confidence, and self-love in a package I kept trying to buy—because your mother had it—a kind of beauty that couldn't be bought. She knew it, but got sick, and gave it away to evil. I had it, but I didn't know it, and your father spent a lot of years trying to show it to me. But before I married Leroy, I found it.

"You know, Imani, the sins of racism have left people so wounded that hate waits for us to embrace it and evil finds its way into us. And then we lose a jewel every day.

"This fine woman that I have become has her days numbered according to the doctors. I have breast cancer, Imani, and less than a month to live. I never followed up on my physical exams. I let things go, 'cause I thought I looked too good to die! I have not decided to die or count until I am dead! I have opened the box of beauty that Mother Zola gave me, and I'm enjoying it more every day. I am no longer Cecelia Jewel Weaver. I changed my name again this year to Cecelia Jewel Taylor. So it's your turn, Imani. Personally, I think your name should be changed to Imani Jewel Brown! That fine young thing, Cayenne, he's a good catch. Don't let him get away. The man is an asset. Fuhtrue!"

Chapter Twenty-nine

I had forgotten about the cold as I banged on Cayenne's door. It was one in the morning!

Calmly, Cayenne answered, "Hey, Jewel. What's up?"

"I have to talk to you. I talked to Autumn. I..."

"Slow down, Jewel. Baby, slow down," Cayenne said as he shivered while closing the door. He was beautiful in black boxers, bare feet, and a body that was well loved.

"I spoke to her. Autumn. She told me..."

"Today?"

"Yes. I went to her house in Silver Row. Carmel got the address for me, even though I found it myself in the phone book."

Cayenne hugged me and whispered, "That's so beautiful, Jewel. You want some coffee or something?"

"Please, no coffee; maybe a sandwich or some food. I haven't eaten all day. I've been filled with so many emotions."

"Okay. Believe it or not, I haven't eaten dinner either. I just got back from a client's house. Their kid spilled soda in the Mid Tower Case, an old model, while they were trying to install more memory. I

had to replace the whole thing. They tried to fix the computer themselves, big mistake! They had wires everywhere, and almost electrocuted each other." Cayenne paused before speaking again. "Earlier today I went to the hospital to see my mother."
"How is she?" I asked.
"She's about the same," he said as he smiled and went on, "So you spoke to the old witch?" He began taking things out of the refrigerator. "What about soup and a sandwich?"
"Fine with me," I said.
"I made some gumbo. I have some left over crab legs, and some French bread. Also have some lunch meat: ham, American cheese, turkey, bologna."
"That sounds fine, Cayenne. You okay?" I asked.
"Cool. So?"
"So? You saw your mother? Did she say anything to you this time?"
"No. I just hold her hands and talk to her. Sometimes I catch a smile she gives me, but that's all. There's warmth, though." He wanted to change the subject, and said, "So, you met Autumn?"
Cayenne kept smiling about Autumn being my great aunt. He smiled even more when I told him she wanted to take me through some kind of family ritual that I had only vaguely heard about when I was a child.
"I'd bring a weapon for protection," he said. "That lady's twisted."
"I think that that's what she wants people to think. I spent the day with her. I think over time, we can become comfortable with each other. She has cancer and probably has a month to live. But she's not counting her days!"
"Oh, I'm really sorry about that, Jewel," Cayenne said as he put his arm around my waist. He then let go to warm up food.
"So, all of a sudden, in one day, you've come to like her?"
"Well, I'm cautious, Cayenne, but she seems to have really changed. To me, she's my encyclopedia to my family's history."

"And, so, what's this ritual thing about?" Those eyes of amethyst wrapped themselves around me as the lavender butterflies slept next to my heart, and I helped him set the food on the table.

"In my family, Cayenne, as far back as slavery, we've kept our unique traditions through the generations. I never got to participate in any of the rituals, except for once when Mother Zola would make the cross over my forehead whenever I was around her, and that used to scare me because I was so young. But Autumn told me that in our family, everyone receives three blessings: a christening with holy oil when we're born, a family quilt that's been blessed and given to us when we're five for our protection throughout life, and the laying on of hands for our 30th birthday to guide us into a healthy age for wisdom."

"That's deep. God, what I would give for something like that, Jewel."

I smiled as I went to the refrigerator to get soda. He was right behind me, so close I felt his breath on my neck, and then the softness of his lips. They began traveling to my ear, and stopped at my lips. And the butterflies were awake, traveling also.

They were so good, the kisses. Kisses I had never felt before. Warm, electric ones darted across my lips and slowed my breathing and made me think I was dreaming until the cave began to haunt me with Blue and Mark's judgment and Bless' eyes and a neighborhood named Jewel Park, and I remembered the word Larry Smith had thrown in my face, "Ho." Then there was whiskey, therapy, two hundred and fifty-seven pounds, a great aunt I used to fear, photographs of white relatives, the longing need for intimate friends, Eva Creek Island, blessings, and family.

He whispered again, slowly, "Tell me all about Autumn." We sat at the table. But there was too much noise already inside of us. For a moment we both listened to the noise that silence eventually found.

I breathed deeply as I kissed him and let the silence we shared sit in a comfortable place in my heart.

And then I told him about Autumn as we sat down and enjoyed gumbo with crab legs and ham and cheese with French bread; ginger ale, and again, coffee for me that I had too much of, tea for him, and the sound of laughter as we watched television until it was time for breakfast, which we ate with more coffee to wait for a new day to begin.

I enjoyed his kisses and the touch of his fingers dancing in my hair.

I remembered Autumn and wondered: Brown. *How could I change my last name to Brown?* But I thought of Mark and Bless.

Chapter Thirty

It was just a half a glassful and I had eaten breakfast with Cayenne and our bodies had had a conversation and Blue was coming over and I wanted to fix this puzzle.

Just a little more, to fight the fear.

Just a little more. Just a little more. Just a little more. I only had one drink today. Just a little glassful. Oh, God. Please help me. I'm so scared. Just a little more to get through. Just a little more.

I filled my glass with ice and poured my favorite drink, as I planned to sip it slowly.

My suitcase was half packed and I was ready to take a ride with Carmel, Autumn, and Leroy to Eva Creek Island for three or four days to see Clara Rogers when Blue rang the doorbell. I adjusted the tee shirt that matched my jogging suit.

"Hey, Sweet! Nice workout gear. You finally started your diet!" He took a step back. "Damn. It's only eleven in the morning. You're drinking?"

"Oh, come on, Blue, it's just a little drink. Want some coffee or breakfast?" I asked.

"Where are you going?" He asked, as he noticed the suitcase on the living room floor.

I carefully placed the glass on the kitchen table and sat down with my hands folded.

"Well?" He looked at me, waiting.

"A lot of stuff's been happening. I'm sorry I forgot about our date. When you didn't pick me up from the Clarke Center, I took a taxi home. Sorry I didn't call you, Blue. I know it's been a while, honey. I just have to clear up all this stuff about my father. Good news though, I met with Autumn, finally."

"Yeah?"

"Yes. We're planning to go to Eva Creek Island tomorrow. But for a few days."

"That's great," he said without enthusiasm.

"Well, you could be happy for me."

I watched as he hung his coat in the closet. I said, "I have some stuff to take care of today, Blue. I'm not going to be able to see you. I'm so sorry."

"Oh, but you had time for Cayenne, right? You were at his place all night."

"I can't believe this. Again? We talked. That's all."

"A whole lot of talking went on all night?"

"What did you do, Blue? Hang out all night, staring at the window?"

The smirk on his face indicated that he had done something like that. Then he said, "Well, if you would keep your legs closed for a day or two, maybe we could get together sometime, Sweet! I mean, since you're giving it up to everybody, I might as well get in line for my turn, right? I mean, after all, fair is fair! Carmel Somebody? Larry Smith? Mark Brown? Cayenne Brown? They're brothers, right? You like that real freaky shit, right? Did you do Redd, yet? Well, I guess Valerie wouldn't have that shit, right?" As he spoke his voice became quieter, and he moved closer to me until his hand was on my shoulder and his eyes were talking to mine. "Right?" He whispered.

Without warning: a slap to the left of my face gave me whiplash. A punch to the right knocked me out of my own kitchen chair. He poured what remained in the glass all over me. I thought he was leaving after that, but he got the entire bottle of whiskey, which was half full, and poured it over me. He took the kitchen chair and placed it over my body so that I couldn't move, and then he sat down. He pulled out his key chain, which had a cigarette lighter in the shape of a car attached to it.

Oh God! Dear God! Please. Please help me. Please don't let him God Please don't let him light it. God please. Help me, God.

I watched Blue as he sat in the chair throwing the lighter from his left hand to his right and then he talked, with great coordination: lighter, left hand. Lighter, right hand. Left. Right. "So, when's my turn? Tonight? Now? Yeah. Sounds good to me. You like that freaky shit, right?"

Lighter, right hand. Left. Right.

"Please Blue. What are doing, Blue? Please, God. Please don't Blue."

I couldn't breathe properly.

"Yeah, I can get with this," he said as he removed his sweater, but kept his pants on. He removed the chair, and then held the lighter to my face without lighting it. I listened to the sound of his zipper. He ripped my tee shirt off and forced my jogging pants down to my knees. I was stunned and couldn't move. He shoved my legs apart far enough to enter me. "Yeah. I can get with this," he repeated, not speaking above a whisper.

I listened to his breathing as I waited for the lighter to heat my face. The weather report was on. Then the news. A commercial. More news. It was 38 degrees outside. It was 11:35 A.M. I heard a car horn. Someone was double-parked. The horn of the car made so much noise.

More breathing. Is the lighter going to heat my face? The weather report is on. Someone got shot. There was a robbery. A cat is singing a song. There is a commercial for tea. A commercial for insurance. A car horn is blowing.

Is the lighter going to heat my face?

More breathing.

Silence. Just silence.

Where are my tears?

I kept trying to find them while Blue spoke softly, "Don't ever call me! Ever! I guess I have to go back to paying for it, now, Sweet." He laughed without showing teeth, then whispered, "Here's something to remember me by, baby," and he threw his lighter at me. I watched a blue flame kiss my kitchen wall, flicker and then quickly disappear, and I rolled into the living room drenched in the smell of whiskey with my legs crossed tightly around each other.

I wanted to sleep forever.

Chapter Thirty-one

Get up girl! Get up! Get up, damn it!
"No. I just want to lay here and sleep."
I was in a puddle of brown liquid and I smelled of whiskey.
"I don't know. I tried to call her. I left a lot of messages Mrs. Taylor. You know, sometimes, she leaves the machine on. I didn't see or hear her go out. I know that her boyfriend, Blue, was here this morning. I called her around three this afternoon. I haven't seen her. Have you, Cayenne?"
"No. She left my house around 8:30 this morning. We had a nice evening."
"Oh, really?"
"Valerie? It was Valerie. She rang the doorbell incessantly this time.
Cayenne went on, "You know, Autumn, she doesn't show it, but she's taking her father's death very hard. I've never seen her so withdrawn. Last night was the first time I saw her laugh and enjoy herself."

Get up girl! You don't want them to see you like this, again! Get the hell up. Let's get it together, girl.

I wiped my face with a damp towel, brushed my teeth and put on a bathrobe after removing all of my clothing. But I couldn't hold it together.

"Jesus. Please help me. I need you." God sent me a river of tears as I opened the door to a familiar look on Valerie's face.

"Lord have mercy, Jesus!" Valerie said.

"For the grace of God, is this the same Imani I just saw yesterday?" Autumn asked God, and she kept glancing at Cayenne and Valerie.

Valerie walked past me into the hallway as she asked carefully, "Girl, you been drinking?"

"Please help me. I don't want to hurt like this anymore. Please," I said. The tears flowed as I tried to breathe normally and walk.

Familiar arms pulled me tightly to a body that was well-loved. Familiar lips kissed me and Cayenne said, "It's going to be okay, Jewel. What's wrong, baby?"

I whispered, and slowly told them what Blue had done.

Now I was lost, and I knew it, but there was a part of me that was still there. I held on to that part, but I screamed until all I could do was sit down on the floor in a corner and cry.

"I don't want to feel this pain anymore," I then whispered.

"Oh, Jesus, honey. Everything is going to be all right. It really is, Imani. Cayenne? Cayenne? Cayenne, where are you going?" Valerie asked. I had never seen her frightened, except for the time her brother disappeared.

"Cayenne! Come back here, Cayenne!" But we all heard the front door slam shut. "Lord, have mercy, Jesus," was all Valerie could say as she held me in her arms. I watched Autumn clean the floor, careful not to get her casual leather flats scented with whiskey. She seemed to be checking out each corner of the house, remembering the times she had there with my father. At Valerie's urging, Autumn then called Dr. Lateesha as I pleaded for her not to.

Soon Dr. Lateesha Clarke and I were seated on my sofa in my living room sipping coffee. Dr. Clarke gave me another card with an appointment on the back of it to see Dr. Renee Alton, and I promised myself that I would not send it to a garbage dump. I whispered to God for help as I went way past the Ogeechee River and the Okefenoke Swamp.

Chapter Thirty-two

On the phone, Valerie explained that Blue had been beaten and taken to the hospital. She and Cayenne kept a careful watch over me by bringing me gifts of words, good food, and aromatherapy, two days after the whiskey shower. Blue had left a message of apology on my answering machine with the hope that I would visit him. I planned to visit him without letting anyone know, but I couldn't get a moment to myself. I just couldn't get away from Valerie or Cayenne, Joy, or Redd. I refused to press charges against Blue, although Valerie convinced me to save the clothes I had had on in a plastic bag in case I changed my mind. There would be some evidence, they hoped.

The photographs haunted me.

No. I would not press charges.

Cayenne had left a message on my answering machine right after Dr. Lateesha left me alone to pray. Cayenne explained that Blue would never bother me again, but when I mentioned Blue was in the hospital, Cayenne feigned ignorance. He then visited me briefly before going to work.

Cayenne had many friends; some were in their thirties and still members of well-known gangs. He only had to call one and instruct them on how to handle Blue. But at this point in Cayenne's life, he would probably handle Blue, himself.

"Sister Imani, would you like me to repeat the question?" Dr. Renee Alton asked.

Dr. Lateesha called her one of the best! For my first session with her, only three days after smelling like whiskey, Dr. Alton sipped green tea and occasionally smiled as she calmly sipped tea from a fine teacup painted with African violets. She wore denim and a comfortable sweatshirt that read, "Fifty and fine!" The harshness of her voice, probably from too much cigarette smoke, and the thickness of her curvaceous body spoiled her image, and that put me at ease.

"I'm sorry Dr. Alton, could you repeat it?"

"Do you love yourself, Imani?"

I hesitated, and then said, "I don't know. I guess so." It was the first question she asked me during our consultation a day ago. I noticed she didn't take notes.

"Well, sister. That's our goal: to find self-love. When you have that, all the pieces of your life will fall quietly and beautifully in to place." After that, her silence made me uncomfortable. Then, "Tell me about Blue," she said, remembering details from my consultation.

The river of tears returned and kept me from talking for a half an hour.

"I'd like you to tell me, Imani, about the relationship you had with your parents." Dr. Alton said, as she shifted to cross her legs.

The pain in my soul was slowly moving, weaving its way through a labyrinth of dirt that I had tried to get rid of, but couldn't. I cried for the remainder of the session.

The pain was wandering within my bones, following my blood cells, and torturing my head. Rape was not something I could make disappear. The memory would stick around for a while.

"Sister Imani," Dr. Alton said, clearing her throat for maybe the fifth time, "Next week, we will return to this place. You've shared with me that you've carried around a letter your father wrote you when you were born, but you didn't get to read it until you were eight. I'd like you to write a letter to your father, and then to your mother expressing how you felt about them. Sit quietly for an hour each day with your journal until our next session, and write down every thought, feeling, wish, hope, and reaction you have ever had concerning your parents. Do the same thing for Blue."

I said, "I don't remember ever talking about my mother after her death. I had a lot of memories, and I didn't want to go looking for them anymore. I realized also that since my father's death, I had not talked about him either. I rarely talked about my parents to anyone. I had always replaced my feelings of abandonment with food and men."

Dr. Alton nodded. She said, "Also, you must attend prayer service this Wednesday, the AA meeting is on Friday, and you might enjoy the Sister Meetings of Sage also on Friday nights at the church. Sometimes they meet at a club or someone's home; and they have a lot of fun in a place where tears are also welcome. You know, people get uncomfortable watching someone cry. One great thing we do at the Clarke Center is return to our African roots and pull out ancient rituals that have sustained and healed our spirits and bodies for centuries, and the beauty of this experience is that other ethnic groups have begun seeking our services. And by all means, I really hope you visit Eva Creek Island. I go every year to a retreat my own family plans for fellowship and renewal. I know it's strange to hear someone like me, a doctor, talk about incorporating holistic healing with traditional healing, but one cannot survive without the other. Sister Imani, we at the Clarke Center are here to support you in every way possible, but you must learn to support yourself. You have the power."

Dr. Alton smiled, sipped her tea, and gave me the church schedule of ministries and services. "Sister Imani, after your six months of counseling, I assess your progress. If there is little progress, I refer you to another doctor offering more intense therapy. For now, sister, let's begin with the thought of self-love. When we meet again, I'd like you to define it for me, okay?"

I smiled.

Chapter Thirty-three

Doo Doo Breath understood that I would be resigning from Jewel Park High School as an English teacher. I left early.

Snow became rain with windy weather, and warmth from the sun eased its way into March, making sure that all memories of February were gone, but I remembered the fourteenth, because 15 pounds had left my body without any help from me.

Valerie and Redd gave a Valentine's Day dinner party for intimate friends: Mark and Bless, Cayenne who became my date, Carmel and Zalia and Winnie and Dr. Lance. And rather than come home to listen to the meditative, healing music of Maxwell daily (I saved his music for weekends now), my life revolved around AA meetings, Sister Meetings of Sage, therapy (which I now called counseling), Valerie, and Cayenne, his kisses had grown intense on the fourteenth of February, and they led to nothing more than talking. But we talked over dinner or over the phone for hours daily, having deep conversations, until I was comfortable enough to talk to him about the way my father made me feel. To my surprise, Cayenne calmly told me that he had had a talk with my father two weeks before he died. He told me that my father wanted me to know that he loved me very much—profoundly. I never gave Cayenne an opportunity to talk to me about my father after Daddy's funeral. The word love danced around the oak trees in my soul.

By the second week in March, after I told Dr. Alton about my family puzzle, which had taken the entire month of February to explain and ate up a week of March, she smiled, and then her raspy voice filled the room with seriousness as she said, "A peculiar name, Blue Greene." We would go back to that place after Easter vacation, which I planned to spend on Eva Creek Island at Clara Rogers's home along with Carmel and Autumn in search of self-love.

And then Dr. Alton wanted to discuss my parents, a place I was still not ready to visit. All I had managed to write in the letters Dr. Alton had requested was, "Dear Mama and Daddy, I have loved you like a daughter should."

I remembered how I felt in my father's house when I had met Carmel. I shared with Dr. Alton the anger I had felt at my mother for taking her life and leaving me all alone. I told Dr. Alton how for years I was afraid to hate my father for not taking me in to raise me after my mother's death and for not checking to see whether my relatives on Eva Creek Island could have taken me.

On a rainy day in March, Dr. Alton gave me a rubber baseball bat and a matching rubber desk and ordered me to talk though my anger and any other feelings I had toward my parents. She then went on to Autumn, Bless, Mark, and of course, Blue.

By the end of March, the bat, desk, and I became great friends. During each session I pounded away at the rubber desk with the bat as angry words that had been hidden in the cave of my soul behind the oak trees poured out of my mouth, words I had been fearful and ashamed to say, words that had helped me form pictures on my mind of unworthiness, self-hatred, and ugliness; words that I had never expressed to anyone, not even out loud to myself; words that left me exhausted at the end of each session with Dr. Alton; words I didn't think I could ever say.

When I managed to say the words, "I forgive you," after beating up the rubber desk, I was able to move on to other projects Dr. Alton had waiting for me. They allowed me to close my eyes and visualize a clear blue sky filled with everything I ever wanted or needed and a way to get each one. They allowed me to see the way I wanted to look, act, and be. They allowed me to create an image of how I wanted to dress, eat, love, and live. They forced me to see myself from the inside out.

Rain drenched my body every other day in March, it seemed, and for a month, I called Blue, just to talk, and told no one; not the new friends I found at the Sister Meetings of Sage, not Dr. Alton, not my AA buddy, Tricia Holt who had named herself a Bitch in Progress, whom I really didn't like that much; I had only known her for three weeks; not a soul at Prayer Meeting; no one at the two church services I had to attend every Sunday, and especially not Valerie or Cayenne.

When Blue showed up at my door with champagne, roses, perfume and Richart Chocolates, I wanted to talk more. I had spent the morning with the bat and rubber desk that now sat on the side of the floor next to my couch.

"You look well," he said, noticing that in addition to the 15-pound weight loss in February, I had lost another ten by March; this was puzzling to me because for the entire year of 1999, I could not even lose five pounds! And that was with exercise and lots of lettuce.

"So do you, Blue."

He had said, "Sorry," for the one-hundredth time for the whiskey shower. But something about the one-hundredth time mixed with the softness of his voice, the insincerity behind it and the memory of a lighter dancing around my face, and rape, made me so angry that I threw the bottle of champagne, roses, and perfume out of my living room window. I also threw every curse word I had ever known or heard at him until he was slamming his car door in front of my house, terrified of raising his hands at me. There was something about the one-hundredth time that made me listen to the beautiful music of the fine musician, Maxwell, and not shed one tear and smile as I soothed my throat with generous bites of Vanilla Ganache, Malt Ganache, Madagascar Cocoa Ganache, Mango/Passion Fruit Ganache, and my favorite, Lavender Ganache. There was something about hearing Maxwell's sweet voice mixed with the taste of Richart Chocolates, and the lavender butterflies returned for the one-hundredth time.

The ecstasy of chocolate almost made me forget to answer the phone.

"Girl, whatchu' doin'?" Tricia asked.

"Eating," I told her, annoyed at her interruption.

"Better not be no alcohol with that entrée, girl," she said. She always sounded as if she had swallowed a balloon filled with helium, although she was 38. Her prominent Boston accent reminded me of the way the members of the Kennedy family talked. She went on, "Just called to say, hey."

"I'm fine," I told her. I could just see her sitting on her living room sofa twirling her waist-length dark brown micro-braids that matched her skin-tone with her manicured fingers, sipping herbal tea. She was a vegetarian, a vegan at that, and annoyed the hell out of everyone whenever food was around with, "Oh, I can't eat that," or "Does that have_____in it?" The blank could be replaced with any item that was a dairy, meat, or carbohydrate product. And she couldn't have been more than one hundred pounds! She had been a professional dancer on Broadway until the alcohol became her personal choreographer.

"Wanted to remind you about tonight's meeting at my house; I'll be nice. And don't worry; it's being catered by the church, not me! You okay?"

"Yes, Tricia."

She went on. "Ain't no time to front, girl. What's wrong?"

I placed the chocolates on the living room table and told her how I had let Blue go. She howled and laughed, slapping her hands against the phone's receiver.

"You go, girl! I did the same thing to my husband Leroy when that bitch Autumn Somebody was up in my house, in my bed, on my fuckin' birthday! That's why I don't live in Silver Row no more. I just couldn't take them people. When people get a little money, they forget how to act. But Leroy's people are from what them white folks call 'old money.' I was glad to be rid of him and his stuck up family. I threw his ass out that very night, and then sold the house and bought me a new one in downtown Jewel Park! Don't if feel good, girl!"

Still in ecstasy with the chocolates, I asked Tricia to repeat herself. She did.

"Was your ex-husband's name Leroy Taylor?"

"Yeah, that's the bastard. I wasn't good enough, so he went out and got some old rich hag that used to be married to a fine looking, rich-ass brother. Dumb bitch. Had more money than Leroy! I bet she took the brother for all his worth!"

"Was her name Autumn Brook?"

"Yeah, girl, that's the bitch!"

"It's a small world, Tricia. God has such a sense of humor! Tricia, Autumn is my great aunt. She used to be married to my father, Matthew Henderson. He passed away this December. But for the record, I assure you, she didn't get a penny!"

"Get the fuck out of here! Amen to that, girl! Ain't this some shit?" We each had a hearty laugh. She went on, "Girl, we gotta' talk! Tonight, at our Sage meeting, okay!"

I smiled and said, "Can't wait."

"We were going to have it at The Blue Zephyr. You know Blue don't own it no more. He sold it to his brother, Rayne. Blue is fine, girl, even though he is an asshole!"

"So Rayne owns The Blue Zephyr now?"

"Yeah, girl. I thought you knew. I would have cut his shit off if he had done what he did to you to me! Blue's opening up another club in Silver Row in June along with his fiancé, Cree. Good riddance is what I say to both of them. They deserve each other. I saw the cheap ass ring he gave her too. The stuck up bitch was showing it off to everybody Sunday in church. But, the club in Silver Row promises to be more elegant. Really, more money! His other brother, Niger, is going to manage The Blue Zephyr while Blue oversees the new club in Silver Row. That's why we changed the meeting place to my house."

"That's fine, Tricia. I didn't know that Blue had another club." More hurt filled my heart at the sound of the word, fiancé. I knew Tricia wanted to do some serious male bashing, but I just wasn't in the mood. Most of her time was spent doing that.

""So, I'll see you at seven, Imani?"

"I'll be there, Tricia."

"Well, girl, let me go. Enchantment is back in that damn litter box, and one of my male friends is stopping by. So I have to go clean up her mess. She's a sweet little thing, but damn, can she smell up a house! Later, girl!" I heard the dial tone.

Chapter Thirty-four

I had not had a drink since Blue's whiskey shower. It wasn't because of the AA meeting or talks with Tricia or The Sister Meetings of Sage or prayer meeting once a week or two services in church on Sunday or counseling or Valerie's comforting food or Cayenne's comforting words or Winnie's comforting prayers. It was because of the combination of all of these people, places, and things that began to create a new way of living for me. Before Blue's whiskey shower, I went to work, came home to eat or went grocery shopping and did it all over again the next day.

The church had another name for the journey toward healing Winnie said when she visited one of our meetings at Tricia's house, "Going Through."

In one meeting, she told us we were all going through a gate of evil, seeking heaven where the goddess inside of us lived. A lot of older members in the church had problems seeing themselves as Christian women who were goddesses. I didn't.

Winnie Clarke had formed this group, The Sister Meetings of Sage, twenty years ago by testifying about her own life. She had been a well-known rapper before she became a pastor's wife and had even participated in some rap videos that she was now embarrassed about.

Dr. Natasha Jones, a clinical psychiatrist and former drug abuser was the group's leader now.

During last week's meeting at Tricia's house, Dr. Jones spoke about forgiveness. I recorded part of a speech Dr. Jones gave at the meeting at Tricia's house because I felt what she spoke about was crucial to my own healing. And I felt it was a good definition for self-love that I had intended to share with Dr. Alton when I returned from my Easter vacation on Eva Creek Island.

Dr. Jones said, "Remember in the bible, the woman who washed the feet of Jesus with her tears and hair? It was the deepest, most holy honor she had, which Jesus found better than money, respect or rituals. That entire section is about forgiveness, most importantly the forgiveness of self. It's like love; you can't forgive anyone else until you've forgiven yourself. This beautiful woman had a faith so profound that she believed that whatever truth she could offer Jesus would allow her to receive the gift of forgiveness and restore her worth. She believed in the holy power of The Anointed One, and she believed that she could be healed. And Jesus saw this. That story comes from the book of Luke, chapter 7, verse 36, to the end of verse 50."

I adjusted the headphones of the MP3 player that Cayenne had bought as a gift to uplift me as I walked toward Dee Dee's Deli to meet Valerie for afternoon coffee. I listened to Dr. Jones on a CD as I walked. "Dear sisters, that ancient woman who went on to do great things for God lives in all women. You are whole and worthy to be loved. And you are loved simply because. You are fine, sweet, delicate earth scented with a godliness that Jesus gave you when He said, 'Your faith has saved you, go in peace.' Faith never left you. It was with you on that day when God gave you as His gift to this world."

I adjusted the headphones and smiled.

For the rest of the month I kept looking for faith, but I found little pieces of it in the perfume of scented flowers. Hiding behind the oak trees, I found pieces of worth, beauty, intelligence, happiness, joy, and love. I saw them for the first time in the cave of my soul, hiding where the lavender butterflies like to dance whenever I played one of my favorite songs from the CDs I loved of Maxwell. I reminded myself to ask Dr. Alton how to get these little pieces to show up in my daily life.

Although the scale and I would never be friends, I managed to do a shimmy when I saw my weight drop to 190 pounds. I had not done anything special, except live. I didn't kid myself though. I had gotten into the habit of eating less and adding more healthy foods to my diet, with Cayenne's help. Valerie on the other hand became a great temptation with all kinds of cakes, pies, and gourmet foods she gave me. She had not gained or lost any weight, and had told me as many times as she could that she would never try to lose any weight again. She felt she was bringing me little pieces of love. And I wrapped that love in aluminum foil and shared it with my new sister/friends at The Sister Meetings of Sage; sometimes, even Tricia gave up pieces of her vegetarian diet to sample a sugary slice of chocolate cake or a finger sandwich laced with turkey bacon, cheddar cheese, baby spinach, and honey mustard.

I glanced at the mirror on the wall at Dee Dee's Deli and fixed my shoulder-length hair that I had box-braided myself and styled into spiral curls. I placed my CD player and headphones into my bag. I was tired of wearing other people's hair. I felt comfortable in designer sneakers, black stretch pants and a lavender jacket with matching camisole, which accentuated my cleavage.

"You depressed, girl?" Valerie asked as we shared a ham and cheese sandwich on a French roll with expensive olive oil drizzled over it from Dee Dee's Deli. She was watching as I poured only one packet of brown sugar into my coffee, and drank the coffee without cream. She repeated her question.

"Why do you think I'm depressed, Valerie?"

"All that weight you been losing. Soon you're going to look like this helpless toothpick!" She pointed to the dressed up toothpick on top of the sandwich.

"I'm fine, Valerie. I haven't had much of an appetite these days."

"Well, you probably won't have much more of an appetite today because I invited Bless here so that we can have a good talk. And here she is!" I half opened my mouth as Bless gave me a look of death, sat down at the table and ordered tea and a grilled cheese sandwich. She had regained all of the weight she had lost nearly a year ago.

"You look good, girl! What's up?" Valerie asked her.

"You know how it is. A good man always makes a good woman look good, sister!"

I washed a bite of my sandwich down with a gulp of coffee.

"Well, that's nice to hear, Bless. You and Mark are getting along fine!"

"Who said anything about Mark?" Bless leaned back in her chair and smiled devilishly.

"Well, ain't he still your husband?" Valerie asked.

"Yeah! So! If he can have a little something on the side, so can I! Shit!" Bless said.

"Why don't you just get a divorce, girl?" Valerie asked.

"Why? I have the best of both worlds. Girl, this is not 1954! Can we please change the subject?"

"You're playing with fire, Bless," Valerie said.

"Says who? Look, I had a nice day so far. I'll be home in time to cook dinner, and my gig last night went good! I sang at The Blue Zephyr, and Rayne gave me a contract to open the Jazz show on Friday and Saturday nights. All kinds of record executives have been hanging out there. It's just a matter of time before I get spotted. Hey, like I said, I got the best of both worlds. And Rayne is paying me some really good money. So, why am I here having tea with this bitch?"

Bless pointed at me, and went on as if I were invisible. "I hear she and Cayenne's got a serious thing going on! She's freaky like that.

First, my man? Then his brother? Well, at least Cayenne's not married."

I sipped more coffee and added two teaspoons of brown sugar. What she didn't know was that Cayenne and I had a beautiful thing going on. We were making love all the time, through poetry, late nights with strawberries and whipped cream in front of his television, and dancing in New York Jazz clubs after dinner. No man had ever taken the time to enjoy my company unless I was in bed with him. But I knew that Cayenne and I were getting deeper, and it was just a matter of time before lovemaking embraced us.

I was no longer afraid to talk to Bless. I had found a piece of worth in the cave of my soul. I had also found some love next to the dancing butterflies that now filled my soul, and I felt loved by Cayenne who I now found amazing, and Valerie who became my confidante, as well as Winnie, Tricia, and all the sister/friends at The Sister Meetings of Sage who kept things real for me. I was now working on the quality of worth. My self-worth.

Dr. Alton explained that experiences of love would lead to a settlement in my soul of all of the others, beauty, intelligence, happiness, and joy. And Cayenne was feeding me so much love that my hunger for men like Mark and Blue was slowly dissolving along with the sugary coffee I had also loved so much.

I leaned back in my chair and looked directly at Bless forcing her eyes to meet mine. I chose my words carefully because Dee Dee's Deli was not the place to cause a scene.

I turned to Bless and said quietly, "I am not a bitch. I will not argue with you today or ever again. I slept with your man and I am sorry. That was almost two years ago. I can't change that. There is no excuse for what I did. I was lonely and wracked with pain. I was depressed, and I wanted someone, anyone to want me, because I felt no one did, except for Mark. It wasn't your fault. Again, and for the last time, I am sorry. Think of me as you wish. But I am not a bitch. And you will never, ever make me feel like one again!" I was calm, and I sipped more coffee.

"Fuck you! Okay. You are a bitch. A fat, ugly, good for nothing bitch. And that's all you'll ever be. Your own father saw that. Your mother didn't want you. And my man just fucked you 'cause he could!" Bless lowered her voice and leaned back in her chair when the waitress brought her tea and sandwich, as well as a "Shit on you" look.

Tears accompanied the hurt she had thrown at me, but a photograph and a letter showed me love. I told her, "On the day I was born, my father wrote me a love letter. He called me Beautiful. Here. I carry it with me every day." I pulled the letter from my journal. Still calm, I told her, to read it. Bless took out a magazine and read that instead.

I said, "On the day I was born, Bless, my father, Matthew Henderson, wrote me a love letter. He called me a medley of beauty and his dearest Jewel. I've been carrying this letter around with me since I was eight. Do you remember the day I showed it to you? I gave you a copy and let you fill in any name you wanted where my father's name was. But you left his name. Remember? That letter was easy for him to write because he loved me. Loving someone is easy, Bless. Hating someone is harder. I haven't been able to sit down and share with you all of the other stuff my father wrote, which was hard, or how he spent his life obtaining property for me so that I would be free. Maybe one day when you learn to love again, we can talk." I wiped tears from my face.

Bitterness was now Bless' sister/friend. It was like a halo around her body. She leaned closer and whispered, "Like I said, Fuck. You. Bitch!" She then leaned back and turned to Valerie. "Girl, the brother I met has got it going on!" She showed Valerie a diamond ring that resembled a medium size rock. She went on, "We're going on a Caribbean cruise for the Memorial Day Weekend. Can't wait, girl! And for my birthday, we're going to Paris! Girl, I have never been to Paris! He's a financial consultant for a mutual fund company. And he's barely 35! As far as Mark is concerned, he's so busy playin' and frontin' he hasn't even noticed. These days, he spends a lot of time with his daughter, who's turning out to be just like him. Malika has his ways, and I don't like it. As long as he's not taking her to meet those little whores he's screwing around with, then I don't give a shit what he does!"

"I'm through," I told Valerie. I finished my food, paid my bill, and left a tip for the waitress. I said, "I'll call you Valerie. Okay?" Valerie nodded and I walked out of Dee Dee's Deli as I watched self-worth manifest right before my eyes as I stared in the mirror to check my makeup.

Chapter Thirty-Five

The Monday after Easter, Autumn, Leroy, Carmel and I, made our way to Autumn's maroon BMW to Eva Creek Island to stay for a week. Cayenne introduced me to Pilates, an exercise routine that was now one of my best friends, along with yoga and meditation; I shared that with them in the car, and everyone smiled.

"You look real good, Imani," Autumn said.

I smiled.

From our last session the week before the holiday, Dr. Alton explained to me the trip to Eva Creek Island could be a lot for me to handle, but would certainly force me to talk about my father and the night of the whiskey shower that Blue had given me, which I still had not talked about with anyone. I believed her.

Autumn's car turned into the walkway of a huge one family home.

"Welcome to Creeksville, Georgia!" Autumn shouted above her favorite Patti Labelle CD. As she parked the car, the smell of fresh clay mixed with roses kissed me and sent a photograph to my mind of peat moss. And it frightened me. The scents of fried chicken, collard greens, and fresh bread welcomed me.

The weather was hot, and dust from the wheels of the car slapped my face as we parked in front of a huge colonial style home with a front porch that snaked halfway around the house. Autumn continued, "To get to Eva Creek Island, we'll have to take that motor boat over there next to that bateau. It's about a thirty-minute ride. This here is where the Wilsons live. They're originally from Eva Creek Island, but they moved here to start a family business renting boats to Eva Creek Island for tourists. It's a shame how the Island has changed. Wealthy white real estate investors are eating up our land and traditions. We hope young people like you and Carmel can salvage some of this land before it's all turned in to resort property. No one person on the Island speaks Gullah/Geechee anymore, least that's what they want us to think! Even though I left at 16, the language never left me. Mahself jus' tummuch hut tuh talk'um! But it's still there! And traditions like basket weaving and quilt making are vanishing, only to be found at walking tours and museums throughout Savannah and South Carolina. Try not to sell Clara Roger's magnificent home, Carmel. Eva Creek Island is 12,000 acres and 9 miles long. Down the road from us, Imani, is Nana Zola Jewel's large house also. Your father bought it. You own it! It needs some work, but it's still beautiful. We need to breathe some life back into Eva Creek Island so our souls can rest. Today, only one hundred and twenty people actually live on the island, and all of them are 65 and older, thank God, they have large families! Can you believe that? Please don't ever abandon it. That's what we're trying to teach the chillun' who went off to Harvard or Howard!"

Autumn smiled and pointed to a large fishing boat that sat several feet away from the house. As she talked, about ten people were streaming onto the porch to greet us, the young and old, toddlers and teens, and the familiar, yet distant Clara Rogers.

Clara was 70, but did not look it. She wore a white uniform similar to the ones church ushers wore in spirit-filled Baptist churches. Autumn told us that there was a praisemeetin' at night and Clara was an usher at The Memorial Heritage Baptist Church of God, which was one hundred and seventy-five years old on Eva Creek Island. Tourist offerings and family members of Eva Creek Island kept the church alive. Clara was reading a story to four toddlers who sat at her feet. She slowly stood when she saw Autumn's car.

Fear sat on my stomach and annoyed me as I watched beautiful people with flawless skin who spoke with rich Southern accents laced with sweetness, and oh, the food they greeted us with! But for the first time in months, I craved Early Times Old Style Kentucky Whiskey.

Carmel, who towered over Clara, hugged her lovingly, and planted a kiss on her cheek. "Mother I missed you so," he said. He kissed the other cheek, and she hugged his waist and showed a mouth filled with ivory teeth and one gold front tooth.

"How you, boy? Ya' home now. Sho' glad to see you, baby. My little man is home, ya'll. Lookit here. He a fine specimen for the ladies ain't he?"

The fine ladies smiled and introduced themselves to him. "I'm Gertrude. How you?"

"Fine," Carmel said.

"This here, my daughter, Ella Wilson. I reckon she 'bout yo' age, and a doctor too, and obstetatrician. Handles babies fine too." Gertrude said, mispronouncing her words in a Southern accent.

Carmel smiled. A very fair skinned black woman about my age with blonde hair and green eyes greeted him.

"Oh Mama!" Ella said. She smiled at Carmel. "Hello, Mr. Carmel. It's a pleasure to meet you. I've heard a lot about you. Maybe we can have coffee when you get back from the Island?"

Carmel smiled. "That would be nice, Ella. Thank you."

"My pleasure," she said, batting her eyelashes at him the same way I had. I wanted to grab his arm and remind him about Zalia, whom I felt was more polished and prettier than this Ella, but I couldn't get to him because another one of Clara's friends reached for Carmel's hand.

"You fine, strong, thing, I'm Bedilia. I used to baby-sit your bad self when you was' bout six or seven, remember?"

"Yes, I do, Miss. Bedilia. You lookin' mighty good."

"Well, I keep myself up now, honey. You know old Chuck wouldn't have it any other way! When them tourists stops by here, he bound to find himself one of them fast city women. So I got to make sure I can keep up with the competition. The other day I just bought myself my first thong! You know, Carmel, I got five children now. My daughter Louise in the back there, baking up some red velvet cake. Remember that?"

"Oh, yes, Miss Bedilia. I can't ever forget that. You make the best red velvet cake I've ever had. I finally learned how to make it like you. My recipe is pretty close to yours. I manage a restaurant in Jewel Park, New York. This here is the owner, sister Imani Jewel Henderson."

Bedilia's eyebrows lifted as she took my hand to shake it. I smiled. She said, "Why yes, Matthew Henderson's child. I believe your mother was Miss Ruby Weaver. You not as light as her though. More like your father."

"Well, we'll just leave all of that alone for now, Mrs. Wilson," Autumn said, glancing at her with that devilish grin. She then said, keeping her eyes fixed on Miss Bedelia, "Tie yuh mout'! Come on, Imani! Carmel! Let's head toward that boat before the sun goes down. Mrs. Rogers, are you coming with us?"

"Why of course, Mrs. Taylor," Clara said. She then leaned in to whisper to Gertrude, Ella, and Mrs. Wilson, "That old hag got the nerve to come back down here after all them years she broke her mother's heart, first with that Henderson fella, now with that fine young thing in the car. Look at him. Leroy Taylor—from the Taylor family with all that good money! I sure hope they pass some of it here. We sure could use it!" Mrs. Rogers said. Carmel and I pretended we didn't hear her.

Bedilia raised her voice to say, "My, Ms. Taylor, It's awfully nice to see you. You haven't changed a bit. We went to the same high school together, remember?"

Autumn was halfway to the boat with her luggage. She turned around and gave the women a wicked smile as she said, "She bad mout' me? Girl, you wear glasses?" She paused and waited for an answer. She then went on, "I know I look good, but I was 16 when I left. You think I still look 16, huh?"

The women wore fabulously fake smiles as Mrs. Wilson said, "Oh, why Autumn, you know I just mean you look fine, that all."

Mrs. Rogers whispered, "The bitch still got that nasty attitude, don't she?" She, along with the other women Carmel and I were standing in front of smiled and waved at Autumn, fabulously fake.

I sighed and wondered what I had gotten myself into. "We're coming, Autumn," I told her. I began walking toward the boat with Carmel. Clara walked between us holding each of our hands.

Clara said, "Imani, it sho' is nice to see you. You look just like ya' mother, Ruby. Just like her! You a rather stunnin' beauty! I saw you at the funeral. I apologize for not speakin'. I sincerely do."

"It's okay, Mrs. Rogers," I yelled, eating up her compliment.

Clara looked at me like I had two heads. She whispered to me, "What you yellin' for, child?"

I looked at Carmel, who just shrugged and whispered to Clara, "Mama, I told Imani you were deaf."

"What the hell you tell her that for?" Clara asked.

"Because that's what you wanted people to think about you, remember?"

"Well, I ain't deaf, and I'm sorry I ever told that damn lie. Ever since I got down here, people don't do nuthin' but shout at me all day. I hears pretty well, thank you. I made that lie up to get the hell out of that school your father worked at in Jewel Park, and to get me some disability. The only reason I ever came to New York anyway was at the request of your father, Imani. First I thought he was gonna' help me get some work on Broadway, but I tired of the auditions and rejections. Either I wasn't the right color, was too old, too young, too sexy—whatever it was—I didn't fit the stereotypes of the mammies they wanted me to play. And I was sure nuf' too old to play a hooker! I didn't realize I had gotten too old for that! Plus, he thought I could help him with research about his family. He was a quiet child. Back then he was sneaky. Course, he never grew out of that! But I tried. I couldn't never help him, though. But he got me a job as a receptionist at that school. Nothing but a bunch of rude, ignant' people would call. And since they thought I was too siditty for them, they complained to the principal about me, and then had the nerve to hire some old heifer named Ella Samuels who didn't do nothing all day but curse people out and eat! Since I wasn't no street woman, they didn't like me. That street woman still work there, Imani?"

"Yes, Clara. Ella still works there," I told her.

"Bet she just as ornery as the devil! Anyway, after a year of that receptionist nonsense, I was through. So I acted deaf. Big mistake! Matthew got me to work at a restaurant. That I loved. Then I found out after he died that I owned it. I like to cook. I don't like to boss people around and tell them what to do. So I gave it to my son. And he passed it on to you. Come to find out, it was the restaurant your mother owned before she died. But she never did manage it well. When I saw it, it was a run-down building, and it stayed closed until your father bought it. I loved working there and became the main cook. Well, anyway, my hearing was never all that bad. I mean, it wasn't that good, but it sure wasn't as bad as I let on. So, Imani, girl, don't be shoutin' at me no more!"

"Okay, Mrs. Rogers."

"And please, child, call me Clara. And please, don't call me Ma'am!"

"Okay, Clara," I said.

"She catches on fast," Clara told Carmel with a smile.

He smiled and filled the air with charm.

Autumn left her car in the Wilson's backyard. Leroy, Autumn, Carmel and I piled into the motorboat run by Chuck Wilson, Bedilia's handsome husband who was at least a foot shorter than Bedilia. He told us that he had affectionately named the boat, Geechie World.

We rocked slowly and steadily pass the Ogeechee River and alligators who remained calm, to Eva Creek Island to the sound of grasshoppers; the sight of red oleander, oak, and tall Georgia pine trees; the smell of peat moss, red clay, fried chicken, collard greens and red velvet cake that sat on our laps wrapped in wax paper on thick Dixie plates sealed with aluminum foil that Bedilia and Ella had brought to the boat for us before we left.

Emerald green foliage guided us into clear blue skies that sank behind white clouds and soft showers of water. We heard birds singing at the sight of squirrels, and raccoons weaving between cedar wood, and the smell of molasses. We approached a sign the color of maple syrup that read, Eva Creek Island. A picture of a smiling brown girl wearing a lavender dress and carrying a basket of flowers was etched on the sign.

"Well, we're here," Autumn said. We watched the sun take its last walk across the sky for the evening. Chuck gave Leroy, who I found extremely quiet, a large flashlight, while he carried a floodlight that slowly waved us, along with our luggage, toward a paved road. Autumn paid Chuck for his service and we all chipped in to give him a tip. I felt as if I was on a deserted island. We reached Clara's house first. Our footsteps sang to the wooden deck as we entered a lovely Victorian style house outfitted with air conditioning and four bedrooms. I was expecting to see an old country shack. I found this house to be awesome with its ceiling fans, brick oven, and a fireplace in the living room. I smelled frankincense and myrrh.

"Well, y'all get comfy. I got some Teacola Tea in the 'frigerator. Y'all want some?" Clara asked.

"Yes, please, I would love some," I said.

She bought a tray of tea and glasses for everyone.

We drank the tea and ate, filling the house with laughter, letting the earth, air, and food fill our souls and soothe our bodies.

Autumn and Leroy went to the bedroom to change to sneakers and comfortable jogging outfits. I did the same while Carmel stayed in the kitchen with Clara remembering old times.

We resumed our laughter in the living room over red velvet cake and coffee that Clara brewed in an old fashioned perculator, something I hadn't seen since I was a child visiting Nana's house in Bedford-Stuyvesant. Later, Autumn asked us, surprisingly, to form a circle of prayer, each holding hands.

She prayed, "Dear Lord, tonight our daughters have come home. Bless this Island, Lord. Protect it. Bless our sons and daughters and guide us to the loving arms of your holy river of peace. Tonight, dear God, we bring you Imani for blessings and protection from evil. We hold her in our arms tonight, dear God, as she begins a new journey with our guidance. Thank you, Lord. Amen."

Chapter Thirty-six

After breakfast we walked up the road past three rivers and through a wooded area next to a Prayers House that smelled of citrus and rosewood to what was left of Nana's house. Autumn opened the door with a key my father had given her before his death, and stepped back.

"I haven't stepped through this door since age 16. I'm not ready yet," she whispered to Leroy, who had his arm wrapped around her waist.

"Don't need to be ready; just walk through," Leroy whispered. Still Autumn would not move as Carmel, Clara, and I slowly entered the house that smelled of rosewood, ylang ylang, and mothballs.

The house was neat, but smaller than I expected from the way Autumn had described it to me, and from the way that I had tried to remember it when I was five.

"Cecelia, love, just take my hand. Ain't nothin' to be worried about," Leroy pleaded. He went on, "First time I seen you here, I was selling boxes of canned food to your people. I seen you sitting on a rock way over there near the water, crying. I come up on you and you cried harder. This pretty fine woman cryin'? Wuffuh? I wondered. And I sat down with you next to the river and took your feet and rubbed water over them, and dried them with paper towels, and asked you your name. You told me you hated it, and then you told me what it was. My grandmamma was named that, Cecelia. And I told you it meant, 'from heaven'. And you was so pretty. And you told me you didn't belong here. I remember, I sat right over there, and told you, you belonged anywhere God was. And since He everywhere, that's where you belonged. So, you belong here, right now. Come on, pretty woman, step through."

Autumn smiled. I had never seen her smile that way. She breathed deeply and stood by a wall near the entrance next to the kitchen as Leroy held on to her hand. Leroy laughed softly. "Damn, I wasn't nothing but a kid myself. And you were so pretty. Just 16. And I asked you where you live? And you said, New York. And I asked why you were on Eva Creek Island in the back of this pretty house. And you said, 'Ain't nothin' pretty about this house!' And I laughed, because it was the prettiest house on the Island. And you went on rubbing your feet, and I didn't see you again until you were 25 and married to Matthew. He wasn't much of a friend to me, but he liked to go fishing with my father and me. He liked to puff himself up and act like he had more than he had. And he never liked me much because I had a lot of stuff that he didn't have, but I never made a big deal about it. But Matthew, every time he got something new, he made a big deal about it. He made you so unhappy. Sort of reminds you of this place, huh?"

Autumn stepped through and nodded as she wiped tears from her face. Leroy led her to the kitchen where we all sat down, but Autumn stood up and asked me to follow her. She showed me each room of the house that I tried to remember.

The house had five bedrooms and three floors. On the bottom floor, there was a small bathroom without a shower or bathtub, just a toilet, and a sink to wash your hands. There was a living room with a ceiling fan, and a separate dining room, and the kitchen was the smallest room in the house. On the second floor, she showed me the room she had slept in. It was large enough to hold three cots. Across the hall was another room that I remembered sleeping in with my mother when I was five. It also had three cots. A bathroom with a shower was down the hall. The top floor had another bedroom, which Nana and Gran'pa John shared. Across from that bedroom was another room set up like an office.

When we entered it, Autumn pointed to the wall on the right-hand side. A poster with the same pink rose petals I had on a love letter that had named me Beautiful on the day that I was born, had been set in a gold picture frame that read:

Nine generations ago, in 1799, Malika was twelve when snatched from her home in Sierra Leone by a Portuguese slave trader.

At age 12 Malika was raped by the plantation owner, Paul Claude Pierre Baptiste, the man she had been sold to in Savannah, Georgia.

Malika gave birth to Linda.

At 45, Malika killed herself. She walked into the Savannah River and drowned.

Linda and Malika became Jewels living in a holy river named Eridanus.

"*Haffuh hol on tuh we'own land; haffuh hol on tuh we'own freedum!*"
From: *The Children of Eva Creek Island*
By Matthew Henderson (1947-1999)
Scholar, Journalist, Teacher

Above the picture frame, from the left side to the right side of one of the walls was a quilt with a rainbow of colors representing the earth along with twinkling stars with the constellation of Eridanus next to it. A large tree had been painted on another side of the wall. It was divided into branches. Each branch had the name of a family member, which went back all the way to 1787 with the name Malika Baptiste. The floor of the bedroom was covered in blue-green tiles that represented a river. On a side of a third wall, next to the tree, there was a bench. Underneath the bench, the floor had been painted a solid shade of emerald green to represent dry land with grass, fallen leaves, fruits, blankets, and a pillow off to the side. Another quilt was folded neatly on the bench, and enough space was left for at least three people to sit and share the space comfortably. Resting against each wall of the room were other benches with emerald green grass and dry land painted under them. These benches were smaller than the one near the tree.

"Who did the art work in this room?" I asked Autumn, amazed.

Autumn said, "Charles Henderson. He's a wonderful artist. When you return to Jewel Park, you should visit the gallery just off of Clarke Road. Your uncle's work is being exhibited there until August of this year. He's been written up in many newspapers and magazines. You should really get to know him, Imani. Visit him in Queens sometimes. He's a magnificent man. Unlike your father, Charles created his own loving family. Many times he reached out to your father. But your father wouldn't reach back. So, Charles just left your father's world alone. It's up to you now to get to know your uncle."

"I will," I told her.

Autumn continued, "This is why you are never to sell this house. Our family tree is painted on this wall. That huge, beautiful oak wood desk by the fourth wall over there is filled with nine drawers of family photos, letters, and memorabilia. That desk and the smaller one next to it is never to be removed from this house, understand?"

I nodded, yes.

"And," she continued, "Every drawer represents a family from our heritage. The bench is special because any time you want to come up to this room to have a quiet moment, you can sit on that bench and pray or talk to one of our ancestors or wrap the quilt around you to feel their spirit. This is a room of peace. This isn't a room for sleeping. That's why we didn't put any beds in here. The bench is enough. We use pillows sometimes just to sit on the floor to pray. We wanted people to feel like they were in a holy river.

"Your father, God bless him now, made a great effort before he died to put things in order. He helped Clara and me create a family website. We hired a computer specialist and set up a web address for anyone who wants to know about our family history. If you have children, you can bring them to this house, and they can see this room.

Anyone can go to the website now to know the story of the family of Jewels. The book your father wrote has been reissued, but not by the publisher—an old friend of his he went to college with who died in 1971. It was reissued because your father hid the only copy he had left in his bank deposit box! He gave me the key back in 1982 after your mother's death. I convinced a new publisher to re-print it. When Matthew died, the publishing company died with him. We got a new publisher from Jewel Park.

"Clara and I didn't know what the hell we were doing. We tried to follow the instructions that came with the computer. I wanted to ask Cayenne to help me, but I was afraid he would think I felt the same way about him that your father did. A few weeks ago, I had had too much champagne and had offered to sell the book for the highest price. Then I changed my mind. I have the only copy left, and it's in the drawer reserved for you and your future family. Well, I hired my own computer specialist after I realized I didn't know what the hell to do with a computer.

"But I lived my life never to treat any human being the way my family treated me. And I cried so much after I turned that knife on you, Imani. For years, I'd wake up crying because I turned a knife on an eleven-year-old child. My God! Girl, I never apologized. Imani Jewel Henderson, I'm sorry. I'm sorry I ever made you feel unloved. I'm sorry I never let you and your father really get to know each other. I'm sorry I hurt you and your mother."

There were no tears this time, as Autumn pointed to the huge tree with branches and read each branch quietly; I joined in:

"An Ocean of Jewels for Imani Jewel Henderson

"Malika Baptiste (1787-1832), one daughter, Linda.

"Linda Baptiste (1799-1826); murdered by mother (asphyxiation), survived by one daughter, Cecelia.

"Cecelia Baptiste (1826-1915); ten children, all died in fire, except one daughter, Marie.

"Marie Baptiste (1834-1846); died in childbirth; one daughter, Sally.

"Sally Baptiste (1846-1935); married Lee White (1835-1915), a free man; two daughters; one, Mary, died mysteriously at birth; one survived, Jewel.

"Jewel White (1858-1958), married a Cherokee named Horizon (1848-1948); five sons: Horizon Jewel (1871-1901), River Jewel (1872-1901), Abraham Jewel (1880-1901), David Jewel (1890-1901), and Malachi Jewel (1900-1901); all died in a fire, murdered by a member of the Ku Klux Klan named James Stalworth; he accused Horizon of raping a white woman named Viola Stalworth, James' sister in Savannah; one daughter (twin of Malachi), Nana Zola Jewel.

"Nana Zola Jewel (1900-1982); married a doctor, John Weaver (1895-1976); seven children: Savior Jewel (1914-1975), Saul Jewel (1916-1944), Malika Jewel (1918-1978), Linda Jewel (1918-1968), Sally Jewel (1920-1990), Solomon Jewel (1924-1974), and Cecelia Jewel (1947–   ).

"Saul Jewel Weaver (1916-1944) married a white woman who was an Orphan Train Survivor and a missionary with The New Jerusalem Baptist Church on Eva Creek Island. Her name was Jurnee Miller Stalworth (1919-1937). Jurnee's mother's name was Judith. Her father, James Stalworth (1871-1942—a wealthy rice and wheat farmer and a Klansman in 1901 set a fire to the house of Jewel White that killed five of her children; one daughter, Ruby Jewel Weaver).

"Ruby Jewel Weaver (1937-1982), never married and Matthew Henderson (He married her great aunt—Cecelia Jewel—They divorced in 1991); one daughter, Imani Jewel Henderson.
"Imani Jewel Henderson (1970–   )"

Autumn continued talking as I finished reading the tree of family names, "Your father and I made a branch for you last year when we came down here. We added Saul's name and corrected the number of children Nana Zola Jewel actually had. We included the deaths and births of the spouses who were directly related to us. In the dresser over there, we have a drawer with the information I told you about when you were at my house. There's a drawer for John Weaver who came from a family of doctors. There's a drawer for Matthew and Charles Henderson to share. For Nana Zola Jewel's children and grandchildren, that smaller dresser has a drawer for each of them, including you, Imani. You have two drawers because I hope when you have your children, you will be able to fill both drawers and maybe even add more dressers to sit throughout this house. There's a drawer for the family of Jurnee Miller Stalworth Weaver to share, that's if we get to meet Eleanor Lowell. She lives on the mainland now in a retirement home. That drawer can be shared along with family members of Judith Miller, James Stalworth, and Eleanor Lowell. On top of the drawer is a guest book for family friends to write important notes that are related to our family, like Clara Rogers, Carmel, Cayenne, Valerie, Redd, and even Mark and Bless. One day, my hope is that this entire house will be filled with a family of Jewels. Here's our family's web address." Autumn handed me a piece of paper with the same web address Cayenne had been looking for: CRFCTFMH. I asked Autumn what the initials stood for.

Autumn said, "C.R. stands for Clara Rogers. C.T. stands for Cecelia Taylor. M.H. stands for Matthew Henderson. F. stands for family."

Autumn continued, "This afternoon, I have invited the residents of Eva Creek Island to meet you, along with your cousins who are the sons and daughters of Nana Zola Jewel's children. Some of them are here already staying at hotels on the mainland in Savannah and South Carolina. I want you to know that you have a large family. Our oldest living family elder is Randolph Weaver. He was the son of Sally Weaver, and he took over John Weaver's family medicine practice. He no longer practices medicine. He's up there in age now. But he had two children, Simone Jewel who is 39 and Albert Jewel who is 36. Simone is a doctor who practices internal medicine in Arizona, and Albert is an entertainment lawyer in Los Angeles. Four of the seven of our brothers and sisters had children, Saul, Sally, Savior, and Solomon. They are expected here this afternoon.

"So take some time Imani to look around the house and get comfortable, because it's yours. When we get back to New York, I'll show you all the paperwork.

"You own Matthew's house in Silver Row, which is paid for. You own this house on Eva Creek Island. Paid for. You own the Eva Creek Soul Food Restaurant. Paid for. Of course you own the brownstone you live in on Dandelion Street. Paid for. And you own the house in Bedford-Stuyvesant, Brooklyn that Nana Zola Jewel lived in because Charles doesn't want any part of real estate. There are still three tenants who live there, and they've been paying their rent to me in the name of Taylor Associates. If you want to change that, you can. Anything with the Henderson name, Charles has spent his life avoiding. I invited him, and he said he's coming this afternoon. So, maybe you can talk to him.

"Your father showed his love for you by making sure that after he died you knew your family and that you knew their love, and that you kept the land! He acquired every piece of property that he felt would be meaningful for you because for so many years he felt that he had let you down. He felt terrible for not sharing joint custody of you with your mother. He never got over a lot of things, Imani. He had a lot of ghosts.

"Eleanor Lowell lives in a retirement home in Creeksville, Georgia. She's up there in age too, but she said she'd make it. So I guess you can say I've organized a reunion. I hope every year you can find it in your heart to continue this tradition of a family reunion. I'll try to help you as much as I can, since I'm retired now. I write sometimes to earn a little money, even though I don't have to because Leroy takes good care of me, and I have my own money. He cringes every time I tell him how much he looks like Matthew." Autumn smiled with some warmth. "So, you go on, Imani. Take a soothing bubble bath, relax, and put something pretty on. Clara cleaned the house, and Bedilia along with Gertrude, her sister, brought groceries and they are through cooking. Chuck installed a phone just last week. God knows what the bill is since those nosy women been here snooping around. But they're going to bring everything over from Creeksville. We've got enough food to feed an army.

"God's been waiting for this day. I'm going to take me a nap. People should start arriving by three this afternoon. I'll be up and ready by then. We got some time."

Chapter Thirty-seven

I wore a lavender knit dress that accentuated my new shape and a pair of black sling-back shoes. I wore my box-braided hair up, letting spiraling curls give me joy, and I added only a touch of lipstick, concealer, and eye shadow. Music and laughter filled the entire Prayer's House as I entered the small, brick building. It was different compared to the time I entered it at age five when I was with my mother. Folding chairs had been replaced with wooden church pews. There was an altar this time, and a small piano near it. Peach colored brick walls decorated with art work from the collection of Gullah artist Jonathan Green gave the room a feeling of love. Everyone paused to watch me, and a little piece of beauty kissed my face as I stared out of the window at the crowd that could not get in to the building. The delicious scent of spring made itself comfortable in the house and I savored the attention.

Autumn was dressed elegantly in a sheer black dress accented with lavender flowers as she greeted my relatives. She spoke clearly, "Welcome everyone."

I noticed that Carmel sat in front with his girlfriend, and nearby Cayenne smiled from a corner of the room where Ella Wilson sat right under him. She was going to be a problem, I thought. Valerie, Redd, and her older daughter, Joy stood near Cayenne. I did not see Mark or Bless.

Autumn continued speaking at the altar, which was decorated with sweet grass baskets; some filled with colorful roses and fruit, "Everyone, this is my great niece, Imani Jewel Henderson. Nana Zola Jewel would have been proud. Welcome home!"

The audience clapped.

Autumn went on, "Today, Imani, Reverend Doctor Lance Scott Clarke has come from Jewel Park, New York to pray with you as you receive the blessings you missed when you were a child. I bought the quilts your mother sold to Mrs. Benson's husband. And although, you are not quite 30 yet, I'm going to start a new tradition that will allow our children to receive their third blessing at any age! How's that? Reverend Lance, please come here."

Dr. Lance, handsome as a sunset, took my hands and led everyone in prayer. He carried a small, decorative bottle of olive oil infused with frankincense and myrrh. He prayed over it as Autumn anointed my head with the oil the way Nana would make the invisible cross on my forehead, except Autumn touched me. I felt the warmth of the oil on the middle of my forehead again as Dr. Lance recited the Twenty-Third Psalm in Gullah. It was in a gold picture frame. After reciting the psalm, he gave the picture frame to Autumn. He ended the prayer by speaking in the ancient tradition of tongues and finished with the word, "Amen."

Autumn kneeled in front of me as everyone watched. Someone sang the spiritual "Amen," and a choir of voices from the congregation hummed along as Autumn spoke, "I bless you with this quilt." Autumn stood, and opened the quilt, and she wrapped it around me so that everyone could see the beautiful designs. She placed the other quilt, the Jewish one, on my lap, and she wrapped a third one around her body.

She continued as I felt the quilts warm my body, "Nana Zola Jewel was an extraordinary woman. She took in children with love. She gave every child love, even me. These quilts are testaments of her love. These quilts are testaments of her mother's love. These quilts are testaments of all of the mothers in our family who went on courageously to find a holy river to believe in when slavery tried to force them to close their eyes to the stars that guided us to freedom. Imani, your mother Ruby was given the quilt you have wrapped around you at age five, but she sold it for a bottle of whiskey that kept her enslaved; today I have freed it and brought it home for you to love."

Autumn continued and pointed to each design on the quilt, "The constellation Eridanus is a winding river of stars. These stars led our family to freedom from physical and mental slavery. These stars led our family to the greatness of Jewel Park, New York. They hang over a holy river where the souls of our ancestors swam to when they were thrown off slave ships headed toward America. Jurnee Miller Stalworth Weaver left it for your mother as a gift. Wrap it around you to feel her love. The quilt I wear belonged to Nana Zola Jewel. She's holding me right now. Look at the stars. These stars led the souls of our people way past the Euphrates, the Tigris, the Niger River, the Atlantic Ocean, the Ogeechee River, the Okefenoke Swamp, the Savannah River, The Horizon River, and The Knowing River. The holy river Eridanus protects the souls of our people. Never sell it. Never, ever, give your stuff away, Imani! Haffuh hol on to we'own!" Wear these quilts wisely and wrap them around you when you need to feel loved.

"Let it be known throughout Eva Creek Island and Jewel Park, New York, that the laying on of hands will no longer wait until age 30 or death. The laying on of hands for this family of Jewels will begin when God sees fit and reveals it to the child, parent, guardian or relative of a Jewel. So be it, Amen. I welcome the laying on of hands, now, to my great niece, a teacher and scholar in her own right, Imani Jewel Henderson."

Although only fifty relatives could fit into the small Prayer's House, at least three hundred people touched me that day with their hands, a blessing, and a prayer. But the most memorable touch and prayer came from Eleanor Lowell who wheeled her motorized chair over to my side at the altar, where Autumn had prepared a comfortable chair for me.

Eleanor said, "Ms. Imani Jewel Henderson, I am sorry for what my husband did to five fine children in your family in 1901. My husband died 58 years ago. But I remember what he did in 1901. He told it to his boys over whiskey and card playing. I remember their laughter. And I remember my shame. I couldn't just leave him. That was unheard of in my family. My family had money earned from the blood of slaves. What do I have to lose in admitting that? I'm 98! A whole lot of folks that are still alive like me know exactly what I'm talking about. But they'll die keeping it to themselves. I was Harvard educated, mind you! But after I got married to James, a very abusive man, I couldn't leave him. My Papa must've turned over in his grave a thousand times when he looked at the life I had chosen for myself. My Papa was what people might call liberal today. He believed I should be educated and follow my dreams. I wanted to be a doctor. But my Papa died the year after I graduated. And my mother, God bless her soul—knew only one thing—how to be a wife. And she felt that that was best for me. She was afraid for me. And she wanted to protect me. And she did. She kept me close to her. We knew that James had this kind of strange respect for elderly white women. There was a line he didn't believe in crossing. He kept a distance from her. Whenever I stayed with her, he wouldn't come after me. We had sneaked Jurnee into my mother's house. But James got home early. So we had to get Jurnee out of our house. But I remember what happened in 1901. In the name of Jesus, I forgive my self for never coming forward. Silence from the witness of murder is just as much a crime as the act of the murderer. I bless your family and pray for your family. May Nana Zola Jewel rest in peace along with my beautiful daughter Jurnee Miller Stalworth Weaver, and may you shine bright and beautiful as the stars that create the formation of the constellation, Eridanus. May God pour his blessings upon you, Imani Jewel Henderson." She touched my hands as I held hers, watching them shake; I felt her tears wet my hands.

The shaking, she explained, was a symptom of Parkinson's disease. In a frail voice, she picked up the box of pictures I had brought with me and kept at my feet, she scanned each one in the box that Autumn had given me.

Everyone in the room went on to sing, "Amen." They whispered as Eleanor called the names of each person I pointed to in each picture—fifteen people, all of the Stalworth family. Five of the pictures were exact copies of the ones I already had of Nana, my mother Ruby, and my father Matthew. As she identified her immediate family members, I wrote the names on the back of each picture. All of them were now dead.

Eleanor kept telling me how James Stalworth had faced a terrible death. He had been working on the family ranch and had slipped and fallen under a group of horses. At age 71 he just couldn't move. He had sprained his left leg. So he lay there in pain for an entire night. A horse he mistreated for years trampled him to death. Several other horses had joined in. When James was found, only pieces of his body could be identified.

Everyone watched Eleanor sadly shake. She said each word with great effort and wiped tears from her face. Eleanor then pressed a button on her motorized chair, wheeled her frail body to the door and waited for a black man whom I learned was a pastor of the church she attended in Creeksville, Georgia where she now lived, to escort her to Chuck Wilson's boat. She wanted to make it back to the retirement home before the sun left the sky for the evening.

Cayenne was the last to lay hands on me. He bent over and whispered, "See, baby, it began with a prayer," and he kissed me on the cheek and let his eyes dance around my body.

I was then greeted by a dizzying parade of cousins. As they all touched me and blessed me with quiet words, all Charles could do was kiss my cheeks and my forehead, smile, and then cry. His wife Eden, a petite, brown-sugared woman, held his waist and escorted him to the porch. I watched him, wondering what kind of life he must have had.

We ate, danced, and toasted a new day as the sun greeted us with beautiful colors, and the sounds of rhythm and blues. The music, musicians Rayne had hired from The Blue Zephyr, entertained us in Nana Zola Jewel's house and reminded me of an old-fashioned nightclub that brought me closer to an ocean of jewels. Blue-green was now the color of a river in my soul. A piece of love touched my heart. This made me smile as a piece of joy comforted me, and happiness paid me a visit because the oak trees in my soul were no longer in the way.

Chapter Thirty-eight

Cecelia Jewel Taylor died from breast cancer on Thanksgiving Day, 2000. She left instructions for the way her name should appear on her tombstone. She felt the name Henderson belonged to me. After her funeral she was laid to rest in the plot next to my mother, Ruby Jewel Weaver.

Between Easter and Thanksgiving, I visited Eva Creek Island every weekend as Carmel provided a ride for me to Savannah, and one of the Wilson family members would meet me and drive me to Creeksville, Georgia, a suburb just outside of Savannah, where Chuck Wilson was always happy to take me to the Island by motorboat, free of charge.

My Uncle, Charles Henderson, and my cousins Simone Jewel and Albert Jewel developed close friendships with me during that time. We kept in touch through emails mostly, and we took turns living in Nana Zola Jewel's house. My heart filled with joy each time I saw them. We shared the same blood and that was powerful.

That first week in December, Eleanor Lowell died in her sleep. The following week, Clara Rogers died in her sleep.

The wise words and comforting love of my relatives helped me write a letter of closure to my parents that had taken me six months to write, even after my sessions with Dr. Alton ended in June. I planned to place the letter in the drawer reserved for me in the room where our family tree lived in Nana Zola Jewel's house.

That June, I read the letter to Dr. Alton, my hands shaking, as she sat back in her chair, content.

June 30, 2000
"Dear Mama and Daddy,
I loved you like a daughter should. I praised your name when I wept for your loving touch. Now I know the truth and I love you more.
Your daughter, a melody no longer waiting,
Imani Jewel Henderson.

Dr. Alton smiled and said, "That's a new beginning! Build on that, Imani."

Our sessions ended that day, and I carried Dr. Alton's smile around with me like a photograph on my mind.

Chapter Thirty-nine

A week before Chirstmas, Blue Greene rang my doorbell.

I couldn't believe it. I opened the door, and then slammed it in his face only to see Cayenne pop out of his doorway. No words were exchanged, and Blue walked to his car as quietly as Cayenne rang my doorbell.

"That brother is vicious," Cayenne said, as he kissed my cheek. I took his coat and offered him tea.

I placed an Earth, Wind, and Fire CD on and we listened to "Drum Song."

I agreed with Cayenne, "Blue is vicious. I heard about what he did to Linda. He knocked two of her teeth down her throat, didn't he?"

"Damn! He did. What's he doing over here?" Cayenne asked.

"I don't know. I haven't seen him in a long time. The last time I saw him, I threw a bottle of champagne at him."

"Oh, yeah! I remember that! Valerie and me saw that through my window. That took guts, Jewel."

I smiled and glanced at him. "The two of you were watching me?" He smiled. So did I.

"We didn't mean to. Valerie happened to see stuff coming from your window, so we watched. That was funny as hell! That brother's going to end up killing someone soon. So, how are you, baby?"

"Happy. For the first time in my life, Cayenne, I am really happy."

"I know. I love enjoying your precious laughter. I love kissing you. I love late nights with that Grand Marnier you add to strawberries and whipped cream. No woman ever treated me like that, baby. I love you. Marry me."

"Yes." I told him without hesitating. There was no fairytale involved. Just like that he asked, and I said, yes, without even thinking. I held him close to me, wanting never to let him go.

"Tell me. You like gold, diamonds, rubies or all three?"

I held him tighter and smiled. "What?" I asked.

He reached into his down jacket and pulled out a bottle of sparkling cider whose wrapping resembled a champagne bottle. In the kitchen he found two wine glasses, filled them with the cider.

"When I saw Blue ringing your bell, I had to hurry up! I didn't want him messing up my day. Now, Jewel, to good loving." We toasted each other and sipped. Back in the living room he whispered to me. "I didn't do it right, Jewel."

"What?" I asked.

I watched as he got down on one knee like men who were proposing in the movies did. From the pocket of his down jacket that he finally took off, he pulled out a gold ring fitted with a circle of diamonds the color of my birthstone, amethyst. He slipped it gently onto my finger. Between kisses, he whispered, Mrs. Imani Jewel Henderson Brown. He repeated it until his kisses were traveling to my stomach.

He worked his way back to my breasts.

"Please don't stop," I whispered.

He murmured, "It still ain't right, Jewel. I want us to get dressed up, and do it right at some beautiful place you like." As the sun greeted us, I tasted his fiery kisses against my body under my softly scented sheets of lavender. For the entire day, we ate fruit and whipped cream, and I inhaled lavender, tender words, and discovered a full piece of beauty.

Chapter Forty

Valerie sat next to Cayenne and me, as Carmel and Zalia sat to the left of us, while Redd offered a toast to Cayenne and me. Redd said, "On this joyous Christmas Eve, with such bittersweetness, Cayenne, due to your mother's passing last month, which I was very sorry to hear, I wish you and Imani health, prosperity, joy, and love. And Mark sent greetings for the two of you. It reads, "Congratulations, Imani and Cayenne." I glanced at the card, and saw that only Mark and his daughter Malika had signed it.

The glasses of apple cider kissed. At midnight, I was greeted with "The Happy Birthday" song and my favorite coconut cake.

Cayenne put his arm around my waist. His tears wet his face and mine as I kissed him. He whispered, "I can't wait until New Year's Day."

"Neither can I," I murmured, kissing his tears, and thanking him for taking me to Nana's house on Eva Creek Island to propose again. He had asked Gertrude and Bedilia to set up the house with romantic candles and cook my favorite meal. He played my favorite music and led me upstairs to the room with the beautiful blue-green river. There he proposed to me. I kissed his lips where the tears had rested and thanked him for making his proposal so special for me.

"So where ya'll going for the honeymoon?" Valerie asked.

"Maui," Cayenne said. "I've been there several times for business. Now I'm so happy I have someone to share the time there with me. That place is like heaven."

"We're leaving right after the wedding reception," I added. "Our stuff is packed, already. We'll be in Maui just for a week, and we're going to spend the rest of the month-long honeymoon on Eva Creek Island in a house that had been abandoned. We'll be renovating next year. We want to live there. We want to have children there. We want our children to grow up there. I'll be renting out my brownstone next door, and Carmel is going to use the house in Silver Row as an office and space for relatives who come to visit. Leroy is two blocks away, so he can pop in anytime also. Carmel is eventually going to turn my father's Silver Row house into a bed and breakfast. I talked Charles, my Uncle, into moving back into Nana's house in Bedford-Stuyvesant. Her house on Eva Creek Island is going to be available for relatives to just come by and relax on holidays and family reunions. You're all welcome to come down, anytime!"

"That's just fantastic, Imani." Redd said.

Valerie smiled as she agreed with her husband. "Now don't be a stranger, y'all. You got to come visit us sometime." Joy and Mocha came out of their room to say hello, but they were more inspired by the cake. She and Redd, along with their staff were catering the wedding and reception at The Temple of Faith Church, and Dr. Lance was the pastor in charge of the ceremony.

After the cake cutting, we danced and laughed as if we were teenagers again, but without Mark or Bless.

Chapter Forty-one

After I said, "I do," Cayenne and I had three hundred and fifty guests, mostly relatives.

The reception served all three hundred and fifty and we grooved to the Electric Slide and to the rhythm and blues of soulful singers. I requested the song, "Whenever, Wherever, Whatever," by Maxwell, and Cayenne and I shared our first dance together as Mr. And Mrs. Cayenne Brown.

This time the feeling of love really embraced me.

There were hours of wedding pictures, greetings, blessings, and the laying on of hands. We looked for Bless and Mark, but we never saw them. We prayed for them, wished them love, and really meant it.

My relatives became Cayenne's relatives as they mingled and danced into the next morning.

Chapter Forty-two

After Maui, Eva Creek Island offered us more rest, like a tired gene pool restructuring itself. The photographs on my mind were exquisite, and the oak trees in my soul were strong and beautiful. There was no darkness, peat moss or dirt to stifle them.

We made love on scented lavender sheets, and watched the sun walk across the sky for the evening.

As he slept, I opened my journal from our night table and created new, powerful words like the ones Nana Zola Jewel offered whenever she blessed someone with the invisible cross. This time, all of the fear was gone, and I thanked Eridanus, a holy river loved by God that offered protection to fugitive slaves named Jewels yesterday, today, and forever.

Chapter Forty-Three

Bless Brown jumped into The Knowing River on January 15, 2001 with a baby in her womb that didn't belong to Mark.

Malika, her daughter, was with her. From the car, she used Bless' cell phone to call an ambulance, but it was too late.

Bless was pronounced dead on arrival at The Jewel Park Medical Center.

A river of cocaine and alcohol was found in her body. How she managed to drive her car twenty blocks to The Knowing River, no one will ever know.

A week after the funeral, Mark sold his house and moved with his daughter Malika to Westchester. He enrolled Malika in a private school, and commuted to the Bronx to work at Montefiore Hospital.

On weekends and holidays, Malika stayed with Valerie and Redd. Mocha and Joy accepted Malika as their foster sister. They became sisters.

Valerie embraced Mark as her foster brother.

One beautiful Saturday, Mark, Malika, Valerie, Redd, Joy, and Mocha visited Nana Zola Jewel's house on Eva Creek Island as guests of Cayenne and me. While adults were downstairs in the living room listening to music and engaging in heated grown folk's conversations, I took a walk to the room with the blue green river to have a talk with my mother, and I found love.

Malika, Mocha, and Joy stood in the blue green river, holding hands. Malika whispered to Bless holy words of love.

And I cried as I listened to Malika sing a sweet love song she had created just for her mother. She had a voice of velvet like the mother whose name she whispered.

Mocha and Joy were her backup singers. I watched as they snapped their fingers, moved like The Supremes, and danced to their own rhythm, unaware of my presence.

When I clapped, they smiled, and then continued rehearsed dance steps and a melody that made me smile.

That photograph will stay on my mind forever.

On a wall next to the dresser was a gold frame with the words of The Twenty-Third Psalm written in the Gullah language. I took my time studying the text and I tried to interpret its meaning by praying to God.

As the girls sang, I read the words and whispered them as best as I could:

The Twenty Third Psalm

De Lawd, 'E duh my sheppud. Uh een gwoi' want. 'E meck me fuh lay down een dem green passuh. 'E Khah me deh side dah stagnant wahtuh. 'E sto' muh soul; 'E lead me een de pat' ob right-juss-niss fuh 'E name sake. Aae doh Ie wark shru' de whalley ob dem grayb yaad Ie een gwoi' skayed uh dem dead people, fuh Ie know de Lawd, 'E duh deh wid me; 'E stick wha' 'E khah een 'E han' 'n de staff een de udduh han' gwoi' cumpit me' 'E fix up uh table fuh me fuh grease muh mout' 'n muh enemies een gwoi' git none. 'E 'noint muh head wid uhl. Muh cup obbuh flo.' Sho' nuff all 'E goodnes,' 'n

'E muhcy gwoi' be wid me all de day ob muh life 'n Ie gwoi' lib deh een de house ob de Lawd fuh ebbuh 'n ebbuh. Amen

978-0-595-40030-0
0-595-40030-2

Made in United States
North Haven, CT
29 August 2022